A LONG LONG WAY

A Long Long Way

Sebastian Barry

ISIS
LARGE PRINT
Oxford

Copyright © Sebastian Barry, 2005

First published in Great Britain 2005
by
Faber and Faber Limited

Published in Large Print 2009 by ISIS Publishing Ltd.,
7 Centremead, Osney Mead, Oxford OX2 0ES
by arrangement with
Faber and Faber Limited

British Library Cataloguing in Publication Data
Barry, Sebastian, 1955–
   A long long way.
   1. World War, 1914–1918 - - Ireland - - Fiction.
   2. Soldiers - - Ireland - - Psychology - - Fiction.
   3. Ireland - - History - - Easter Rising, 1916 - -
   Fiction.
   4. Historical fiction.
   5. Large type books.
   I. Title
   823.9'14–dc22

ISBN 978–0–7531–8438–7 (hb)
ISBN 978–0–7531–8439–4 (pb)

Printed and bound in Great Britain by
T. J. International Ltd., Padstow, Cornwall

For Roy Foster,
in friendship

Acknowledgements

The following books are part of a growing shelf of pioneering works on the First World War and Ireland, and this novel could not exist without them:

Ireland and the Great War by Keith Jeffery, Cambridge, 2000

Irish Voices from the Great War by Myles Dungan, Irish Academic Press, 1995

They Shall Grow Not Old by Myles Dungan, Four Courts Press, 1997

Orange, Green and Khaki by Tom Johnstone, Gill and Macmillan, 1992

Ireland's Unknown Soldiers by Terence Denman, Irish Academic Press, 1992

A Lonely Grave by Terence Denman, Irish Academic Press, 1995

Irishmen or English Soldiers? By Thomas P. Dooley, Liverpool University Press, 1995

Ireland and the Great War edited by Adrian Gregory and Senia Paseta, Manchester University Press, 2002

Dividing Ireland by Thomas Hennessey, Routledge, 1998

Far from the Short Grass by James Durney, 1999

I would also like to acknowledge the immaculate instincts of my editor at Faber, Jon Riley, who suggested this book to me.

PART ONE

CHAPTER
ONE

He was born in the dying days.

It was the withering end of 1896. He was called William after the long-dead Orange King, because his father took an interest in such distant matters. On top of that, an old great-uncle, William Cullen, was yet living in Wicklow, across the mountains as they used to say, where his father himself had been reared.

The winter sleet bit into the Dublin cab-men, where they gathered in their mucky gabardines by the Round Room in Great Britain Street. The stony face of the old building remained indifferent, with its strange decoration of ox-skulls and draperies.

The new babies screeched inside the thick grey walls of the Rotunda Hospital. Blood gathered on the nurses' white laps like the aprons of butchers.

He was a little baby and would be always a little boy. He was like the thin upper arm of a beggar with a few meagre bones shot through him, provisional and bare.

When he broke from his mother he made a mewling sound like a wounded cat, over and over.

That was the night of a storm that would not be a famous storm. But, for all that, it rattled the last leaves out of the regal oaks in the old pleasure gardens behind the hospital, and it drove the wet harvest along the gutters and into the gaping drains and down into the unknown avenues of the great sewers. The blood of births was sluiced down there too, and all the many liquids of humanity, but the salt sea at Ringsend took everything equally.

His mother took him to her breast with the exhausted will that makes heroes of most mothers. The fathers stood well away, taking a beer in the Ship Hotel. The century was old and weak, but the men spoke of horses and taxes. A baby knows nothing, and Willie knew nothing, but he was like a scrap of a song nonetheless, a point of light in the sleety darkness, a beginning.

And all those boys of Europe born in those times, and thereabouts those times, Russian, French, Belgian, Serbian, Irish, English, Scottish, Welsh, Italian, Prussian, German, Austrian, Turkish — and Canadian, Australian, American, Zulu, Gurkha, Cossack, and all the rest — their fate was written in a ferocious chapter of the book of life, certainly. Those millions of mothers and their million gallons of mothers' milk, millions of instances of small-talk and baby-talk, beatings and kisses, ganseys and shoes, piled up in history in great ruined heaps, with a loud and broken music, human stories told for nothing, for ashes, for death's amusement, flung on the mighty scrapheap of souls, all those million boys in all their humours to be milled by the mill-stones of a coming war.

* * *

When Willie was six or seven the King of Ireland came from England to visit Ireland. The King was as big as a bed. There was a big review over at the barracks in the Phoenix Park. Willie stood there with his mam because the King as big as a bed, a brass bed mind, for two people, wanted to see the gathered men of the Dublin Metropolitan Police. And why wouldn't he? They were as grand and as black as an army, marching and drilling there. His father, though only an inspector at that time, was put up on a big white horse, so the King could see him all the better. His father on that horse looked much finer than any King, who after all had to stand on his polished shoes. Like God Himself, or the best man in God's kingdom.

For years after, till he put away such childish ideas, he thought his father always went out to do his work on the white horse, but of course it wasn't so.

Such a singing voice he had. His mother, who was a blunt woman enough, one of the Cullens herself, daughter of the coppicer on the Humewood estate in Wicklow, got only good from it. She set him on a chair to sing like any woman might, and he threw his small head back and sang some song of the Wicklow districts, as might be, and she saw in her mind a hundred things, of childhood, rivers, woods, and felt herself in those minutes to be a girl again, living, breathing, complete. And wondered in her private mind at the power of mere words, the mere things you rolled round in your mouth, the power of them strung together on the penny string of a song, how they seemed to call up a hundred vanished scenes, gone faces, lost instances of human love.

His father, right enough, was a dark policeman in dark clothes. Willie Dunne was washed every night of his life in an enamel bath set beside the big fire in the sitting-room. And six o'clock every evening prompt, his father would come in and grip the wet little boy and lift him to his breast, where the silver buttons were, and Willie would lie up there like a scrap, like a featherless pigeon, still damp from the bath, his mother straining up with the towel to dry him, and his father perpetually frowning, all six foot six of him, and saying what a fine policeman he would make in time, a fine policeman.

And year by year his father measured him, standing him up against the wallpaper by the old marble fireplace, and putting a volume of operettas on his head, The Bohemian Girl and Other Popular Operas, and marking off his height with a stubby official police pencil.

And then Willie was twelve at last and a proper boy. And his youngest sister Dolly was born in the house in Dalkey and his mother was killed by that. And then it was his father only and the three girls and him, and at last into Dublin Castle with them in 1912, it was the winter of that year, and the memory of his mother was like a dark song that made him cry in his bed alone, strong though he was and all of sixteen, and the steam of his sisters' cooking turned to tears on the chilly glass of the old windows.

And then there was another thing to make him secretly cry, which was his "damnable" height, as his father began to call it.

For his growing slowed to a snail's pace, and his father stopped putting him against the wallpaper, such was both their grief, for it was as clear as day that Willie Dunne would never reach six feet, the regulation height for a recruit.

Willie cursed his very bones, his very muscles, his very heart and soul, for useless frustrating things, and shortly after he was apprenticed to Dempsey the builder, which in the upshot was unexpectedly very pleasant, and gave Willie secret joy. Because it was a pleasure to work at building, to set stone upon stone by gravity's rule.

Gretta was the secret he kept from his father, he loved her so much. It had happened by accident that he met her. During the terrible lock-out the year before in '13 his father had had the responsibility of keeping order in the streets of Dublin, as being high up in B Division of the Dublin Metropolitan Police. He had led the baton charge against the crowd gathered in Sackville Street, that time the Labour leader James Larkin had spoken to them.

Many heads had been smacked with those batons. And indeed a few of the DMP men themselves, the batons wrenched out of their hands, had been thumped in turn with their own weapons. But it was considered generally by the government that the police had acted bravely and had won the day.

One of the thumped citizens was a man named Lawlor, who Willie's father knew from around Dublin Castle, because he was a carter there. And Lawlor's head was done in good and proper, and Willie's father had tried to make it up to him, coming to visit in the evenings with apples and the like, but Lawlor was outraged and would scarcely speak to him, even though the policeman wore an ordinary suit to protect Lawlor's feelings and was inconspicuous. But the fact was Mr Lawlor was passionately in Larkin's court. The old policeman could never even countenance such a possibility, and for many months continued to court the man's friendship. Why him among all the others Willie did not know, unless it was a question of neighbourliness, an important matter to a Wicklow man.

Now Willie was nearly seventeen by this time, and when his father's conscience ached and yet he was too busy to go and see Lawlor, Willie was sent. The first time he was given two pheasants to take that had been shot on the Humewood estate, and sent up by the old steward, Willie's father's father, to his son in the castle. Now Mr Lawlor's rooms were in a tenement under Christ Church Cathedral, so it wasn't a long walk for Willie. Nevertheless, he carried the two birds with an inexplicable shame, though in the event not even the critical urchins in the streets mocked him.

When he got to the house Mr Lawlor was not in, but Willie went up to his room anyhow, just intending to leave the birds inside the door. They had beautiful feathers, those cock pheasants, like something you would see in the hat of the Viceroy's wife — or mistress.

8

Willie always enjoyed the scandalous stories told by Dempsey's men, when they would be having their breakfast all together at some site or other at six, lovely sausages and hot tea and the scalding scandals of the day. He was as plagued as any other boy by desire, trying to put manners on the endless erection of his sixteen years, and the laughter and passionate disclosures of the men delighted him well enough.

Willie went in through a dirty, heavily scratched door into an old room with a high ceiling. All around the edge of the ceiling were musical instruments in plaster, violins and cellos and drums and flutes and fifes, because it had once been the music-room of a great Protestant bishop connected to the cathedral, long ago. There was an elaborate marble fireplace at the top of the room, as yellow as a hen's leg from the damp and the soot. The room itself was divided here and there by long rags sewn together, so that the inhabitants of the place might have privacy. Indeed, there were four families in the room, so each division was a separate kingdom.

And in one of those kingdoms he saw for the first time his princess, Gretta Lawlor, who truly was one of the beauties of the city, there would be no lie in that. Dublin could show many beauties, skinny and destitute though they might seem. And she was among the finest, though of course she knew nothing of that.

She was sitting by a window writing on a piece of paper, though he never found out what she was writing. Her face made his stomach weak, and her arms and breasts made his legs of poor use to him. She had the strange look of an old painting, because the light was on her face. It was a neat, delectable face and she had long yellow hair like something caught in the act of falling. Maybe in her work, if she had work, she kept it tied and pinned. But here in her privacy it was glistening with the secret lights of the old room. Her eyes had the green of the writing on a tram ticket. Her breasts in a soft blue linen dress were small, thin, and fiercely pointed. It was almost a cause for fainting on his part, he had never witnessed the like. He held the pheasants up in the gloom and noticed for the first time that they had a curious smell, as if left hanging too long, and they were starting to decompose. She was just thirteen in that time.

As he stood there a man came in behind him and pushed past into the curtained space. He was wearing a long, black, threadbare raincoat. The man laid himself down on one of the rickety beds and swung his feet up wearily, and it seemed only then noticed Willie.

"What you want, sonny?" he said.

"I was bringing these up to Mr Lawlor," said Willie.

"Who are they from?" said the man.

"From my father, James Dunne."

"The chief super at the castle?"

"Are you Mr Lawlor, then?"

"Do you want to see the scar on my noggin?" said the man, laughing not entirely agreeably.

"Can I put them down somewhere?" said Willie, uneasily.

"So you're his son, are you?" he said, maybe noting his height.

"I am," said Willie, and then he knew the girl was looking at him. He raised his eyes towards her and she was smiling. But maybe it was a smile of mockery, or worse, pity. She's thinking, he thought, I am small to be a policeman's son. He was hoping still in those times he might make a last spurt of growth. But he couldn't tell her that.

"So what do you think, son, about Peelers rushing in on passers-by and knocking the bejaysus out of them?"

"I don't know, Mr Lawlor."

"You should know. You should have an opinion. I don't care what a man thinks as long as he knows his own mind."

"That's what my grandfather says," said Willie, expecting to be mocked for his words. But the answer wasn't mocking.

"The curse of the world is people thinking thoughts that are only thoughts which have been given to them. They're not their own thoughts. They're like cuckoos in their heads. Their own thoughts are tossed out and cuckoo thoughts put in instead. Don't you agree? What's your name?"

"William."

"Well, William. Don't you agree?"

But Willie Dunne didn't know what to say. He could feel the eyes of the girl on him.

"Yes," said the man, "if Gretta here, my daughter Gretta, was to elope to Gretna Green tomorrow with some young fella, with you even say, I would ask her as she went out the door, 'Gretta, do you know your own mind?' and if the answer was yes, I couldn't stop her. I might want to stop her, but I couldn't. And I might beat you just for the sake of it. But if it was a thought put in her head by another, you for instance, why, I would bolt her leg to the floor."

This was peculiar, embarrassing talk for Willie and, he believed, for anyone in his position at that moment. And while he was reluctant truly to move away from the girl, he was longing to move away from Mr Lawlor.

But Mr Lawlor had stopped talking and closed his eyes. He had a bushy black moustache but his face was long and thin.

"Mother of Jesus," he said.

"It's all right," said the girl, and she had a low, deeply pleasing voice, Willie thought. "Leave the birds there. I'll cook them for him."

"I don't want the birds," said Mr Lawlor. "And I don't want his jars of lamb stew and his jams and his — Do you know, William, your father sent me in a live chicken last week? I'm not going to be wringing the necks of hens at my time of life. I sold it to a lady for a shilling only because I couldn't watch the creature starve to death, for the love of God."

"He's only trying to make it up to you. You're his neighbour," said Willie. "He didn't like to see a neighbour hit on the head."

"But it was him hit me on the head. Well, not him, but one of his lads. Wild, big, feverish-looking fellas with big black sticks knocking sparks off of my skull. See, does he know his own mind? Now, does he? If he knew his own mind, he could give a man a belt and not think twice about it. And I suppose could be quite easy in that same mind about the four men killed that day."

Willie Dunne stood there marooned by these truths.

"I'm being a miserable old so-and-so, hah?" said Mr Lawlor. "Yes, Gretta? I expect so. Put down your birds, sonny, and thank you. But don't thank your father. Tell him I threw them out the window into the street. Tell him I did that, William."

Four men killed that day. The phrase sat up in Willie's head like a rat and made a nest for itself there.

Although he protested, Mr Lawlor was brought further treats in the coming times and Willie ferried them for his father. Mr Lawlor had lost his work as a carter because of the blow to his head; it was thought by his employer that he was a dangerous man if he had been agitating in Sackville Street. But thousands had forfeited their jobs for the duration of the lock-out and when it was over many found it impossible to get them back. So Mr Lawlor was one of many. And like many another he joined the army so he could get food for himself and send his pay to Gretta. And so he was away for days on end, and although there were women in the other parts of the room that looked out for her, it was easier for Willie to come and talk to her. And they talked about everything that was in their heads to talk about.

He kept it all a secret from his sisters on instinct and no doubt it was a good instinct, because the truth was that Gretta was a slum dweller and Willie knew what

Maud and especially Annie thought about such things, and they would immediately tell his father. And he did not wish that to happen. And he confined himself to going when his father gave him a parcel or a little bit of beef, so it all seemed normal and straight. But he supposed it wasn't normal and straight exactly. He was in love with Gretta like a poor swan was in love with the Liffey and cannot leave it, no matter how often the boys of Dublin stone her nest. Her voice to him was just music, and her face was light, and her body was a city of gold.

One day he came and she was sleeping. He sat on a broken chair for two hours watching her breathing, the gappy coverlet rising and falling, her face dreaming. The coverlet fell away and he saw her soft breasts. There were angels on the O'Connell Monument but she was not like them but he thought she looked like an angel, at least how an angel ought to look. It was as if he were being shown the heart of the world, such beauty in that shabby place. The weather was evil beyond the window, a harsh sleet pinning the darkness with a million pins. He loved her so much he wept. That was how it was for Willie Dunne, and maybe they were matters that could only be taken away from him.

By the time he was seventeen and she was nearly fifteen, they had been almost a year dodging both the fathers. Gretta was an extremely straightforward person and she knew herself when she saw Willie that first time that he was for her, young though she was. Her world became things before Willie and things after meeting

Willie, like the world designates things before and after Christ.

Perhaps merely by some rough chance he never slighted her or grossly offended her, though they could have a row like the best. She wasn't so wedded to the idea of his erection as perhaps he was.

"Well, you boys are all the same," she said.

Her father was going to put her to service in one of the Merrion Square houses if he could, or failing that, he thought he might send her down the country to a good family. And he might have done so already except he was fond of her, and his wife had died of a galloping consumption many years before, turning to a wet stick in the goosedown bed at his side. And he had no other companion in the world.

Willie, for his part, was going to grow rich at the building with Dempsey, and marry her. He felt he could carry the day with her father when the time came.

But then that other queer time of the war came suddenly and, much against Gretta's desires, he wanted to go to the war.

It was difficult for him to explain to her why it was so, because it was difficult to put it into words for himself. He told her it was because he loved her he had to go, that there were women like her being killed by the Germans in Belgium, and how could he let that happen? Gretta did not understand. He said he would go to please his father also and though she did understand that, she thought it a poor enough reason. He told her her own father would be in the fight now, and she pointed out that he was part of the garrison at the Curragh, and she didn't think he would be sent to France.

But he knew he must play his part, and when he came home he would not be remorseful, but content in his heart that he had followed his own mind.

"Your Da said himself we have to know our own minds," he said.

"That's only a thing he got out of a little book he reads. St Thomas Aquinas, Willie. That's all," she said.

CHAPTER
TWO

Willie Dunne was not the only one. Why, he read in the newspaper that men who spoke only Gallic came down to the lowlands of Scotland to enlist, men of the Aran Islands that spoke only their native Irish rowed over to Galway. Public schoolboys from Winchester and Marlborough, boys of the Catholic University School and Belvedere and Blackrock College in Dublin. High-toned critics of Home Rule from the rainy Ulster counties, and Catholic men of the South alarmed for Belgian nun and child. Recruiting sergeants of all the British world wrote down names in a hundred languages, a thousand dialects. Swahili, Urdu, Irish, Bantu, the click languages of the Bushmen, Cantonese, Australian, Arabic.

He knew it was Lord Kitchener himself who had called for volunteers. And John Redmond the Irish leader had echoed the call, down at Woodenbridge in Wicklow. There was a long account of the matter in the Irish Times. A fierce little river flowed under him as he spoke, and a countryside all beautiful and thunderous with wood-pigeons and leaping waters flew up about his ears, for he spoke his speech in a ravine. The Parliament in London had said there would be Home

17

Rule for Ireland at the end of the war, therefore, said John Redmond, Ireland was for the first time in seven hundred years in effect a country. So she could go to war as a nation at last — nearly — in the sure and solemnly given promise of self-rule. The British would keep their promise and Ireland must shed her blood generously.

Of course, the Ulsterman joined up in the selfsame army for an opposite reason, and an opposite end. Perhaps that was curious, but there it was. It was to prevent Home Rule they joined — so his father said, with fervent approval. And many to the south of them in those days felt the same. It was a deep, dark maze of intentions, anyhow.

Willie read about these things in the company of his father, because it was their habit to read the paper together in the evening and comment on the various items, almost like a married couple.

Willie Dunne's father, in the privacy of his policeman's quarters in Dublin Castle, was of the opinion that Redmond's speech was the speech of a scoundrel. Willie's father was in the Masons though he was a Catholic, and on top of that he was a member of the South Wicklow Lodge. It was King and Country and Empire he said a man should go and fight for, never thinking that his son Willie would go so soon as he did.

Willie had never reached six feet. How proud he was now to go to the recruiting officer who was lodged just outside the castle yard in quite a handy way, and be signed up, his height never in question. For if he could not be a policeman, he could be a soldier.

But when he came home that night and told his father, the big, blank, broad face of the policeman wept in the darkness.

And then his three sisters, Maud, Annie and Dolly, lit the candles in the sitting-room and they all felt part of the tremendous enterprise because Willie was going to be in it, and they were proud and excited, though it might last a few weeks at most, because the Germans were known to be only murderous cowards. Dolly at that time was just a mite and she ran around the castle sitting-room shouting and singing, till her eldest sister Maud lost patience and screamed at her to stop. Then Dolly cried unrestrainedly and her brother Willie, like he had done a thousand times before, took her in his arms and comforted her, and kissed her nose, which she especially liked. She had no mother but she had Willie to mother her a little in those days.

Royal Dublin Fusiliers,
Training Depot,
Fermoy,
County Cork.
December '14.

Dear Papa,

Please thank Maud for the under-drawers which she sent for my birthday. They are just the ticket for keeping out this dark weather. We were treated yesterday to a route march of twelve miles and we know the back lanes of Fermoy better than the postman now. Tell Dolly this army life is not as hard as the schooling though! I hope she is getting on fine now in High Babies. We are hoping we will be finished men by Christmas. And then I am sure we will be sent over to Belgium to the war. Lots of the men were fearful it would be over but our sergeant-major always laughs when he hears that. He said the Germans are not finished with us yet, not by a long chalk, and we better be careful to learn everything we can about soldiering. He has us going on like the poor lunatics above there in the Dublin Lunatic Asylum, flinging our arms about. There is stabbing of bags full of straw, with pretend bayonets because we have none of the real thing. My friend Clancy says we are lucky the food is not pretend too. My friend Williams says he is not so sure it is not. I keep thinking of that time in the singing competition a few years back in that hall at the back of Prussia Street and you were in the audience that time. And I was to sing the "Ave Maria" by Schubert, but I learned the two verses separately, and I never heard the peculiar bit on the piano that comes between and joins them up until that very moment. I fell at that hurdle. I don't know why I keep thinking of that! I wonder how the other lads in Dempsey's are doing and what are they building now? It is six o'clock now and I suppose Maud is beginning to get the tea. Annie will be helping, but Dolly will be at her tricks. Dolly, Dolly, you scamp, I will kill you. That is Maud shouting! I will sign off now, Papa. I wish that I could have a taste of those sausages that I am sure are sizzling on the pan. I miss my home right enough.

Your loving son,
Willie.

The time came when the new recruits were changed into something they had despaired of, trim, polished soldiers, though they had never seen battle.

It was past Christmas now and the new year had come and still the war was there. They had got used to the novelty of the number 1915 on their forms and chits and thrown the old number into the back of their minds with all the other years, in the manner of a young man's easy way of thinking. They had all heard the stories of the lads on both sides at Christmas coming out of the trenches and singing together, and playing a bit of football, and exchanging black sausages and plum puddings, and singing, and now they all knew that "Silent Night" was called "Stille Nacht" in German. So it didn't sound all bad, though of their own regiment hundreds had died and many taken as prisoners by the vile Hun.

The most difficult thing in barracks was to find some quiet spot to masturbate, because if he didn't masturbate, Willie thought, he would explode worse than any bomb. That was the principal difficulty anyhow.

Stille Nacht, Heilige Nacht . . . It didn't sound so bad at all, really.

Much to Willie's delight, they were to head off from the North Wall in Dublin, so it was a chance to be waved off by his own people. They were carried up from Cork on the train and were to be marched from the station to the ship. And indeed faces lined the road to the North Wall like a thousand blowing flowers.

Little scuts came out of the back streets and shouted God knew what at them.

He looked everywhere in the crowds for his own Gretta. Gretta the secret he kept from his father, he loved her so much.

He couldn't see her anywhere. But girls in their dresses and nice coats waved at him, and the soldiers large, thin and small looked all puffed up with the excitement, and they were cheered from the station all along the Liffey and all the way through the docks. All those Dublin people loved to see them go, it seemed, they looked proud.

Annie, Maud and Dolly had told him they would be standing at the O'Connell Monument, up on the first plinth below the angels, and he was to look over that way when he crossed the bridge and not to forget.

They marched like great experts of marching and indeed they had been well drilled and perfected in Fermoy after all. The boredom had become ability. They kept good time with their boots and kept themselves stiff, though they couldn't help a little tincture of swagger. Soldiers after all, who had freely signed up for the duration.

Not long now, of course. And they would be lucky if the war was still there when they got to France.

Everyone hoped to see a bit before they were turned back victorious.

The men marched with the knowledge that they had the bit of money now and the bellies of brothers and sisters wouldn't go empty. You could write it down in a special book, or have an officer write it down in a special book, who the pay was to be sent to, if you didn't want it yourself. And any young wives now would have the allowance to fend off the evil days and keep that wolf from the door.

But he didn't see sight nor hear sound of his sisters. Maud wrote to him later to say that Dolly refused to go. In fact, she refused to be found, and hid herself in the labyrinths of their castle quarters. It was half-four before they found her in the great coal-cellar, weeping, weeping. And it was too late to set out then. Oh, they asked her what the matter was, and why she had been so bold as to run off. She couldn't help it, she said. If she had to see her own lovely Willie go off to war, she would die.

It was a strange England they moved through. Not the England of stories and legend, but the real, plain land herself. Willie had never seen those places in true fashion. Now he was required to see them as they were, through the bright glass of the troop train.

In little villages and towns the people there also came out to cheer his train, his very train. They lifted their hats and smiled. Even at daybreak the sleepy inhabitants came out. The young soldiers were all weary so it was very cheering. Private Williams rather bitterly decreed that they were just people going on their own journeys, and would probably just feel embarrassed if they didn't cheer when they saw soldiers. Williams was a tall, soft-looking man with hair as yellow as wall-flowers, all spiking up.

"They certainly don't know we're Irish," he said.

"Would they not cheer as loud if they knew?" said Willie Dunne.

"I don't know," said Private Williams. "They more than likely think we're little lads from the collieries of Wales. Yeh, because they see you sitting there, Willie. They think we're all midgets."

"They think we're from the circus. A battalion of pals from the circus, I bet," said Clancy. He was as plump as the day he had come in, despite the training, and as confident as a robin in winter.

"You can't tell a man's length sitting down," said Willie agreeably.

"That's not what Maisie says!" said Private Clancy. Clancy was from south Dublin somewhere.

"I don't think there's anyone called Maisie where you live," said Williams. "They're all Winnies and Annies there!"

Now, Willie Dunne's middle sister was Annie, so he didn't quite follow the friendly insult here. But he thought it might be a rural reference.

"Ah well," said Clancy. "It's a saying. I pay no heed to anyone but Maisie — she bakes the currenty cake. Did you never hear that, Johnnie?"

"What in the fucking world does it mean?" said Williams.

"I couldn't tell you. A saying isn't supposed to mean anything. It's supposed to — what in the name of fuck is a saying supposed to do, Willie?"

"Jesus, don't ask me," said Willie Dunne.

"Too many cooks spoil the broth," said Clancy inconsequentially.

24

"There's no hearth like your own hearth," said Williams.

Willie in his mind's eye saw for the thousandth time his three sisters milling in the pantry, Annie getting under Maud's elbows and Dolly getting under any elbows going. And his father shouting from the front room not to be roaring at each other. And the fire of Welsh coals roaring in the big black iron grate, speaking of the collieries. And the chimney howling in the wind, and the skies blowing about outside in the deep winter.

And it was not a world he had thought he would ever leave; you didn't think that at the time — you didn't know.

He thought he knew what a saying was supposed to do, despite his denial. A saying, since a saying arises always from the mouths of adults when a person was just a listening child, was supposed to carry you back there, like a magic trick, or a scrap of a story, or something with something else still sticking to it. But he had no inclination to bother his pals with such a winding thought.

The seats of the train were made of wood; it was really a fourth-class carriage in its civilian days. There must have been a hundred trains rushing across all the old shires of England, coming down out of the highlands, from the dirty north, from the sedate south, bringing all the boys to the war. And some were more than boys, men in their thirties and forties, even a few aged ones in their fifties. It wasn't all a young fella's game.

When he went to the jacks to piss he thought he was pissing with a new dexterity. He could think of only one word to describe everything, bloody manhood at last.

In that strange six o'clock when the sun just began to mark the dark horizon.

"See," said Clancy, "they don't mean a blessed thing, bloody sayings. They're not supposed to."

They went through from the French port in real transports, big, groaning lorries the like of which he had not seen before.

As they approached the war, it was as if they went through a series of doors, each one opened briefly and then locked fast behind them.

At first it was the miraculous and shining sea, like some great magician was trying to make a huge mirror out of dull metal, and half succeeding, half failing.

Then the salty farms and then the flat chill fields, with little modest woods and high straight trees along the grey roads. Well, the roads were almost white, because the weather had been unusually dry. So one of the lads said it looked like home except with the mountains flattened out and the people were in queer clothes.

It was thrilling to travel through that foreign place. Willie Dunne was ravished by the simple joy of seeing new places of the earth. He sat up in his seat so he could peer out through the planking of the truck and thrummed with pleasure. He found himself comparing this serene landscape to the country place he knew best, the fields and estates around the home place of his old grandfather in Kiltegan. There was nothing here to compare to the mysterious heights of Lugnaquilla, the folds and folds of its great hills, like a gigantic pudding not ever to be entirely folded in, that would bring a traveller at last into the city of Dublin.

But sober as it was, the landscape overwhelmed him.

He sat with his new companions Williams and Clancy. Across the gap sat his company sergeant-major Christy Moran, a wraith of a fellow from Kingstown with the face of an eagle. If there was fat on that body, Willie was not a Christian. The man was all sinew, like a carpet at the mills in Avoca before they start to work the loom at it. He was all long threads going one way only.

Willie had been pleased to discover also as they had boarded the Dublin train at Limerick Junction that their platoon leader was a young captain from Wicklow, one of the Pasleys of the Mount, and Willie's father when he wrote to tell him was pleased also, because everyone knew the Pasleys and they were highly respected people and had a lovely garden there around their house. Willie's father indeed was sure the captain would be a chip off of the old block, just as he himself was a chip off the old block of his father, who had been steward of Humewood in his heyday, and just as Willie was a chip off him.

The big transport lurched on towards the war. He felt so proud of himself he thought his toes might burst out of his boots. In fact he imagined for a moment that he had grown those wanting inches, and might go now after all and be a policeman if he chose, astonishing his father. The men of the decent world had been asked by Lord Kitchener to go and drive back the filthy Hun, back where they belonged, in their own evil country beyond the verdant borders of Belgium. Willie felt his body folding and folding over and over with pride like the very Wicklow mountains must feel the roll of heather and the roll of rain.

It was this country he had come to heal, he himself, Willie Dunne. He hoped his father's fervent worship of the King would guide him, as the lynchpin that held down the dangerous tent of the world. And he was sure that all that Ireland was, and all that she had, should be brought to bear against this entirely foul and disgusting enemy.

The blood in his arms seemed to flush along his veins with a strange force. Yes, yes, he felt, though merely five foot six, that he had grown, it was surely an absolute fact, something in him had leaped forth towards this other unknown something. He could put it no clearer than that in his mind. All confusion he had felt, all intimations that troubled him and unsettled him, melted away in this euphoria. He was full of health after the nine-month slog in Fermoy. His muscles were like wraps of prime meat to make a butcher happy. The lecturers at Fermoy had described the cavalry engagements that would soon be possible, and there would be no more of that miserable retreat that had made the beginning of the war a horror, killing indeed so many of the old Dublin Fusiliers and making prisoners of heroes. The enemy lines would be burst asunder now by this million of new men that had come out at Lord Kitchener's behest. It was obvious, Willie thought. A million was a terrible lot of men. They would smash the line in a thousand places, and the horses and their gallant riders would be brought up and they would go off ballyhooing across open ground, slashing at the ruined Germans with their sabres. And good enough for them. Their headgear would stream in the foreign sun and the good nations would be relieved and grateful!

"Why are you lashing your arm about?" said Clancy playfully.

"Was I, Joe?" he said, laughing.

"You nearly had my head off," said Joe Clancy of the village of Brittas in County Dublin — not the seaside place, mind, as he often was driven to point out. The other Brittas. Without the sea.

"The other fucking Brittas!" Williams had said when this litany was first rehearsed. "For the love of God!"

"I'm sorry, Joe," said Willie. "Isn't it a fine, long-looking country?" he said.

Then suddenly a hand of fear dipped into his stomach. What a curious thing. One moment as brave as a young bird. Well, he felt as if he might even throw up his breakfast, truth to tell. And that had been three gristly black sausages murdered into life by the cook, so he didn't want to see them again.

"Jaysus, what's the matter, Private? You have gone very green," said Christy Moran, the sergeant-major.

"Ah, just the rocking about, sir."

"He's not used to travelling in style, sir," said Clancy.

The truckload of men laughed.

"Don't be puking this direction," said another lad.

"Someone open a window for the poor bollocks!"

"There's no fucking window!"

"Well, you'll have a lapful of warm puke if you don't!"

"No, no," said Willie, "it's all right, lads. I feel better now."

"Poor fucker," said Clancy and gave him a bang on the back. "Poor bloody fucker."

And Willie brought up the sausages, though they didn't look like sausages, and they spread like a little plate of guts on the wooden flooring.

He'd have been fine if he hadn't been banged on the back like that.

"Oh, you little bollocks," said the sergeant-major.

When they came into their trench he felt small enough. The biggest thing there was the roaring of Death and the smallest thing was a man. Bombs not so far off distressed the earth of Belgium, disgorged great heaps of it, and did everything except kill him immediately, as he half expected them to do.

He was shivering like a Wicklow sheepdog in a snowy yard, though the weather was officially "clement".

The first layer of clothing was his jacket, the second his shirt, the third his long-johns, the fourth his share of lice, the fifth his share of fear.

"This fucking British army, I hate it," said Christy Moran, in the doubtful glamour of his own mucky British uniform.

They were all gathered, the platoon, around a small brazier with weakling coals. But the murky twilight was fairly warm and the bombardment had stopped.

The last three murderous, racketing hours Christy Moran had been on watchful duty with a fiddly mirror. It had been enough to drive a sane man to madness. The angle and catch on it had been driving him spare, some patented piece of genius to serve the brave man in the trenches. He had been trying to scope out across the tormented acres for any sign of grey figures rising from the reasonably distant trenches. Those mysterious strangers, but in the same breath neighbours, the fucking enemy. And now on top of that there was no sign of the hot grub that would make the long night bearable, not to mention the rum ration, the most essential bit of kit outside tobacco, chewing or smoking.

Christy Moran was talking now to himself, or the mirror, or the men of the platoon. It was to put something against the dirty silence. A sort of whining silence it was. He was white in the face from lack of sleep.

Willie Dunne couldn't even hear him right; it was a muddle and a trickle of words. But it did a good thing, it dispelled that fog of panic that he had begun to know, at all turns of the days.

It was Christy Moran's heartfelt creed, his inner understanding, his root of joy. It was not talk for captains or second or first lieutenants and not meant to be, either. It was for the ordinary Irish philosopher that the generality of enlisted men in this stretch of forlorn torment were, men of the Dublin back streets, or the landsmen of some Leinster or Wicklow farmer, the latter being fellas that might not even understand the thrust of Christy Moran's argument, being often loyal, unthinking and accepting sort of men.

"The same fucking army that always done for us. Held me head down in all of history and drownded me and me family, and all before, like fucking dogs, and made a heap of us and burned us for black rebels. English bastards, bastards the lot, and poor people like me and the father and his oul da and his again and all going back, all under the boot, and them just minding their own business, fishing out of Kingstown Harbour till they were blue in the teeth."

But Christy Moran had no truck with diatribe just for the sake of it. He paused, dug a hand into the seam of his jacket, pulled out a pinch of lice, crushed them in a hopeless manner, and said: "And I'm out here, I'm out here fighting for the same fucking King."

And indeed it was a known fact that Christy Moran's da had been in the army before him, and in a different mood the sergeant-major might tell them about that same da in the trenches under Sebastopol in the Crimean War.

But it was quite pleasant eating the tinned maconochie then, instead of good hot grub, all of them there, and shaking their heads at the sergeant-major's energy and lingo. Because you could be shot for less, they knew. But they knew it was just the fiddly bloody mirror and the noise that had annoyed him, and the fact that the ration detail hadn't showed — or the blessed rum.

"It's fucking stand-to in five minutes, Willie," said Christy Moran, "so lug your arse to the latrine and do your business, and then mount the fucking fire-step for a lookout before the captain comes out of his fucking dugout and has your arse for a handbag."

"Yes, sir," said Willie Dunne.

"Williams, Clancy, McCann, all you buggers, likewise," he said. And the men of the platoon stirred like disturbed woodlice. "I've a horrible feeling the captain has plans for us tonight, I do," he said.

McCann was a quiet sort of a sourpuss of a man from Glasnevin, with a face that looked like it was spattered with smuts of soot, but that was only because it was perpetually unshaven.

So while one man kept a watch, the rest went round the traverse to the latrines. There were four nice big buckets there with wooden planks above for seats and the men eagerly took their turn. It was like a drug, when the shit left them, the body seemed to race high into happiness. It might have been the poisonous, but hopefully nutritious, stuff in those tins.

Christy Moran however merely suffered. He sat like an afflicted saint on the wooden seating. He scowled and moaned. Little lines of red and blue seemed to gather on his thin cheeks. He looked like a whiskey drinker that hadn't had a drink for ten days. He was the very picture of suffering.

"If a man could have a wash and steam his poor bollocks in a tub of hot water, that would be some

33

recompense for this fucking torture of pissing fire," he said.

"Yes, sir," said Clancy helpfully.

"I didn't fucking say anything," said Christy Moran, genuinely surprised.

"You did, Sarge," said Clancy, "you said —"

"I never spoke," said Christy Moran.

"You did, sir," said Clancy, in a friendly way.

And Sergeant-Major Moran looked at him with real fright. It was a fact that the sergeant-major had a little problem. He thought he was only thinking his thoughts and not speaking his thoughts. It was odd. But they were beginning to get a handle on their sergeant-major. They certainly liked him, all guff and gristle that he was.

"Mother of the good Jesus," said Christy Moran, and he pissed at last like a free man, and his bowels mercifully opened.

"Hallelujah," said McCann, quietly, and lifted up his big square hands to the skies.

Now at least they understood the purpose of the bombardment. That night not a crumb of fresh grub reached them from the rear.

The unwearying Boche had worked out where those supply trenches were, not merely because they had been their own trenches in a previous time, but because a watchful airplane passed over yester-eve. That pilot must have bollocking returned the information to his artillery, like a gillie guiding huntsmen.

34

Now those bombs had fallen, right on top of the supply boys. Not only were those lads incinerated, blown out among the atoms of Flanders, but the vats of soup had been spilled and ruined. The rum was roasted. The tobacco was turned to ashes.

By the fucking boys of East Bavaria.

CHAPTER
THREE

In those days, as chance would have it, or the striving plots of generals, they did not rise up and crest the parapets.

They were dug in God hardly knew where, although wise maps had their numbers, and the river was said to be not too far off. But what river Willie never was sure. His ear wasn't attuned to the strange, harsh names. Their trench was called Sackville Street anyhow; that was enough to be going on with.

Willie and the other lads knew there had been a great battle hereabouts, because coming up to the line they had passed little clusters of graves, on fenced-in patches of ground, and oftentimes little posies — a man's idea of a posy, a few wilting wildflowers — left on the gradually sinking mounds. So they knew companions had briefly mourned there, and gone on, maybe to death themselves.

So they wondered about that in their private minds. They had their own company padre, a long, pained-looking man called Father Buckley, who darted among them like a spaniel dog, his back bent like an old woman. He petted them like sons.

But grief was as common as whistle-tunes in that place. It wasn't just their own crowd.

Willie knew that the French soldiers in the defence of their beloved country had lost half a million souls already, young fellas like himself who had leaped forward into bullets and bombs with the passions of loyalty and youth. He supposed they lay all about their afflicted homeland like beetroots rotting in the fields. He tried to imagine what it would be like if this war were being fought in Ireland, across the plains of black Mayo, across the mountains of Lugnaquilla and Keadeen.

Later that night Willie Dunne's hands were shaking. He was looking at them, these hands of eighteen summers. They were shaking slowly, but he was not causing them to shake.

Willie was not thinking of the killed supply party exactly. But his hands were.

"Jesus," said Christy Moran, "I wish I was meeting some girl at the monument on Kingstown promenade."

He lit a lovely woodbine and sucked at the skinny cigarette. He hoped tomorrow some weary bollockses would make it up to them with supplies, because he had only thirty fags left, and that wouldn't do a man a night.

"If I was, I tell you, I wouldn't be minding if it was skelting down rain, mud or anything, because I'd be thinking of the dress on her, and how clean and good and sweet-smelling and everything, and the neat coats that girls do have."

There was another violent pull of the fag.

"And I wouldn't be failing myself to have polished boots that I'd have spat on for a good ten minutes and racking the elbow at them, you know? Ah fucking yes."

He scratched his inner thighs in a concentrated manner.

"Not that I'm against soldiering, no. I like these white bastarding lices crawling around my bollocks, and the fucking rations blown to kingdom come and general muck and mayhem, and pissing into a thunderbox that smells of all you bastards' shite."

The fellas near him laughed.

"But it's a nice enough thing to meet a girl and go and have a cup of tea in the Monument Creamery, and try not to talk with curses, and working up to a decent kiss at some point in the proceedings."

Christy Moran had himself wedged in under a bit of an overhang to try to keep himself out of the cascading rain that had suddenly fallen. Willie wondered if he put his head above the parapet, would he see the rain walking across the buckled and wrenched fields, or would he just get his face shot to pieces?

The rain stopped as suddenly as it came and Captain Pasley emerged from his dugout. The men bestirred themselves.

"Evening, Sergeant-Major," he said.

"Evening, sir," said Christy Moran, saluting nicely. "What can we do for you, sir?"

"Did the lads get their food?"

"It didn't come up, sir."

"Ah, did it not, lads?" said Captain Pasley, and looked around at the faces. But the faces were smiling encouragingly enough.

"We had the few tins left, sir," said Christy Moran.

"I'll phone down for double rations tomorrow," said Captain Pasley.

"That'll hit the spot, sir," said Christy Moran, taking a last drag of his woodbine and flicking it away into no-man's land. It soared like a firefly. Willie Dunne half expected a shot from the other side.

"All right, Sergeant-Major," said Captain Pasley. "Anyone stirring over there?" he said.

"Divil a one," said Christy Moran.

Captain Pasley incautiously stepped onto the fire-step and raised his capped head with alarming indifference so he could peer out.

"Careful, sir," said Christy Moran, flustered despite himself. "Don't you want to use the mirror, sir?"

"I'll be all right," said Captain Pasley.

So Christy Moran was forced to stand there, his brain rattling a little, expecting a shot.

"Such beautiful country," said Captain Pasley. "Such a beautiful night."

"Yes, sir," said Christy Moran, who had not noted particularly the beauty, but was willing to allow it might be there.

"You can see the river glinting away over to the right. I am sure it is absolutely full of trout," said Captain Pasley in a dreamy, distant voice.

Christy Moran was further disconcerted. "I hope you're not planning to go out there and try your luck with a rod, sir."

Captain Pasley stepped down again and looked down at his sergeant-major. "Do you have everything you want?"

"Everything we want, bar stew," said Christy Moran, immensely relieved. "Isn't that right, lads?"

"Yeh, yeh," said the lads dutifully.

"It is a lovely night, a lovely night," said Captain Pasley, leaning back his head now, and lifting the rim of his cap, and gazing upwards. "Would you look at those stars?"

"At least we can look at the stars still, sir," said Christy Moran, on the brink of euphoria.

"I take your point, Sergeant-Major. I'm sorry if I gave you cause for concern."

He smiled. He was not a handsome man and he was not an ugly man, the captain, and Willie was not in any way against him because he had an air of confidence, which was a good air when you were all stuck out in foreign fields, and even the birds did not sing the same run of notes.

No man in truth regretted being raised above his fellows, that was a human fact, Willie supposed. But the raised-up ones needed to be of the ilk of Captain Pasley for it to make sense.

You couldn't take against Captain Pasley.

"We'll have to go out later anyhow," he said, with a sigh.

"Oh, yeh, sir? Ah, we thought so, sir," said Christy Moran. "Didn't we, lads?"

"Ah, we thought so, we thought so," they said in chorus.

So they rose up like shadows of the dead from their lair at the bulking of the night, a fierce frieze of stars rampant above.

Willie saw the sudden vista of no-man's land, the dark openness of it, the lurk of the old fences and field corners. There was barbed wire everywhere, put in by scores of successive wire parties, going out on nights like these, under stars like these, with hearts like these, German and Allied, pounding and leaping into throats.

Willie didn't know where the enemy trenches lay exactly, but he hoped Captain Pasley did, from his map and the numbers on the map.

Up the moist clay they went, Captain Pasley ahead, Christy Moran quietly following like a scowling wife, and Joe Clancy was in this group and Johnnie Williams, and also a red-haired lad called Pete O'Hara.

Willie knew they were to check their own wire along a four-hundred-yard stretch because the captain thought during the day he had seen a gap here and there. And they didn't want even jack-rabbits or rats getting through. Or, slipping with horrible creeping murderousness upon them in the dark, great muscled engines of Germans who would leap down on them and drive their fine-honed Dresden bayonets into their Irish chests. They didn't want that.

So now they had to creep along themselves, slightly hunched, arms sloping, being so careful, as indeed signally recommended in their soldier's small-books, not to betray themselves by a snapped twig or a cough or a stumble.

And Captain Pasley, who was a small man, a miniature man in some ways, with a head like a nicely rounded turnip, he walked quite erect and purposefully, getting them to follow with little shakes of his right hand. O'Hara and Williams carried a light enough roll of wire between them for repairs, and Willie Dunne had big wire-cutters like something you might imagine a mad dentist would possess to torture you with, and he had to carry his rifle also. It was up to Clancy to dart along carefully in his captain's wake, peering into the murky tangles, like sad brambles that would never bear berries in any known September of the world.

Meanwhile, the Boche threw up, now and then, the dreaded star-shells, festive enough things except they banished the night-time. But when these shells were heard going up, at least the little party knew their sound by now, and flung themselves into the grasses and the clays, Captain Pasley too, like a fellow diving off the rocks at the Forty Foot swimming place in Sandycove, in Dublin, in that vanished world behind them.

Then they went on, and now they found one of the captain's gaps, and set to, Willie snipping off a length and them all pulling the awkward, snake-like object like a mythical creature out of a Greek story into its place. And Christy Moran bound the new to the old, and it was a wonder no one else heard him cursing, although maybe now the German lads were grown used to his cursing and thought it was some kind of wild bird's calling, out there in abandoned Belgium.

"The fucking cunting thing is after biting the thumb off me," he said, "the fucking bastarding cunting piece of English shite."

"Moran, leave off the giving out, man, a bit of god-forsaken ciuneas, if you will," said Captain Pasley.

"A bit of what, sir?" said Christy, sucking the little berry of blood off his finger.

"Quiet, quiet. Do you not speak any Irish, Sergeant-Major?" said Captain Pasley in a friendly way.

"I don't fucking speak Irish, sir, I don't even fucking speak English."

"Whatever it is you speak, Moran, don't."

"All right, sir," said Christy.

"God bless you, Sergeant-Major," said the captain, perhaps humorously, they didn't know. "Wait, wait, wait," now he said, hunkering down. "Whisht, lads, down."

And they all dropped like Wicklow sheepdogs. The mucky ground was decorated with red pebbles, Willie could see them. He had slightly pissed himself; he didn't mean to. Now when he looked up he could see, much too clearly, a few heaps of figures passing along a hundred feet beyond them, like fellas out for a starry walk, unconcerned, but silent, and Willie felt the warm piss seep again onto his legs, and he cursed himself for a fool.

He could feel Christy Moran lying in against him as tense as a piece of dried timber, ready for God knew what, to spring up and gain a Victoria Cross, some awful act of valour that would get them all killed, and only a medal left of them to clank in a biscuit tin with other cherished nonsense. Might he not smell the smell of the piss anyhow?

But no, Christy Moran stayed where he was, maybe as afraid as Willie in the upshot, and they could all hear Joe Clancy's slightly chesty breathing as if miniature pigs were living in his mouth, and it was not a relaxing sound. Then Willie became conscious again of his rifle in his hands, and he gripped the smooth wood and the oiled barrel, and suddenly, despite the pissing, he knew he was not afraid. He was afraid but he knew he could rise now and meet the danger and wrestle with the enemy party and do what was called for.

It was a wonderful feeling; he was entirely surprised by it. He had not been out before on the cold night land, the blotchy skies with a touch of forgotten frost, still with a breeze of doubting cold. He was grinning now like a real fool, but a happy one.

The unknown figures passed on and away, themselves at some similar task put upon them by fate, ordered as one might say to wander in that dangerous nowhere for an hour or two, and risk everything for that, a roll of wire, a scrap of intelligence about a hole other men had maybe dug afresh.

Willie grinned and grinned, he put a hand down into the clay and scrabbled a cold fingerclasp of it, and put it to his damp cheeks and rubbed it in gratefully. The little red stones rasped along his skin. He had hardly a true idea who he was in that second, what he was thinking, where he was, what nation he belonged to, what language he spoke. He was as happy in this absence of fear, fear that he had feared would stop him dumb and numb, happy as an angel, as a free bird, as that doomed man to the right of Christ must have felt when the King of the Jews Himself said that for his kindness he would be saved, would be seated at Christ's right hand in heaven, that though the three would die, two would not die, bound one to the other by kindness.

"What in the name of the good fucking Christ are you grinning at, Willie Dunne?" said Christy, lying now on his side on an elbow, quite in the country and at his ease. Willie knew Christy Moran was itching to unhitch the fag in his ear and have another pleasing smoke. Have a pleasing smoke and fuck the world and her wars and her cares.

"I don't know, Sarge, I don't know."

"Fuck me to heaven," whispered Christy Moran, "if I didn't think I was going to have to drop dead from the fright those buggers gave me. Can they not make a bit of noise when they're going about so someone can shoot them?"

"Come on, lads, we'll shimmy back and have a can of evil-smelling tea," said Captain Pasley.

"Just the job, Captain," said Christy Moran. "We'll come with you, right enough. No bother, sir."

"Everyone shipshape?"

Shipshape, and alive.

CHAPTER
FOUR

Now Willie was gone all those months. Dublin he supposed was just the same, and he wondered what spring would be looking like, sitting in the trees along Sackville Street, the real Sackville Street and not just a trench, and cheering up the starlings.

He thought how beautiful Gretta was, like the statue of the Grecian lady in the Painting Museum in Merrion Square. But she was no great hand at the letter writing, that was sure. The fella would come by with the letters and if he was lucky there'd be one from his father. Weeks and weeks and weeks he had waited for a letter from Gretta. It could be said that just now and then he was angry about it, humiliated. Even Christy Moran's wife, never mentioned by Christy, wrote to Christy, because Willie had seen him hunkering down hungrily to read such letters. Joe Clancy had a girl that wrote to him right enough and regularly into the bargain.

He knew the captain had to read all the letters that they themselves wrote, so that an eye would be cast over everything, for information that might give help to the enemy, in case the letters were lost in an attack. He was always a bit nervous so writing to

Gretta, to declare those few words that had been said he knew those countless times in all the languages of mankind. But it had to be risked. He loved her. And he knew, he hoped, she loved him because she had said so at their parting. And though the occasion may have driven the words into her mouth, he knew and hoped and prayed that they had started their journey in her heart, as they had in his.

Sometimes he could manage quite a long letter and sometimes for some reason when he tried to fetch out the proper words, there were only a few of them.

He thought how young she was in truth and how young he was and all their possible long days ahead, if they could only get their hands on them, and nothing standing between.

Of course, he remembered that she had not been able to give her word that she would marry him. He had felt awkward asking her in the dark of the stairwell of her father's tenement, but she had not felt awkward saying no.

"No, Willie, I won't undertake such a thing," she had said, like a lawyer or the like.

And well he understood why not, what with her so-called beau going against her wishes and off to war with him seemingly without a care. That was the story then.

But it was every day now he cared, for her and for all the things he had left behind.

How beautiful she was, he thought, how beautiful.

Royal Dublin Fusiliers,
Flanders.
April 1915.

Dear Gretta,

I am thinking and thinking of you, Gretta. There are
Chinese diggers everywhere and black lads and the
Gurkhas looking fierce, the whole Empire, Gretta. And I
don't know what nation is not here, unless it is only the
Hottentots and the pygmies stayed at home. But maybe
they are here with us too, only we can't see them so low
in the trenches. I should talk! I am longing for furlough
so I can go home and tell you all that I have seen here at
the war. I love you, Gretta. That's a fact.

Your loving friend,
Willie.

He wrote that. And then he tried to erase the "friend"
and put in something better. But it became a smudge,
so he wrote in "friend" again and hoped it would do the
trick. He was very nervous writing the letter all right.
The captain might think it was stupid; and worse than
that, she might think it was stupid.

Some toiling days later they were on the move again,
pushing on further up country to near St Julian. He
was getting the hang of the new words, and anyway St
Julian wasn't much of a mouthful, it was almost
English.

At first they considered things to be much improved. There was a river near the reserve lines where they were billeted, waiting to go up into the line, with weeping willows along the banks, and the same river was known to meander out between the lines eventually, and to carry into the German lines themselves, so it amused them to set little paper boats on the water, with violent messages written on them in bits of German, in the hope that somewhere a German hand would fish them out.

They supposed they would have to say it would soon be summer, as summer was said to come early in those parts.

Clancy, Williams, O'Hara and Willie Dunne asked permission one fine day to swim in the river, and Captain Pasley didn't say nay, in fact declared he would join them.

It was a pleasing stretch of country there when they reached the elected spot. The glistening blue bullet of a kingfisher fired along and away under the lowering trees. The water was dark black silk.

Once the uniforms were stripped off, no one was so obviously a private or an officer. It was curious to Willie and his pals how slight and young Captain Pasley looked.

They ran about in their long-johns kicking a sick-looking football, and there was a fresh and excited laughter in their voices under the trees.

It was a laughter almost painful in their throats, and the willows seemed to float now in the breeze, like green clouds, and the river water was a piercing blue, the blue of old memory, and although being young they did not know exactly the privilege of being young, yet even after long hardships their bodies felt fine, and the blood was flowing round them well, and after all in the horrible mathematics of the war, they were alive.

Then Clancy did a running dive into the river, and Williams arrowed in after him, and then Willie, and then Captain Pasley went in with a belly flop.

Then they were out again smartish as the water was still quite chill and they lay back on their uniforms, arms behind their heads. They were naked as babies. A little breeze played about in the willows. The five penises lay like worms in their nests of pubic hair. It was like, thought Willie, an old painting in the window of a pricey shop in Grafton Street that a person might gawp at in surprise.

It was not that the war receded; they could hear it clearly enough, coming over to them in the still air, the shocking repetition of the high-explosive shells, and shrapnel bombs that even at that distance made a mean little insect noise.

An airplane careered overhead, going about its business of photographing and intelligence-gathering. The head of the pilot was quite plain, jutting up from the canvas of the craft. The colours and the big letters of the Royal Flying Corps gave the airplane an air of the circus.

But it was quiet otherwise along those fields.

"How long will the war last, do you think, sir?" said Clancy, scratching his ankle with his other foot. His nails were as long as Methuselah's, yellow and bony looking, and they had begun to curl back under the toes. They had been long days in their snug boots.

"I hope not too long, anyhow," said Captain Pasley.

Then nothing for a while.

"It's the farm I miss mostly," said Captain Pasley, as if the words arose from a private thought of his own. "It makes me jittery to think of all the work that needs doing at home."

He pulled at the grass under his hands.

"And my brother John's in now, South Irish Horse," he said.

"Is that so, sir?" said Clancy idly.

"And the father's not getting any younger, I suppose," said the captain. "You know, he needs us there really, to be seeing to the liming of the fields, that's a big job just now. We only have one or two labouring men left, everyone else gone into the army, like the men of Humewood and Coollattin and the other estates. By Christ, boys, I am jittery to think of it."

O'Hara nodded sagely enough. They liked him talking about his home place somehow.

Captain Pasley stayed peaceful enough, despite what he said about being jittery.

The kingfisher went firing back up the other way.

"That liming is a big job," he said, pensively.

But soon enough they were wearily in the line again — wearily, because they took over twenty yards of a trench that had been in the possession of some sad-looking Frenchmen, and by heavens their idea of a nice trench

51

was a strange one. At least they had decent spades up here, and regulation army wire-brushes to get the clay that stuck like toffee off their boots.

It was foolish to make too many banging noises in a trench. In this position the enemy was a comfortable three hundred yards distant, and there was no sense in waking them up to their duty. Willie Dunne's spade bit quietly into the ragged trench. The spoil was thrown up conveniently behind to make a better parados, a line of heaped earth to prevent fire unexpectedly coming in from the back. Other loads were heaped into sacks and stacked up in front for a decent parapet. A fire-step was put in place below so a fellow could stand on that and make some fist of firing out into no-man's land, or, in the worst case, stand there by the ladders before going over the top.

The Algerians were just over to his right. The Algerians sang fine, strange songs most of the day, and at night now he could hear them laughing and talking in a sort of endless excitement.

The trench was soon looking fairly smart.

"That's fucking better now," said the sergeant-major religiously.

They did all that and then lurked in the perfected trench, getting muggy like old boxers. The poor human mind played queer tricks, and you could forget even your name betimes, and even the point of being there, aside enduring the unstoppable blather of the guns. What day oftentimes it was, Willie would forget.

Then a different day arrived. Everyone had had a lash of tea, and there was a lot of farting going on after the big yellow beans that had come up around twelve. As usual after they had eaten, they were beginning to look at each other and think this St Julian wasn't the worst place they'd been in. It was the essential illusion bestowed on them by full stomachs.

A breeze had pushed through the tall grasses all day. There was a yellow flower everywhere with a hundred tiny blooms on it. The caterpillars loved them. There were millions of caterpillars, the same yellow as the flowers. It was a yellow world.

Captain Pasley was in his new dugout writing his forms. Every last thing that came in and every last thing that went out was accounted for. Items and bodies. Captain Pasley, of course, was obliged to read all the letters the men sent home, and he did, word for blessed word. He thought it might break a man's heart to read them sometimes; there was something awfully sad about some of the soldiers' letters. They didn't mean to make them sad, which gave their efforts to be manly and cheerful a melancholy tinge. But it had to be faced. God help them, they were funny enough efforts sometimes. Some men wrote a letter as formal as a bishop, some tried to write the inside of their heads, like that young Willie Dunne. It was a curiosity.

The yellow cloud was noticed first by Christy Moran because he was standing on the fire-step with his less than handy mirror arrangement, looking out across the quiet battlefield. That little breeze had freshened and it blew now against the ratty hair that dropped out of

Christy Moran's hat here and there. So the breeze was more of a wind and was blowing full on against Christy's hat and mirror, but it was nothing remarkable.

What was remarkable was the strange yellow-tinged cloud that had just appeared from nowhere like a sea fog. But not like a fog really; he knew what a flaming fog looked like, for God's sake, being born and bred near the sea in fucking Kingstown. He watched for a few seconds in his mirror, straining to see and straining to understand. It was about four o'clock, and all as peaceful as anything. Not even the guns were firing now. The caterpillars foamed on the yellow flowers.

And the grass died in the path of the cloud. That was only Christy Moran's impression maybe; he hoiked down the mirror a moment and wiped it clean with his cleanish sleeve. Back up it went. The cloud didn't look too deep but it was as wide as the eye could see. Christy Moran was absolutely certain now he could see figures moving in the yellow smoke. It must be some sort of way of hiding the advancing men, he was thinking, some new-fashioned piece of warfare.

"Would you ever fetch out the captain," he said to O'Hara. "All right, boys, stand now in readiness. Get those rifles up here. Machine-gunners, start firing there into that bloody cloud."

So the gun detail leaped to their machine-gun, Joe McNulty and Joe Kielty the loaders as ever, Mayo men and cousins too, that joined up somewhere against the wishes of their fathers they had confessed, and the bullets started clattering away from them, the water-man keeping the gun well cooled, the shooter firm on his knees and expecting all the while to have the top of his noggin shot off.

But this was a very curious advance. Captain Pasley came out and stood contemplatively by Christy Moran, who had abandoned his mirror and was standing up on the fire-step, such was his puzzlement.

"What's going on, Sergeant-Major?" said Captain Pasley.

"I couldn't tell you, for the life of me," said Christy Moran. "There's just this big fucking cloud about fifty yards off, drifting along in the wind. It doesn't look like fog."

"It might be smoke from fires the Boche are burning."

"Might be."

"You can see them coming on?"

"I thought I could, sir. But there doesn't seem to be anyone. No shouts, no cries. It's as quiet as a nursery, sir, and all the babies asleep."

"Very good, Sergeant-Major. Cease firing, men."

The Algerians to the right were a little ahead of them, as the trench twisted away there in a slight salient. All the Irish were on the fire-step now, all along the length of the trench, some fifteen hundred men showing their faces to this unknown freak of weather, or whatever it might be. The commanding officer was rung up and told what was afoot, but there wasn't any coherent order he could think to give, except to be cautious and shoot anything that came creeping.

There had been no warning barrage and the dense smoke didn't look too threatening. It was beautiful in a way, the yellow seemed to boil about, and sink into whatever craters it was offered, and then rise again with the march of the main body of smoke. There were still birds singing behind them, but whatever birds had been singing in front of them were silent now. Captain Pasley removed his hat and scratched his balding pate and put the hat back on again.

"I don't know," he said. "Like a London fog, only worse."

The big snake of turning yellow reached the parapet of the Algerian stretch of the trench far over to the right and now strange noises were heard. The soldiers seemed to be milling about haphazardly, as if invisible soldiers had fallen in on them, and were bayoneting without restraint. That wasn't a good sound. The colonial men were roaring now, and there were other frightening cries, as if the unseen horde were throttling them. Of course, the Irishmen could not see into the trenches as such, but in their mind's eye ferocious slaughter was afoot. Those men from country districts must have thought of pookas and fairy hordes because only such tales of childhood and firesides seemed to match these evil miracles. Horrible laments rose from the affronted Algerians. Now they were climbing up the parados and seemed to be fleeing back towards the rear. The smoke came steadily on.

"It's the smoke," said Captain Pasley, "there's something wrong with the smoke, gents."

56

Now, in his old house at home in Wicklow there were seven fireplaces, and two or three of them were as leaky as old buckets, and when they were lit, smoke poured forth into the bedrooms above them. And that was an evil smoke, but it would not drive you back as if you were cattle, as was happening to those poor men of Algiers, now for some reason tearing off their uniforms and writhing on the ground, and howling; howling was the word for it.

The Dublin Fusiliers took the smoke at the furthest right tip beside the Algerians. Exactly the same thing happened. Now the men were possessed of an utter fear of this dark and seemingly infernal thing creeping along, seeming to make the grass fizz and silencing birds and turning men into howling demons. On instinct the men pushed down along the trench, as anyone would do in the same circumstance, crowding into the next stretch suddenly, so that the men there for a moment thought they were being attacked from the turn of the trench. These men in turn were panicked and poured on into the next section, and because the line of the trench was at only the slightest of angles to the line of the smoke, they had to move proportionately faster to keep ahead of it. Soon the third and fourth stretches were in a hopeless tangle and the smoke poured in upon them. In the sudden yellowy darkness awful sounds sprang up like a harvest of hopeless cries.

O'Hara started to scramble up the parados behind and it was only Christy Moran's bark that made him stop. The sergeant-major looked to the captain. Captain

Pasley's face had turned the colour of a sliced potato; there was the same bloom on it also of damp.

"I need to ring headquarters and ask them what to do. What is this hellish thing?"

"No time for that, sir," said the sergeant-major. "Can I let the men fall back, sir?"

"I have no earthly orders for such a thing," said Captain Pasley. "We are to hold this position. That's all there is to it."

"You won't hold nothing against that smoke, sir. Best to fall back to the reserve trenches anyhow. There's something deathly and wrong."

But before such a sensible conversation could continue, the smoke was slipping down the parapet about a dozen yards ahead, itself like dozens and dozens of slithering fingers, and there was a stench so foul that Willie Dunne gripped his stomach. Joe McNulty came tumbling down from his emplacement, gripping his Mayo throat, like a dog done in by poison meant for rats.

"Get the fuck out," said Christy Moran.

"All right," said the captain. "I'll hold the fort here, Sergeant-Major."

"You will on your fuck, sir, begging your flaming pardon. Come on."

Willie Dunne and his comrades scaled the parados and everyone started to stumble back across the broken ground. It was astonishing to be up, out of the trench and going along at the level of normal things. Ghosts of soldiers plummeted out of the smoke up to the right and tottered screaming along, falling to their knees, their hands around their throats like those funnymen in the music halls that would pretend to be being strangled and it was their own hands at their necks doing the throttling. Now there was no question of order or retreat; the soldiers that had not had a dance with the smoke just went tearing away towards what they hoped was safety. After some hundreds of yards they reached one of the advance batteries who without a word caught the horror in their faces and began to shout and pull and jostle to try to get up the horses quickly to bring off the guns, for it would be a fearsome disaster to let guns be captured. But it was all aspiration, when the scores and scores of suffering men were beheld, staggering towards them like an insane enemy, the artillery men scarpered too; there was nothing else to be done. Anyone that lingered tasted the smoke, felt the sharp tines in his throat raking and gashing, and he was undone. Now and then miraculously a man seemed to run unscathed from the gloom, running all the faster for his escape. Rifles were scattered now across the pounded fields, as if some proper battle were being fought after all.

Willie Dunne ran with the rest. There was a bottleneck ahead where the ground had been fought over a few weeks back and the men had to get up on a rough road to make any progress at all. This, of course, engendered the wild fear of being prevented from escaping at all, and still the vile smoke came on behind. Men were slushing into craters to try to swim across and could not get up the other blessed side. No act of virtue or rescue was possible; every man had to do for himself.

Now three or four battalions seemed to be mixing themselves together: there were the remnants of the Algerians and some regular French soldiers and the Fusiliers themselves and there were lads from some Lincolnshire regiments that must have been driven across from the left. Everyone was gripped by the same remorseless impulse: to flee the site of nameless death. If it were a battle proper, these men would never have turned tail. They would have fought to the last man in the trenches and put up with that and cursed their fate. But it was the force of something they did not know that drove them shoving and gasping away from that long, long monster with yellow skin.

There were officers now along the road trying in a bewildered and puzzled fashion to get the men to turn around. They did not know what was happening and all they saw was men that seemed to be deserting wholesale. A rout like this was unheard of, unless a man was a veteran of the terrible push back from Mons to the Marne in the first months of the war. Battalions in reserve had to conclude that there had been some mighty breakthrough by the Hun, but this seemed entirely mysterious, as no one had received the least message in this direction, and no massed bombardment had been heard and endured. Furthermore, no bullets even followed the retreating and desperate men.

Now a weakened version of the stench seemed to be everywhere. It was getting into every niche and nook in creation, into ears and eyes, into mouse-holes and rat-holes.

But the danger then was at last passing. Men dropped where they found themselves, soaked in sweat, already exhausted men further exhausted by such a hard gallop across ruined ground. Willie Dunne was visited by a tiredness so deep he lay where he had fallen and plummeted further into a dreamless sleep.

He awoke to a yellow world. His first thought was that he was dead. It was the small hours of the morning and there were still torches and lights being used. Long lines of men were going back along the road, with weird faces, their right hand on the right shoulder of the man in front, about forty men in a chain sometimes. He thought horribly of the Revelation of St John and wondered if by chance and lack he had reached the unknown date of the end of the living world.

Smeared across the faces was a yellowish grease, the men's uniforms had turned a peculiar and undesirable yellow, and all the acres of the world had been seared and ruined afresh. Even the leaves of the trees, so fresh the day before, seemed to have gone limp on their natural hinges and twisted about sadly, not making the usual reassuring music of the poplars along the roadside, but a dank, dead, metallic rustling, as if every drop of sap had been replaced with a dreadful poison.

It was two days before this shocked stretch of Flanders could be restored to ordinary war. All the first day for seven miles it was said there was not a soldier in the trenches. The reserve battalions were marched up as quickly as it could be done, and the survivors went back to see if they could group up again with their platoons. Willie Dunne, frightened as he was, felt doubly distraught that he was alone in all this crowd of dour-faced men. It was then that he felt slight enough in the world, a creature of low stature. He wanted his sergeant and his captain and his mates the way a baby wants its home, no matter how provisional. And he felt a fool for feeling like that, but there it was.

He wandered back along the way of fear and no one said a word to him. Soon there were bodies everywhere strewn about, and burial details were busy composing them into sudden little graveyards. He passed through the wretched bottleneck and the drowned men in the craters floating face-down, and though he was fearful of what he would find he pushed his legs on to the lip of his trench. He half expected despite everything to see his pals crouched down and easy, drinking their tea, scuttling along to take a crap in the latrines, someone on sentry duty, someone singing, but all he saw was a place that had turned into a mere pit of death.

The hole was filled with bodies, and to him they looked like dozens and dozens of garden statues of the sort you might see in Humewood, where his grandfather had worked, fallen down like figures from some vanished empire, thinkers and senators and poets unknown, with their hands raised in impressive attitudes, their stone bodies for some reason half clothed in the uniforms of this modern war. The faces were contorted like devils' in a book of admonition, like the faces of the truly fallen, the damned, and the condemned. Horrible dreams hung in their faces as if the foulest nightmares had gripped them and remained visible now frozen in direst death. Their mouths were ringed and caked with a greeny slime, as if they were the poor Irish cottagers of old, who people said in the last extremity of hunger had eaten of the very nettles in the fields. And still the echo, foul in itself, of that ferocious stench hanging everywhere.

And down on the fire-step across the chasm of the trench, quite naked, his uniform cast all about him like the torn petals of a flower, with a face to match the other faces tortured eternally in a last agony, that decent man who did not wish to leave his post, heaped about everywhere with Algerians and Irishmen equally, a man that knew well the hard task that was in the liming: Captain Pasley.

"God rest his soul," murmured Willie Dunne.

Then Willie found John Williams, Joe Clancy, Joe McNulty. A dozen men and more who had been bound to him by some bond he didn't know the explanation of. Willie's very stomach was torn by sorrow, his very eyes were burned by sorrow, as if sorrow itself were a kind of gas. He was so disgusted somehow he thought he might puke like a dog. In the disgust was a horrible push of anger that dismayed him entirely. Like an old man, he walked back over to stand stupidly by the captain's body.

Father Buckley was down among the dead also, going from stiff head to head, choking himself from the residues of the smoke. Now they knew it was a filthy gas sent over by the filthy Boche to work perdition on them, a thing forbidden, it was said, by the articles of war. No general, no soldier could be proud of this work; no human person could take the joy of succeeding from these tortured deaths. Father Buckley muttered quickly at each set of unlistening ears; he was anxious it would seem to include them all in the roll-calls of the saved, to get them, in particular after such an utter ruin of things, to possible paradise.

"Is that you, Willie?" said Father Buckley, when he reached Captain Pasley.

"It is, Father," said Willie.

"Isn't this the saddest thing you've ever seen?"

"It is, Father," he said.

"Who is this man here?" asked the priest.

"Captain Pasley from Tinahely."

"Of course it is, Willie," said the priest, kneeling to the naked form. He did not seek to cover him up; maybe he respected this simple aspect of a ruined man. "I wonder what religion is written in his small-book?"

"I think he wasn't a Catholic, Father. Most of the strong farmers in Wicklow there are Church of Ireland men."

"You are probably right, Willie."

Father Buckley knelt in close. Of course, you cannot take a last confession from a voiceless man. But there must have been some small ceremony that could be offered, because the priest was mumbling in his little singing voice.

"Do you know his family there in Wicklow?" said the priest then, rising stiffly.

"I think I would know the house. The Mount it is called, I think. He used to talk about the work there. I think he loved the bit of land they have there. My grandfather will know them, I am certain."

"He's a farmer there, your grandfather?"

"He was the steward on the Humewood estate. He is one hundred and two years old now. He knows all that world."

"Well, if chance should bring you down that way, Willie, will you go in and tell them how he died? Not this dreadful end. But that everyone knew he elected to stay so that no one could say he left without orders."

"I will say it to them if I am down there because that is what happened, Father."

"It is."

"How are you yourself?" said Father Buckley.

They stood quite carelessly, not really thinking of their safety. They knew the Germans would not shoot today. Christy Moran opined that the gas had shocked even them. They were ashamed, he said, and would let them bury the dead. The awful gap in the line that the gas had made, which had the general shouting, it was said, back at headquarters, and swearing, was not molested again in any way by them. They did not seek to take their advantage. It was as if in the laden baskets of tragedy of this war, this one act had the weight of a boulder that no man's strength could shift. Everyone was amazed and afrighted.

"How are you yourself, Willie?" said the priest again when he got no answer. He wanted to say that Willie would feel the death of his first captain the most sorely, that after this it would be easier, but he didn't say it somehow.

Willie could find no useful words to offer. He wanted to say something, at least not to show him discourtesy or roughness.

They stood there two feet apart in all that vale of tears, one man asking another how he was, the other asking how the other was, the one not knowing truly what the world was, the other not knowing either. One nodded to the other now in an expression of understanding without understanding, of saying without breathing a word. And the other nodded back to the other, knowing nothing. Not this new world of terminality and astonishing dismay, of extremity of ruin and exaggeration of misery. And Father Buckley did not know anything but grief, and Willie Dunne on that black day likewise.

Five hundred men and more of Willie's regiment dead.

As they stood there a strange teem of rain fell down from the heavens. It rattled, veritably rattled on their human shoulders.

That evening Father Buckley was around asking if anyone wanted communion. He had a little travelling communion thing he carried. And the priest asked Willie if he wanted communion and Willie said he didn't and then the priest took his right hand and shook it and when that was accomplished Father Buckley went on his way.

After that battle where no one fired on them and not a shell was lobbed over at them, the survivors thought their thoughts.

Willie kept thinking a queer thought. That he was only eighteen years of age, nineteen this coming birthday.

"He should have run like the rest of us," was Christy Moran's comment. "Not run — I mean, withdrawn."

"How do you mean, sir?" said Willie Dunne suspiciously.

"He was a fool to stay there like that, Willie; he was a fucking eejit, as a matter of fact."

Willie was steaming about that. He couldn't bear to hear the sergeant-major say such things. Captain Pasley had made his decision and they had made theirs. It was a sacred matter really.

Willie wanted to say this as vigorously as he could. In fact he wanted to strike the sergeant-major for himself. It was the one time he thought maybe the sergeant-major was not just a bit of a bollocks, but a bollocks through and through. It never occurred to him that the sergeant-major might have spoken only out of his own version of sorrow.

They buried their five hundred men, five hundred vanished hearts, in yet another new yard in the general mire of things.

It was a while before they could fetch a lot of them in, because the Hun soon perked up, but they managed it. The Royal Army Medical Corps boys were fearless, and there was no glamour in the job at all. And the chaplains came and said their say. Father Buckley uttered familiar words, and the Protestant chaplain likewise. The little rabbi came out also, and said a few Hebrew words for Abrahamson from Dublin and a fella called Levine from Cork. Willie Dunne and his friends sang a hymn, "Yea, though I Go through the Valley of Death". Christy Moran's voice truly sounded like a kicked dog. The men who wielded the spades were thankful enough the summer was nearly there and the earth had dried but not hardened. They were small Chinese men with little moustaches and pigtails; coolies, they were called, a race of diggers that kept themselves apart or maybe were kept apart. The Chinamen dug the holes, five hundred of them. They were filled with Catholic, Protestant and Jewish Irishmen.

Soon the places were filled with new men from home. Flocks and flocks and flocks of them, thought Willie. King George's lambs. It was just a little inkling of a thought.

Now summer was spent in the rearrangement and building up of their battalion — that was the official plan anyhow. Their sector quietened down. They blew the blue smoke of their fags up to the blue sky. They ate like dogs and shat like kings. They stripped to the waist and got black as desert Arabs. The white skins were disappearing. Mayo, Wicklow, it didn't matter. They might be Algerians now, some other bit of the blessed Empire.

They knew violent battles were afoot in other parts of the line and they all heard the hard stories of the Irish soldiers in the Dardanelles. Again and again was rehearsed the horrors of the landing in April, when lads had tried to get out of the ship The River Clyde onto the beach, and been gunned down in their hundreds as they emerged from rough holes cut in the bow. Dublin lads that had never seen a moment of battle till that moment of their death. The story always ended with the detail that the water had turned pink with the slaughter.

"So you can get yourself rightly bollocksed in any corner of the earth now," said Christy Moran.

"Is that right, Sergeant-Major?" said Willie Dunne.

"Ah, yeh, it's not just here, Willie, boy. Sure you have a choice now."

"Well, that's handy," said Pete O'Hara jocularly.

"You see," said Christy Moran — he happened to be trying to pull a big stain out of his tunic with old tea, which was more or less making the stain worse — "you cannot keep news from an Irishman. In the old days, a new song could cross from London to Galway in a day and a night."

"Is that a fact, Sarge?" said Pete O'Hara, after a moment.

"Anyhows," said Christy Moran, looking suspiciously at O'Hara, "a good song would cross from London to Galway, because the bellhops in the hotels would be singing it, from heart to fucking heart. It would be in Galway by nightfall. But now it's not songs, but bad news that crosses, and crosses the world at that. From Irishman to Irishman. The fucking British army is full of us. It should be called the fucking Irish-British army."

There was a long silence then as the listeners imbibed this notion.

"Well, there you are, Sarge" said Pete O'Hara.

And winter came in then like a hawk to afright the mice in the fields, like a wolf to test the stamina of his foes. Like a travelling salesman it brought all its white cloths and laces and spread them everywhere, on mucky trench sides, on battered roads, on the distant stubbled fields, it laid its stores of rime and frost in little luckless pockets, in turns of earth, it tried to go one better than the spring, giving the girlish trees long coats of glistening white, tenderly and murderously gilding the lily of everything, the autumn's wildflowers bravely putting out a few mad flags of red and yellow. Thunderously without a whisper it drove the sap back in every green thing such as remained after the long destruction of the warring men.

Now Willie's lot were shunted back almost to the edge of the true world where there were quite peaceful-looking farms all frosted and beautiful under the moon, crisp and familiar as some stretch of Irish midlands under the struggling light of day. Even woods were impressively standing. The roads were all cobbled with mere fieldstones as you might find in a Wicklow yard, and they were rough ways to walk upon, in your hobnailed boots. But they marched the roads in three stages, and although they were weary from the stretch in the trenches, nevertheless they took some pride in their marching. Exhausted boys were carried by their pals, so as not to hinder the rate of progress. It was good to get the blood going round and it was better than sitting in trenches with the frost threatening fingers, toes and noses without cease. There was a timetable for everything and it pleased the men to make their distances on time.

Maud had sent him out a sheepskin jacket for his nineteenth birthday and Willie wore it gratefully in the fierce air. His legs thumped along the roads. He thought time and again of the gangs of men that would have lain these cobbles in. He wondered did they batter up a mix of clay and ashes like they would at home, and spread out the slush till it rose about two inches from the required level, and then on their knees, had they pressed in the cobbles and tamped them level with a decent floor beam? He didn't think there could be a hundred ways to do such a job. He began to think indeed that the methods of building were common to men everywhere, the ways of the ants and the ways of the bees were known to ants and bees wherever they might range about. He saw that the roads had been given a nice camber, so that the rain would run off quick and not cause mischief. There were miles and miles of it, with oftentimes highly pleasing stands of poplars for miles also.

The people in the farms seemed indifferent to them.

O'Hara marched beside him, and O'Hara wasn't a bad fellow by any gauge. His red hair burned out from under his helmet.

Captain Sheridan, the new man in after poor Pasley, had a very merry way about him. He might have been thought handsome but that he had two queer-looking blooms of red, broken veins or the like, on his cheeks, which gave him the air of a circus clown at first sight. But he liked to hear the men singing anyhow.

And it did Willie Dunne more good than food to open his mouth and heart and sing "Tipperary", the long line of men bawling it out.

Every man Jack of them knew "Tipperary" and sang it as if most of them weren't city-boys but hailed from the verdant fields of that county. Probably every man in the army knew it, whether he was from Aberdeen or Lahore. Even the coolies sang "Tipperary" while they dug; Willie had heard them.

The men near to him liked to hear Willie sing because his voice reminded them of the music hall. It was as good as any of those tuppenny tenors they had there. Pete O'Hara too, it was noted, had a decent voice.

Then they sang "Your Old Kit Bag". And they sang "Charlotte the Harlot", which was a good song, and they sang "Take Me back to Dear Old Blighty", even though none of them were from dear old Blighty, but how and ever.

"Keep the Home Fires Burning" was a favourite but not on a march; that was for some quiet evening in the reserve trenches.

Then, by request of the captain, they sang "Do Your Balls Hang Low". It had been a revelation and an especial delight that Captain Sheridan, unlike Captain Pasley, who had been a little restrained in such matters, favoured this song above all other marching songs:

72

Can you sling them on your shoulder
Like a lousy fucking soldier
Do your balls hang low?

Like Dan Leno dancing the fucking clog dance, Willie sang it — with infinite passion. It was a wonderful odd thing to see Captain Sheridan up on his horse, his head thrown back, bawling out those happy words to the lowering winter sky. Under his hat he looked like a boy, did Sheridan. And that passed a mile or two just nicely.

The only thing different now was that when Willie sang too mightily he felt a dire need to cough. It was the little bit of gas remaining, he thought, in his chest, some little whirling marble of wretched gas that was upsetting his means of singing. But the men didn't mind a bit of spluttering and for the most part he got through without too much impediment.

He was gay enough, in such singing times. But he couldn't shake off the feeling of being knackered, knackered somewhere deep in himself — something going wrong, in the very centre. In the corner of his eye there was always a black shadow now, something, someone, some afflicted figure looming there, like an angel or a meagre spectre. He couldn't quite make out the features of the spectre but he thought it might be Captain Pasley. It chilled him. And in general terms now he found it impossible to get truly warm, which was, he knew, an affliction of old men.

The sorrow he had felt at the death of his captain, and Williams and Clancy, something had happened to that sorrow. It had gone rancid in him, he thought; it had boiled down to something he didn't understand. The pith of sorrow was in the upshot a little seed of death.

Sometimes he wanted to cry out against his officers, his fellows, even his own heart, and he didn't know what stopped him, he didn't.

CHAPTER
FIVE

They were adjudged to have been through a bit of bother and then a long time left in trenches and were being rested conscientiously in Amiens. It would not last more than a few days, and they had to make the most of it.

Willie Dunne and O'Hara went forth one evening from their billet to see what they could see. The sun was falling off the edge of the world like a burning man. The sergeant-major had given them good directions and they had a scrap of paper with the name of a street on it, which brought them to the best estaminet in Amiens, for a private soldier, anyhow. And it was bursting with private soldiers, of many different regiments, strangers to Willie and Pete O'Hara, but also, being marked by the shadows of the same war, not strangers. The drink of the place was a shit-coloured beer.

Willie Dunne had not been a man for drinking in his short life and yet he had taken his ration of bleak rum now every day this last few months, and he found the beer was like water in his mouth.

But he liked the bolts to be loosened on his concerns like any other soldier. He liked the warm swill of the beer and the heat in his stomach and the thoughts it prompted.

"Well, Pete, this is not so bad now!" he shouted to O'Hara above the din of the estaminet.

"What's that?" called O'Hara.

"Not so bad now!" shouted Willie.

"Not so bad!"

This wasn't a spot he could have brought Gretta, anyhow. He wished so deep in his heart that she had been able to take up her pen more often — or even once, for the love of Jesus — and write to him. Maybe she had written and the letters had gone astray, as any letters might in the strange "streets" and "avenues" of the trenches. The first time he ever saw her she had been writing, so he knew she had the alphabet and all the rest; of course she did, she had brains to burn.

"More beer, Willie, more beer!" shouted O'Hara.

"More beer, more beer!" called Willie.

The ruined face of Captain Pasley hung over all like a moon. The man in the moon was Captain Pasley with his twisted arms and his dancing hands.

Willie's head was rushing now.

Maybe there was a poison in this tepid water. Maybe there was worse than poison, maybe there were dead men's destroyed dreams milled down into powder and scattered in these bitter glasses.

Now the room was a wash of colours, as if the room itself were a glass of suspect beer. The khaki jackets smeared in long trails, the laughing, shouting faces likewise, like the balls of comets foretelling neither good things nor bad, empty omens, horribly empty men.

How could this estaminet be spinning like a great wheel, the songs going round and round, in a great trail of stars and colours? It was beautiful, after a fashion. O'Hara was dancing now with a girleen, it seemed so gay and good, and now Willie was being dragged to his feet, "No, no, I do not wish, I do not, non, non," but he was laughing, the truth must be told, he was kind of raging within, he was laughing and crying, Gretta was dancing in his daft head with Captain Pasley in a silver trail of stars, in the tail of a comet that promised heaven to the world, and good purpose to all things, and the loving chanting of God.

They were danced, O'Hara and himself, into a deeper room. Willie went crashing down onto a mattress that had lived a long and ruinous life — there were fearsome gashes in it all over and the hair of a dozen horse tails was spewing out. The room stank of powder, something like oil, and other odd, fierce smells.

But the girl who had pulled him up to dance was a beauty right enough. Truth to tell she was. He lay on the ancient bed and looked up at her. She wore only a loose shift and a long petticoat like a queer metal, and he glanced hastily at her fat, trim breasts, in case she would take offence at his staring. From the crown of her head dropped hair as black as a dark corner. Thick, thick black hair like a smudge of night she had, and clear, clever eyes the colour of the dark blue feathers in a magpie. My God, he thought, she was like a goddess.

She seemed to Willie more beautiful than any woman he had ever seen.

"Money for fuck?" she said.

"Hah?" he said. But he knew what she had said, because she had said it very clearly, through her small, sharp teeth.

"Shillings," she said. "Fuck shillings?"

He looked over at O'Hara and he had wasted no time at all and had climbed up on the other girl. His bare arse was pumping in and out, but his trews were pulled only down to his knees. Two little footballs of lard, it looked like. Two other soldiers were at the same work indistinctly in other corners. The girl leaned down and took the hem of her petticoat in her brown hands, and slowly raised herself again, her breasts tumbling about a little in a way that made Willie's pecker so hard it was trying to strangle itself on his under-drawers. As she straightened, the hem was raised, and her thighs revealed, the skin as white as eggs, and then the pitch-black shiny hair between her legs.

"Mercy," said Willie.

She smiled and dropped the petticoat and he smelled the heat from there blown out at him. She unfastened his belt and trousers, and pulled trousers and drawers down with a rough yank. Willie glanced down at himself, the flattened wig of his hairs there, and his pecker lolling to one side but blatantly uncovered. He was suddenly afraid that O'Hara would see him naked but he had no need to worry about that. O'Hara was deep in his own pleasure, and was gasping and giving out little shouts. The girl as beautiful and rare as a black rose hoisted her petticoat again and climbed neatly onto him, and leaned her face to his, and laid her soft cheek on his. She manoeuvred his pecker into herself and suddenly he felt that graceful heat.

It was remarkable, he thought, how tender he felt towards her. He sort of loved her for that while. He tried to gaze into her eyes right enough, but she wasn't a one for gazing it seemed. When he came it felt like what he thought being shot in the spine might feel like.

Then he seemed to sleep and awake. It wasn't like proper time passing.

The girl was over in the corner, sluicing her crotch out at a chipped enamel basin. He felt as if his brain were loose in his skull. O'Hara looked very glum and was sitting wearily on one of the awful beds. He stared over at Willie now.

"Will we go, Willie?" he said.

"Why you call Willie?" said the beautiful girl, giggling.

"Let's go back to fucking billets and forget this ould shite," said O'Hara. "It's all shite."

The woman beside O'Hara had a long purplish rash down the inside of her leg. Willie could glimpse it through her torn stocking. She grinned at him, as if wondering if he was the boy for a second lap.

"All right, Pete," said Willie.

They careered out into the bleak night. Amiens was teeming. The clanking matériel of war inched along the road, the men of the army passed like a river. There were new faces in the backs of trucks, all white from the sea-voyage and raw with ignorance, their eyes burning brown and blue and green under the awnings.

When they went back to the billet the sergeant-major was awake. He didn't say anything to them. He was lying on his army bed staring out of the window.

Royal Dublin Fusiliers,
Belgium.
January 1916.

Dear Gretta,

I hope this letter finds you and yours well. I hope over the Christmas you were happy and peaceful. Here is another year! I am sitting in these support trenches and the wind is coming howling over Flanders like a lot of old ghosts. There is a very quiet sector ahead of us with little or no bombardment and I think it is true that everyone begins to be dying off from the boredom. Not that we want to hear the bombs, but I tell you a tin of maconochie is not like a friend, not a welcome thing under your nose day after day. But at least we have proper latrines here which makes a change from other arrangements we have put up with. But you won't want to be hearing about latrines. I wish I could write to you about roses and flowers and love, and that I am coming home for good. We all do wish the war was over now, though make no mistake we will stand up to the Hun no matter what. I do feel I have seen the inside and the outside of war and you do end up here as hard as a nut, which is all to the good. Say hello to your father for me.

The wind is howling tonight. I wish you could see the frozen snow that lies over everything, it is quite something when you lift your head a moment above the parapet, which of course is a very foolish thing to do as there are still snipers everywhere, but we have the front line ahead of us for protection. Somehow we seem to be going through a time of peace more or less. The land is locked fast in winter and generals as a rule wait for the spring to be thinking of further things. We live day by day, my friend O'Hara and me get through the night-times chatting away like lunatics and when we have to go out to do this and that up on no-man's land in the darkness, we try and stick together. He is a nice sort from Sligo, you would like him, and I hope after the war you might meet him. He is what is left of our little group of mates now. He has a reasonable voice and he likes to sing with me in the daytimes. We are mostly sleeping when not on guard duty but you can't sleep all the hours of the day and when we are awake we are repairing the trench walls which is work I alone in this army quite like, because it reminds me of the work I did with Dempsey's, trenching for pipes and the like, and it keeps my spirits up. Then we are grubbing down and O'Hara has read his soldier's small-book and likes to boil everything in his tin till the colour has gone out of it. I fear to tell you that I haven't had a proper wash now for a week and God alone knows when we will get one, because we are told we will be going up into the front line in another week or two and then we will beaway from washing rightly. Even the line officers smell like old clothes. This is all farms hereabouts, with little stone farmhouses here and there, and we are billeted in the nooks and crannies of our own trench. I have carved out a happy niche for writing to my girl in. That girl is deep in my heart. I wish, Gretta, I had words for what I think of you. How high you seem to be, like an angel in the high sky. Luckily in dreams I see you, all bright and yourself. I am afraid you do kiss me then and often, and I am glad of it. Do you dream of me? I will sign off now and just to let you know I am always thinking of you.

Your Willie.

He didn't think "Your Willie" sounded very good and he crossed it out and put, "Your loving Willie." Then he crossed that out and put, "Yours lovingly, Willie." He always had trouble with the ending of letters, certainly.

It was a long letter though, and every inch of writing it he thought should he say something about the fallen girl of Amiens?

A couple of days later Willie and Pete O'Hara were at the latrines together. Poor O'Hara was yelping as he tried to piss.

"Jesus, Jesus, Jesus Christ," muttered O'Hara, with an oily sweat on his brow.

"What's wrong, Pete?" said Willie.

"It's just like — oh, mother of fuck — someone's lost a razor in my belly, and the bastard's trying to pull the fucking thing out through my bollocking willie — Oh, mother of the good Jesus, save me. Oh, mother of the good Jesus."

"You need to get permission to see the good nurses, Pete."

"Oh, yeh, that's great, Willie, I'll go and bring this to the nurses. Nice Irish girls. They'll be only thrilled. Of course. I just didn't think of it."

"Well, Pete, what'll you do, so?"

"I'm after telling the sergeant and he's going to fix it for me."

"Fix it for you?"

"He'll get me the necessary."

The sergeant-major had laughed apparently and said that those women were dangerous girls, that had been driven out of Paris and Rouen and other points for one reason and another. "But aren't they very fine girls?" he had said, laughing.

"All right," said Willie. "Well, that's good, Pete."

"Fucking bitches. I should go back and slit their throats for themselves. Of course, of course, lucky fucking Willie with his lucky willie, not a bother on you."

"Ah, here, don't be giving out to me."

"And I'm after peeking into my fecking long-johns and haven't I a rash the shape of fucking England all down my leg?"

"Ah, Jesus," said Willie. "That's bad luck all right."

And so things went on and so they arranged themselves.

His company as promised went into the front line shortly but it was quiet in that cold sector of the world. About four or five men a day were lost to snipers.

One morning just after stand-to a lad from Aughrim put his nose above the parapet, not three feet from Willie. Willie Dunne was drinking a tin-mug of dreggy tea so he was not minding, trying to soak in every essence of surviving tealeaf. To think it had come from China just to be boiled to death in Flanders. The lad from Aughrim had been only one day with them so far; he had been sent up among a group of replacements for what was called the natural wastage. Willie thought his name was Byrne and he meant to ask him shortly if he had any news of Captain Pasley's family, because Aughrim was only a few miles from Tinahely where their house was situated.

As Willie drank his tea a shot rang out from over the way and for a moment Private Byrne stayed where he was, and then fell back onto the bottom of the trench. Willie stopped sipping a moment. Then he saw from the boy's left eye, right from the centre of the eye it looked like, a bloom of red like the bud of a rose. Then it started to pump out fiercely, like a painter might try to paint vision itself, a conical jet of crimson.

The Royal Army Medical Corps could only come up slowly and after a couple of hours the boy still lay where he had fallen. He was alive and screaming non-stop. But Willie could not immediately give himself to the fact. He stayed put in his niche at first. After a while he couldn't accommodate the screaming any longer and he crossed over to the lad and knelt beside him. But no one had any morphine and the ruined eye must have hurt like a coal. What could Willie do? He wished he had had the composure to stay in his niche and drink his tea. He was doing the lad no good and he was certainly doing himself no good.

The tea was long cold and forgotten in his stomach when the private disappeared on his stretcher around the corner of the traverse, the bearers cursing every inch of the way. This lad from Aughrim would be bumped down now to the Aid Post and then on to the Clearing Station if he lived that long. Then on to a hospital and if that bullet hadn't done for him, he would be in Charing Cross Station before long, heading for an English hospital among all the thousands upon thousands of wounded and destroyed that passed through London. Men with half their faces gone and limbs lost and really and truly, ruined men, and then those more lightly wounded with their cherished Blighty, a wound that would take them out of the war for a little, maybe for good.

But Willie felt nothing but a cold despair as he watched the stretcher disappear. There were pains now and things now that no compassion could help. There needed now to be fellas brought up with guns, to shoot the most horribly wounded, like you might a horse. You'd never leave a fucking horse with an eye like that; you'd feel pity maybe, as much as you'd like, but you'd shoot it, to put it out of its misery. There needed to be a new sort of line officer like a veterinarian, he thought, because there was too much of this screaming and suffering. There was too much of it, too much of it, and it wasn't love or anything close to it to leave a young fella screaming on the ground for three hours. It wasn't love and it wasn't even like being at a war and it wasn't fucking right.

Christy Moran was strangely jubilant a few weeks later. They were back in the reserve lines, billeted on a right old so-and-so in a freezing and dilapidated farmhouse, not like their favourite old woman in Amiens.

"I think they're planning to give you a few days' furlough, Willie. Proper leave, home leave," he said.

He said it with as much pleasure as he might about furlough of his own.

"Jesus, when, sir?"

"In a couple of weeks or so."

"Oh, that will be mighty."

"Try and stay alive till then, Willie."

"I will, I will, sir."

CHAPTER
SIX

The sentry at the castle gate gave him a right look as he walked in, like the ghost of the war. The sentry, of course, was in the same uniform, but a hell of a lot cleaner.

Willie knocked at the familiar door of his father's quarters. After a good wait the door was opened by Maud. She looked like she was in a dark mood; her face didn't brighten to see him.

"What is it, what do you want?" she said, and he laughed at the fierceness of it.

Of course, she didn't know him.

"It's me, Maud — Willie."

"Oh mercy me, poor little Willie, oh come in, come in."

And it was with unusual joy that she pulled him into the rinsed room. It was all scrubbed floorboards, and there was a dresser of blue and white delph and really it was very shipshape, he thought, altogether shipshape.

After the long journey through the reserve lines, across England and over the Irish Sea, he would have been grubby even if he had started clean. But he had started in the state that ten days in trenches will leave you.

"I think before you are kissing me and the like, Maud, you had better fill a tub for me, and maybe give these clothes an awful seeing to, and if you had something to disinfect them well and good, and me into the bargain."

Maud drew back.

"Annie, Annie!" she called. "Annie will help us. Don't you worry, Willie, we'll get you clean all right."

And she rolled up her black sleeves and went down the back stairs for the zinc tub that was stowed in its place under the lower landing. She nearly collided with Annie in the door.

"Annie, dear, you will need to boil up some bathwater promptly and we will be washing Willie Dunne immediately."

"Willie, Willie," said Annie. She rushed forward and was about to put her arms around him.

"Don't touch me, Annie, I'm all lousy and God knows what."

"Well, we had better clean you off before Dolly gets back from school, because you won't be able to hold her off!"

"I'm sure that's right," he said.

Annie had the polio as a little girl herself and was left with a bit of a hump, but it wasn't anything too grievous and everyone hoped she would be able to get a husband.

"To leave you standing there like that," said Annie, desperately. "Without a kiss. But I'll warm the water in the scullery. Do you want a nice big lump of cheese in a bit of Maud's bread?"

"I do, I would heartily like that!" he said, laughing.

"Well, heavens, it is a nice thing to have you back, and that laughter, and you will sing tonight, won't you, some of those wicked songs of the war?"

"I will not, Annie," he said, "they are much too bad, and you wouldn't understand them anyway. I hope not!"

"And who will we have to wash you? My heavens, I will have to send for Papa, I don't know if I won't. You can't get rid of all those creatures yourself. And he was always a great man for the nits."

"He was always the king of the nits."

"He was!" cried Annie.

Soon the water was warmed, and the bath dragged over to the big window that looked out on the blind wall of the chief secretary's department, but that let in a wonderful stream of sunlight, as good as a fire. Dark, deep, rich Dublin sunlight, he thought, that would roast the back off you if you lingered. For the windowglass didn't let in the April breeze; it admitted only the sun itself. The blind planet sat above the city and you must not stare into it, his father taught him that years ago, when he used to wonder what the sun might be. But his father was ordinary and rigorous in his own mind, he considered the sun in a scientific manner, what its light might do to his son's young eyes.

And Willie stood there and thoughts he didn't welcome began to unsettle him.

He couldn't stop his mind going back to that year, '13, when his father faced the crowd in Sackville Street.

His father went into a shop in Sackville Street. He had his men massed at the O'Connell Monument, and he telephoned headquarters to see what should be done, because there were hundreds of fellas out from the back streets, milling about, and there were scores of respectable people, and children, trying to make their way through the strange crowds. And headquarters told him to clear the streets.

Oh, Willie knew all the details, and they were like embers now in his head, hurting him strangely. The darker details he had from Gretta's father, of course, the dark, hard details that had seemed bad enough going into his head, but had grown and spread there since.

Four men left killed. It was odd that those four men meant so much, when he had seen now so many others killed. But they did.

Dempsey the builder of course would never employ a union man, and they had worked all through the General Strike, and so might be said to have the characteristics of scabs. That was a bother to Willie too now, looking back.

Willie remembered coming home that night to this very room and his father was sitting alone in the dark, in his uniform still. Willie went up to him and asked him how he was, and got no answer. That silence in the dark room puzzled him that time and it still puzzled him. It terrorized him.

And he wondered at himself that he couldn't stand in his father's quarters without rehearsing the story over again. He felt like a traitor really.

Now his father came up from the yards with little Dolly led by the hand.

And Dolly broke from her father's grip and came running without a word to Willie and hugged his dirty legs. Willie stroked her head gingerly, adoringly. She was adding her happy tears to the soiled uniform.

"There you are, Dolly," said Willie. "There you are at last."

"Ah, Willie, Willie," said his father, all the great height of him, and the wide waistband straining as ever. "The veritable hero returns."

"How are you, Papa, and I've missed you. I hope you got all my letters?"

"And I hope you got all mine?"

"I got many, and I suppose it was all of them, and you were very kind to think of writing to me."

"My God, Willie," he said. "It was my honour to write to you."

"Willie, Willie," said Dolly, "what are you after bringing me?"

"He hasn't had a chance to do anything, I'm sure," said his father. "Leave the lad be."

"We'll go down to Duffy's after, Dolly, and see what big gob-stoppers she has for us," said Willie, a little abashed.

"You will of course," said his father.

Then he cleared out the bigger girls and Willie stripped out of his uniform and his long-johns and his father bagged them up and opened the rear door and flung them out to Maud and Annie for ginger boiling. Dolly sat on an old chair. It was a finely carved one but very spindly, that had been their mother's special chair in the bedroom of old, a dress chair. Dolly watched the show gleefully, swinging her legs like a clock gone mad.

"Can we not come in?" Annie teased, and her father roared back at her, like she was a rascally hen advancing into the house against the wishes of the yard woman.

So James Patrick, a man of six foot six, stood his son William, a man of five foot six, into the steaming zinc bath, as indeed Willie's mother had done a thousand times while Willie was a boy. And it was a strange enough thing, to see the policeman throwing on the accustomed moleskin apron kept for the purpose no doubt of washing Dolly still, and fetching in close the basin with the big sponge and the carbolic soap. And he lathered the sponge up mightily, and he started to lave his son from head to foot, cascading the water neatly over everything. And the lice must have been flying from Willie Dunne just like those poor men in Sackville Street from the batons, and soon the water was speckled with them, little writhing white creatures. He saw under the suds or through them that his skin was all blotched with red circles so he supposed he had the ringworm into the bargain. Certainly the nits must be in his head because it was terrible itchy now in the steaming heat. But his hair was only recently cut as short as the Viceroy's lawn, so the nits had not much chance against his father's nit comb, which he wielded now like a delicate surgeon, combing out the eggs.

Then he asked his son politely to step out and he fetched the big sheet from the range in the scullery and came back in and wound it round and round his son, till he sucked the wetness off him.

Then a pair of clean long-johns of his father's was fetched and the legs had to be rolled up and the arms, and then Willie put on his old working suit from when he used to go out building. His uniform would be a while drying, what with the heavyish material in it.

Then, when he was all shipshape, his father put his big arms around him, and held him close to him for a few moments, like an actor on the stage.

It was not a thing you would see in real life anyway, and there was a faraway look on his father's face, like it was all years ago and otherwise and maybe they were still in Dalkey and he was a little lad.

But he was a soldier now of some nineteen years and for all that he was glad of his father's arms around him, strange as it was, strange and comforting as it was.

"Come on and get a hat on, Willie, and we'll go, and we'll go!" shouted Dolly Dunne.

His furlough slipped by and seemed like only a handful of minutes. He spent some pleasing hours with Gretta, walking about the place, and she was very friendly to him really. Her father was thinking of deserting the army, that was the main news. He didn't intend going to France, anyhow.

His last evening Willie sat by the fire with his own father. He might rather have been out up the road to see Gretta, but he had a strong desire to linger near the bulk of his father. Whatever hard thoughts he had about him, his love for him was entirely undiminished. And he could hardly get enough of his breathing presence. The two chairs were pointing at the flames; there were four or five lumps of wood blazing generously. It was a plain dark blue fireplace made of slate.

"That wood came up from Humewood," said his father. "The old fella sent me up a good load, and that's the last of it."

It was pleasant though to think the very logs had grown up in the woods of Humewood.

They said nothing for a little while. It was an easeful heat creeping out and into their bones, for all that it was April. Just to the right of the fireplace on the old wallpaper were still the ancient marks of the measuring, when his father used to put him up against the wall like a fella to be shot at dawn, and place the volume of Irish operettas on his head, and mark the height religiously with a thick-leaded policeman's pencil. He could still in his mind's eye see his father lick the lead and peer at the new mark, delightedly or not, as the measure of progress might warrant. Even in the murky firelight now he could make out the marks clearly, for if the wallpaper pattern was fading, the pencil marks looked freshly made. But it was a few years now, of course, since they had abandoned that ritual. Plain as day were the last ones, two or three marks from different dates, but one virtually on top of the other, where his growth had ceased. There was an angry look to those last marks.

"I'll be retiring now in a few years, Willie, so we won't be here that much longer in the castle."

It was astonishing for Willie to think of his father retired. And old maybe too in due course. He could not imagine it at all.

"How many years will that be in the force, Papa?"

"Forty years, Willie. It was a good life till recently."

"How do you mean, Papa?"

"Ah, it's not the same now. There's all sorts of new villainy now that you could barely be keeping up with."

"You'll go back to Kiltegan, Papa?"

"I will, of course."

"The girls will like that. Annie will like that in particular."

"She will, unless I get her married off first!"

"You think?" he said, laughing.

"Well, sure, why not? She deserves her chance too."

And indeed and indeed, you never knew, and never mind the humped back.

"And you might like it yourself, when the war is over," said his father.

"Oh, yes," he said.

Then there was another lengthy silence. Willie stared almost surreptitiously at his father, the big, serious face. Willie jumped when his father fixed his eyes on him suddenly.

"It's rough out there, is it, Willie?"

"Out where, Papa?" he said. "Do you mean out in Belgium?"

"Aye, I do, aye."

"It is," Willie allowed.

"I gather it is, all right. That's what everyone does be saying."

Then nothing for a while.

"I think about it, Willie. I think about it. I think about a great deal of things. I pray for you."

"I'll be all right, Papa."

"Of course you will, of course you will."

"The only thing I wish you'd get going at is the letter writing," he said to Gretta the next morning. He was walking her down to Capel Street where she worked as a seamstress.

"I haven't been good at that," she said. "I will improve now mightily. I do think of you all the time, Willie. I'm tired in the evening when I get home and have to make a supper and then I just sit in my chair like a ghost or fall into the doss."

"And I wish I could be in that doss beside you."

"Well, some day, maybe, Willie."

"If we could get an understanding, between ourselves, a kind of engagement, Gretta, do you know?"

She stopped on the bridge, and stopped him, and turned him towards her, and surprisingly shook a finger at him.

"We have to wait, Willie."

"For what?" he said, a touch desperately.

"For the war to be over and you to be home and you to know your own mind. There's never any sense in a soldier's wedding, Willie."

"I know my own mind. There's nothing in the world more important than this matter, Gretta. I would like to be your husband."

"And I would like to be your wife, of all the lads in Dublin. Of all the lads in Ireland. Leave me here on the bridge, Willie."

"Why?"

"I don't want the bossman Mr Casey seeing us. He's like a bishop when it comes to his women courting."

"All right."

"Don't look so sad. I'll come tonight to the barracks gate and see you in safe, Willie."

"I do love you, Gretta," he said, feeling glum and unhappy in that moment.

"And I do love you, Willie," she said, and of course he was happier then, how could he help it?

And she was there that evening, as good as her word, and kissed him under the big Lombardy poplars along the grand canal, where the gates of the barracks were. It was like a brief furlough in heaven, kissing Gretta. Then she drew him back into the deeper dark, till he was aware of bulrushes and the light stink of water. And they lay down together like ghosts, like floating souls, and she drew up her skirt in the greeny dark.

CHAPTER
SEVEN

It was in the very seam of night and morning, and Willie woke with ease and freshness. His body was warm and his limbs did not ache. It was very odd really.

His brain was merely human nonetheless, and for the first few moments he didn't know where he was. The long room with its iron pillars stretched away and a fine muslin-looking light pierced in wherever the window shutters were not snug.

The room was full of breathing, those private breaths of human sleep. His comrades lay in the iron beds like prison men. There was a smell of polish and the pleasing murmurs of men dreaming. His pecker was hard and had a powerful desire to piss. If it was not one thing it was another.

Then well he knew where he was. He was in bloody barracks. His leave was over. Back he must go.

He scouted under his bed and fetched out the pisspot and pissed into it.

"What's up?" said a Southern Irish voice, and the soldier in the bed adjacent lashed upright, his travelling Bible falling off his pillow towards the floor, and into the wretched pisspot.

"Oh, my God," said the soldier, obviously disorientated, "the Word of God's in the bloody bucket. Who put that bucket there? Isn't there hooks for those buckets?"

He had a hollow face of uneven eyes and a twisted nose like a damaged bolt, and two queer little yellowshot eyes like the eyes of an ill-intentioned snake.

"Listen," said Willie, deeply embarrassed, "I'll fetch it out for you."

It was in a very sorry state. The paper of the Bible was that thin sort they put in Bibles, to fit in all the stories and suchlike.

"Look it, I'll give you my own," said Willie Dunne, though his own had been a present from Maud, with the same thin paper, and stuck in everywhere the letters sent to him, and a sacred photograph of all of them, made in a shop in Grafton Street before his mother had died.

"Ah, don't mind it," said the soldier.

"What?" said Willie. "You can't still be wanting this one?"

Now Willie Dunne held up the other ruined little Bible pragmatically in his right hand, the urine dripping off it. He could see that every page had been claimed by the wetness. Now the soldier also was gazing at it, as if reconsidering his reaction. The first instinct of a comrade was to be agreeable, because the life of a soldier was chancy, and this fellow after all was probably a new man. Nevertheless, the plain vision of his Bible seemed to overcome him suddenly, and he sat up roughly in the bed and swung out his stubby legs.

"You fucking midget, you," he said.

"What?" said Willie Dunne.

"Ah, you manky midget, you," said the man, now ferociously, and because his mouth of teeth was bad, he spluttered. What a change round. He had a Cork accent like an illness. And who indeed was he calling a midget? He wasn't much taller than Willie.

The little man launched himself from the bed and put his two hands around Willie Dunne's neck and squeezed. It was so sudden Willie might have laughed if he hadn't been choking.

Now most of the other poor men were awake and a few were ignoring the first event of the day and were dutifully setting up their shaving gear, and the doors were being unlocked and shortly the barracks orderlies would be bringing in the tepid water and the like. Willie Dunne was not fighting back one ounce and his face was going red now, and the other little man working away to strangle the living life out of him.

Suddenly the Corkman stopped and looked at Willie Dunne, as if they were sitting at a bar and sharing a drink.

"What?" said Willie again, half dead.

"They won't let me go to France if I kill you," he said, smiling now.

"Definitely not, no, they won't."

"And you'll give me your own Bible then?"

"I will, if you want."

"Get it for me, so."

So Willie stooped to his pack and reluctantly ferreted out his fine Bible and looked at it and offered it to the man.

"Ah, you're all right," said the man, laughing. "I'm not taking your Bible, even if you did make a hames of my own."

The man smoothed his hollow cheeks with a hand and looked about for to see if the hot water was coming. And Willie put the Bible back in his pack.

"Do you have a bet on?" said the man, at ease now, in his shirt, the sleeves rolled up. "I have a little be on 'All Sorts'."

"How's that?" said Willie.

"The Grand National," said the man, surprised.

"Oh, yeh, no, I don't."

"The Grand National is the poor man's friend," said the man, "and I'm the poor man."

Willie Dunne laughed. It was a fair joke.

"Kirwan's the name, Jesse Kirwan, Cork City."

"William Dunne, Dublin," said Willie Dunne, and they shook hands, despite the general presence of urine on Willie's greeting hand. "Who are you with?"

"The Dublins, like yourself. All the lads I came up with are mostly. We might have joined the Munster Fusiliers, but we decided to be awkward."

"Come on, the Dublins," said Willie lightly.

"Come on, the Irish," said the little man. Then he turned on a sixpence and said, "What did the Irish ever do?"

Willie laughed. There was a bitter tincture to that laugh.

"Lost a lot of lads at Mons, that's what," said Willie. "And Ypres, and the Marne. Loads and loads of young lads. That's what we Irish did, lately."

There was good hot water fetched in now, and he was setting-to to lather his own cheeks, and have a decent shave for himself.

"Well, then," said Private Kirwan, very pleasantly, "that's my answer."

Now the doors were rattled and the shouts went up.

Private Kirwan was still looking now and then at Willie Dunne, as if he was thinking on what had been said to him.

The girls of Dublin were out in force again at any rate, just like the year before, waving little Union Jacks. The soldiers in the transports were laughing and shouting at the talent on offer.

Willie Dunne strained above the heads of his taller fellows to see if he could catch a sight of Gretta. It would be difficult to see her among the crowds, but she had told him exactly where to look for her, if she managed to concoct an excuse to get away from her work. The bossman Mr Casey was a pious bastard and if he thought she was going to wave off a soldier there'd be no chance at all.

His new pal Jesse Kirwan had somehow got himself on the same lorry but he didn't seem to want to be gazing out much on the passing sights. He was hunkered down against the side of the lorry, not even perching his bum on the rough benches.

"Won't you look out at old Dublin?" said Willie Dunne.

"Ah, it's not my town."

"Can't you take a gander at it even if it isn't? There's rakes of girls just as pretty as anything."

"Are there now?" said Jesse Kirwan, and hauled himself up after all, and peered out across the planking. "Well, by God and all, Willie, you're right there."

"Now, see, you were missing the sights," he said.

"I was, boy. How are you, girls?" Jesse Kirwan called out. "Never mind these Jackeens! Don't you know the better thing when you see it? Up Cork!"

But there was little chance such raillery could be heard above the engines of the transports. Black smoke as ugly as death belched from the fretting engines. The transport boys were notorious for letting any type of engine out of the garages.

Well, Willie saw no one he knew. Of course, his father had told his sisters not to risk coming down to see him off. These were different days, he said. The spring sun ran along the river like a million skipping stones.

Then he saw her, just where she had said, on the steps that led down to the ferryboats. Gretta, Gretta! He waved like a maniac now, screaming her name, Gretta, Gretta. My God, she looked everywhere but at his transport, everywhere, and he was sick at heart suddenly to think she wouldn't spot him.

"Look, look," he said to Jesse Kirwan, "there's my girl!"

"Where, where?" said Jesse. "Give us a look, boy!"

"There," he said, "there, your one there with the yellow hair!"

But it was no damn good, they were past, she hadn't seen him, and Jesse hadn't seen her either. Oh Jesus, he thought, strike him dead. But just as she nearly vanished from sight, she saw him, and jumped up and down in her drab blue coat, maybe calling, he couldn't tell, but he waved again, he waved and he waved.

But happiness was general. There was a happiness in the new men, who had been released from what were truly the dull repetitions of the camps. Now they had the elation of actors on a first night, all hope and effort in their faces. Willie Dunne smelled the spit and polish on their boots, their uniforms in many cases just cleaned and ironed by careful mothers, their chins shaved whether requiring shaving or not, their different-coloured hair all sleeked and ready for the adventure. Many of these men had been born and raised in these very streets, played marbles along these very gutters, kissed those very girls maybe.

Gretta had come out to see him go, and that was as good as a letter — as good as ten letters.

"I'll tell you something, Willie Dunne, you have beautiful girls in Dublin."

"They're famous for it," said Willie.

"They ought to be," said Jesse Kirwan. "Lord above, they're beauties. Euterpasia or Venus bright," he sang briefly. "You know that one?"

"I don't," said Willie, "and I know a powerful lot of songs."

"Or Helen fair, beyond compare, that Paris stole from her Grecian's sight . . ."

"It's a good one," said Willie.

"I don't know, boy, it's just a song that my father sang."

104

"Well, you must teach it to me some time. Some of the old songs have very complicated words, that's true enough."

"Ah, it's not a singing song, not a singing song for soldiers, I'd say."

"What does your old fella do, Jesse?" It was very hard to hold a conversation over the noise, but Willie was intrigued by the man who was almost the size of himself.

"Well, what does *your* old fella do?" said Jesse, countering, and the transport swayed them both, making Willie bite his tongue from the crazy swaying.

"Policeman," said Willie, through the pain.

"That's a queer sort of a job," shouted Jesse Kirwan.

"What's queer about it?"

"My father wouldn't think much of that. My father doesn't hold much with laws and policemen and the like."

"What the bugger is he then, a robber?"

"A lithographer."

"And what in the name of God is that?" shouted Willie.

Jesse Kirwan slapped him on the shoulder then and they laughed like proper eejits, enjoying the general mayhem.

The open sea showed its dancing vistas, the wooden lighthouse in the sound of the river, the drowned man all swollen with salt water that was the peninsula of Howth. Willie could well-nigh feel pity for Jesse Kirwan, coming from mere Cork.

105

But in the next second Willie's head was banging. He feared, he feared to tell Jesse Kirwan what awaited him. He feared to tell himself.

The officer in charge, a florid-faced captain with a patch on one eye, lined them up, ready to embark.

Willie remembered he used to be down here as a little fella with his father, to watch the Irish lambs being loaded on, for the English trade, his father checking the manifests so that the numbers tallied. It was a caution against smuggling.

The one-eyed officer was very dissatisfied. He was shouting now at the corporals and the sergeants as if it was all their fault. The boys of Ireland were willing to embark, but it was mighty awkward hauling everything up the gangplanks. There were whistles and shouts and the civvy dockers were putting their hands to the ropes suggestively, and the engine-room was thrumming as if a thousand giant bees were milling there.

Suddenly Willie didn't feel so bad. Things were as they were; if you couldn't change a thing you had better lump it. All the din and to-do was strangely cheering. The sea air filled his lungs and unexpectedly he found himself ready enough to go.

Then an army messenger came up on horseback, from the city itself it looked like. His horse made a noise on the wharf like shipbuilders working at rivets. Eyes fell on this flustered soldier, with his air of urgency and a dispatch bag flapping on his leather coat.

Then soon there were officers re-emerging from the ship's bowels, and the soldiers were ordered back out onto the dockside. Had they been rejected at the last minute? Was the war over maybe?

"What's going on?" said Willie to another baffled private, one of the older men, his head as bald as a spoon — he had knocked his helmet back to scratch it.

"Don't know, bless me," said the man.

In minutes there was a haphazard, thrown-together column marshalled on the dock.

Suddenly Willie got an elbow in the ribs, but it was only Jesse Kirwan, appeared out of nowhere, and put in to make four.

Now here were the soldiers, marching back! You might think they were arrived at last in France, thought Willie, with a sad laugh, as he marched along himself.

They approached the city like very ghosts. Few citizens could be seen and the crowd that had cheered their passing had melted away.

"What's afoot?" said Private Kirwan, as if Willie Dunne, being not a recruit but an experienced man, might know.

"I haven't a notion," said Willie.

"Do you think they're to disband us or what?"

"I don't know."

"I'm one of Redmond's men, the Volunteers. You know?" he said, as if maybe this was something else that Willie wouldn't understand, something in the line of lithography.

"What's that got to do with the price of bacon?" said Willie.

"If the war's over, I'm not staying in the army," said Jesse Kirwan. He sounded quite angry. "I only came in as a Volunteer."

"Sure we're all volunteers," said Willie, a touch sardonically.

There was the O'Connell Monument now where his father paused just three years ago, ready to charge the mob. The bank-holiday crowd looked something similar to the crowd that had come out for Larkin. It was very peculiar, anyhow. Some of them were actually running from the direction of the Rotunda Hospital. At the same time there were groups of a dozen or so gathered in spots, looking back up the street.

Their column was fiercely halted and things took place now that no one could understand the purpose of.

For here now, as real as a dream as one might say, a little contingent of cavalry was drawn up just under the awnings of the Imperial Hotel, and at a shout from the officer in front, they drew their swords, pointed them forward, and went clattering and hallooing up Sackville Street.

It was the most astonishing thing Willie Dunne ever thought he would see in his native place. It was one of those dragoon regiments, with all the old plumage of the last century in place. But this was just Dublin in the modern day with all of modernity raging peaceably there in the principal street of the country, the second most important street in the entire three kingdoms. The wonderful short jackets of the dragoons clasped their waists, the dark black plumes streamed from their polished helmets, they looked like old Greeks, they were shouting now their calls of battle, the officer in front, who had the bent aspect of a heron about him, by far the loudest.

The groups of Dublin citizens suddenly broke out into cheers, as if moved beyond silence by being spectators in a battle. On they galloped like heroic figures in a vast painting.

Then, even more bizarrely, rifle shots crackled out from the General Post Office, in a most queer moment of ill-fitting likelihood, and then horses and riders started to go down, just as if it were some old battlefield, and there were Turks or Russians in the portals of the Post Office. With roars of pain from the riders and strange shrieks from the wounded horses, which hit the cobblestones with that shocking implication of bruise and broken bone, the charge broke up, and the surviving riders careered away down Henry Street or crossed back madly into Abbey Street, presumably to take their horses and themselves out of the range of fire.

The officer himself rode on regardless, never looking back, and it must have been three or four bullets were needed to bring him down, the skittering horse shot out from under him.

"Jesus, are there Germans in that big place, or what?" said Jesse Kirwan.

"I don't know," said Willie Dunne. "I suppose there must be."

Now Willie Dunne saw some Dublin Metropolitan Police men here and there, and he called out to one he knew.

"Here, Sergeant, hello!"

And the sergeant wheeled about and stared at Willie Dunne.

"Ah, Willie," he said. "Little Willie."

"What's going on?" said Willie. "Is my da anywhere around?"

"I haven't seen the chief at all," said the policeman.

"And is it the Germans have invaded us?" he said.

"I don't know, Willie."

"Look it here," said another man, a mere citizen, proffering a printed sheet to Willie.

Willie took a step towards him, which seemed to excite the captain leading the column.

"Step back in, Private," called the captain. "Don't parley with the enemy."

"What enemy?" said Willie Dunne. "What enemy, sir?"

"Keep back away, or I will shoot him."

And the captain hurried down and put his Webley against the poor man's temple, a very grievous thing, it appeared, because a horrible rank sweat broke out on the civilian's forehead. But the captain was content when Willie stepped smartly back.

The column was told to go on then, and they wheeled about across Sackville Street Bridge and on towards Nassau Street. They were hearing shots now in other sections of the city. Willie Dunne could not bring himself over the strangeness of it.

110

In proper order they were marched right through Trinity College, where there were students hanging from the windows, cheering them. But that mystery was ignored also, and on they went, out onto the lower corner of Merrion Square, then away along the swanky square towards Mount Street Bridge.

Here for the first time the familiar noise of rifle bullets passed overhead, and skipped up from the cobblestones, and as far as Willie Dunne could see they were being fired on from a premises just to the left of the bridge. They could see now others of their own troops coming up from Ballsbridge direction, marching.

His column was instructed to build a barricade across the street, and men smashed their way into the dwellings and pulled out nice sofas and hall tables, perambulators, mattresses. They made themselves as safe as they could behind these objects. Then they knelt to the gaps and were told to commence firing.

Meanwhile, the troops on the other side of the bridge continued to advance, line after line, and a machine-gun opened up from the premises and began to mow down the soldiers.

Willie Dunne could clearly see two second lieutenants urging them on from the front, and they were the first to go. Willie stood up now with open mouth. His own companions were firing as they had been bidden, and he was certain that some of the fire was going straight on over the bridge and adding to the murderous business afoot on the other side. The captain ordered them to stop firing.

111

Now they crouched among the furniture. "Made in Navan", Willie Dunne read on the underside of a chair. Navan right enough was well known for its furniture making. Whose bottom sat there usually, he wondered? Private Kirwan was just beside Willie, sheltering behind a plump cushion wrapped in an antimacassar, probably not made in Navan, Willie thought. Somehow or other Private Kirwan had got hold of one of those pieces of printed paper blowing about here and there and was intently reading.

Actually he was intently weeping.

"Are you hit?" said Willie.

The little Cork man looked up at him. He didn't say anything immediately.

"Are you hit, are you wounded? Will I call out for the stretcher bearers?"

"No," said Private Kirwan. "Oh, Jesus, Jesus."

"What is it?" said Willie.

"It's our lot," said Private Kirwan.

"How do you mean?"

"It's our fellas. James Connolly is out. And Pearse the schoolmaster."

"I don't follow you. Who are they?"

"It's here," he said, rattling the sheet, "it says it here, you poor gobshite. What sort of a man are you? It's a notice. To tell the people."

"What people?" said Willie. About forty more soldiers across the bridge were added to the dead or wounded, and the rest were now lying in among the gardens of the huge houses on that side of the canal.

"Here, give us a look at that," said another soldier, with a raw Dublin accent himself. And he started to scan it quickly. "Our gallant allies in Europe," the man read. "Who the fuck are they? Is it us against us? What in the name of Jaysus is going on?"

Now a sort of noisy silence descended, and Willie heard the groans and distant screaming of wounded men.

"What's going on, for the love of God?" said Willie Dunne. "I have three sisters up at home."

They were told to be ready now to charge, to relieve the men the other side.

"All right, boys," said the captain. "We won't be long mopping these lads up."

Willie's arms were weak and his rifle felt like an iron girder for some enormous roofspan. He lifted it painfully. They were poised to go, and Willie chose a convenient enough footstool to clamber over.

"All right, boys, advancing now. Pick your targets. Watch out for the men on the other side. Fire at the building only."

A machine-gun, which had been brought up unnoticed by Willie and positioned in a house on his right, started firing into the building some hundred yards away, as covering fire.

Just as they were all ready to go and in fact some strength was returning to his arms, suddenly from Warrington Place appeared six horses being led by a groom. They were beautiful horses, Willie could see, and he could also see the horror on the face of the groom who, whatever his mission was, was not expecting a war at the intersection of the canal and the Ballsbridge road.

The two horses in front reared up. For some reason the machine-gun started firing on the group. The groom went down immediately, his golden outfit blooming with red, and his horses in their panic started galloping up towards Willie and his fellows. Their order to advance was repeated, and over they went, running now towards the building, which was itself all bullets vomiting out of the windows.

Men were going down all around him. He had to dive into a doorway halfway down, and others were doing likewise. Of the hundred men who had come out with him there were three just at his boots lying dead almost on top of each other, their faces bizarrely staring at him. It was hopeless. The officer himself had been wounded in the shoulder. There was a little pipe of bone sticking out through his jacket. The charge broke up entirely.

He was standing there in the portico straining his eyes to the building. They would need guns bigger than machine-guns to get them out. He knew intimately the secret nature of that building, the two layers of granite in the walls, the brick facing, it was like a medieval tower for strength.

He heard something behind him, a clicking. Someone had come up behind him in the gloom. He turned about with his rifle raised and found he was facing a shivering man, a very young shivering man in a Sunday suit and a sort of military hat, and an ancient-looking revolver held in both his hands, raised towards Willie's chest.

"You're my prisoner," said a trembling voice.

"I'm not," said Willie Dunne.

"I need you for a prisoner, Tommy," said the youngster.

"No," said Willie.

The wounded captain behind Willie sort of reached in over Willie's shoulder and fired his pistol. The bullet tore into the young man's neck, and he fell to the marble floor.

"Rifle jammed, Private?" said the captain.

Willie stared at him a few moments. "No, sir. Yes, sir. No, sir."

The captain issued a sardonic laugh and pulled away again.

"Oh, God," said the man on the ground. It was a definite wonder he could speak still. There was a huge hole in his throat where Willie imagined his speaking equipment would be.

Willie thought it would be heartless not to attend to the man in some fashion. The old revolver had slipped from the man's hands and had slithered along the floor, and the fellow was eyeing it hopelessly.

Willie knelt down to him.

"I'm not going to shoot you," he said. "Are you a German?"

"German?" said the man. "German? What are you talking about? I'm an Irishman. We're all Irishmen in here, fighting for Ireland."

115

There was dark red blood leaking from the terrible hole, it was pouring onto the flagstones and soon it would be running out of the door and down the granite steps. It would cross the pavement, thought Willie, of Wicklow granite, and sneak along the cobbled gutter, and into the dark drain. It would leak down into the great Victorian conduit and go away and away to the river and the sea. It was his life's blood, Willie knew, well he knew it. The young man gripped Willie's arm nearest him through the khaki sleeve, but it was pain that drove him to it, animal pain.

"Oh, God," said the boy.

"There ought to be medical fellas around somewhere," said Willie, but he hadn't seen any himself.

"I have to say an act of contrition," said the man. In truth the blood was beginning to bubble in his throat, it was pretty horrible to hear. "Are you Scottish, Tommy?"

"No."

"Well, whatever you are, Tommy, can you hold on to me while I say an act of contrition?"

"Of course I can."

So the young man said his act of contrition. It was as sincere and contrite as any priest could wish.

"That sounded grand," said Willie. The man's hand had a fierce grip on his arm; it was surprising, the strength left in him.

"I only came out to win a bit of freedom for Ireland," the man said, laughing miserably. "You won't hold that against me?"

"No, no," said Willie, bizarrely, he thought.

116

"I'm only fucking nineteen," said the man. "But what odds?"

His blood was vigorous and generous. It started to fill his throat in the wrong way and the young man began to splutter and choke, spraying Willie's face and tunic. He was coughing now for dear life, for dear life itself. The grip began to loosen, to loosen and loosen, till the fingers fell away entirely. The man's head tipped back and he was gurgling, in a nasty, metallic way, like a banging lid. Choke, choke, choke. The blood was thrown over Willie again and again like a fisherman's net, again and again, and then the man was as still as a dead fish.

There was still a light in his eyes, just for a moment, and the eyes were staring into Willie's. And then the light was gone, the eyes merging with the deep brown shadows of the hallway. Willie bent his head and muttered a quick prayer.

They were moved back out of position and then shunted back to the ship. They boarded it in the confused dark, as if perhaps there were also urgent things to be done by them elsewhere. They were all and everyone stunned and horribly hungry and thirsty. No one seemed to have the story straight at all. When Willie had come out of the hallway, he had not seen Jesse Kirwan anywhere about, but he found him again on the ship. Not everyone on board it seemed had been called back into Dublin, and there were a hundred strange conversations going on, people asking each other what the ruckus was, why there were fellas with light wounds being tended to by the nurses, what in the name of Jaysus had been going on.

When Willie found him, Jesse was away near the second funnel of the ship, sitting as alone as he could on a crowded troopship. The huge funnel reared above him, sending quite a timid streak of smoke into the darkening sky. There was that sense now of the deepening sea, and unfriendly cold, and the realms of other things besides mankind. But whether Jesse was aware of this Willie could not tell.

Willie sat down beside him as casually as he could. The chill off the sea was making his nose run, and he was wiping at the snots that started to seep down. Jesse turned his head and gazed his gaze again.

"Snotty bollocks, aren't you, boy?"

"It's cold, isn't it?" said Willie.

"Do you want a fag?" said Jesse Kirwan, pulling a clutch of small cigarettes from his tunic pocket.

"No," said Willie Dunne.

Jesse Kirwan drew a nice old Lucifer box from his britches pocket and got the contraption to make a flame and lit his meagre little cigarette and pulled on it with a great movement of his lungs. He nearly pulled the red tip the whole length of the cigarette in one blast. Then he let out the dark blue smoke.

"These Volunteers you mentioned, your crowd," said Willie, "were they the crowd was firing at us?"

"What? No, you gammy fool, that's the other Volunteers. You got to keep up, William. We were one and the same up to the war breaking out, and then some of us said we would do what Redmond said and fight as Irish soldiers, you know, to save Europe, but a few of them — well, they didn't want that. You know. A handful really. But the names, you know, I know them well. Some of the best of us."

"I don't understand this volunteer thing," said Willie. "You're volunteers, you say — but, you know, I'm a volunteer too — I volunteered for the army."

"Ah Jesus, Willie. That's different altogether. You're a volunteer for fucking Kitchener. You can't be this thick. Look it, boy. The Ulster Volunteers were set up by Carson to resist Home Rule. So then the Irish Volunteers were set up to resist them, if necessary. Then the war came, as you may have noticed, and most of the Irish Volunteers did as Redmond said and came into the war, because Home Rule was as good as got. But a few broke away and that's who you just saw on the lovely streets of Dublin! Of course, Willie, the Ulster Volunteers came in too, but not for Home Rule, for God's sake. But for king and country and everything kept as it is. You see it now?"

Well, it was a veritable tornado of volunteers, that was the truth. If he never heard the word volunteer again it would be too soon.

"So where does it leave you, Jesse?"

"I don't know, do I, Willie? Where does it leave you?"

"Well, I'm not one of those Volunteer fellas. And do you know, Jesse, I'd like to ask you, because I can't work it out, did that bit of paper they gave out, did it mean the Boche were their allies, or what in the name of God did it mean? Our gallant allies in Europe. What does that mean?"

"What do you think it means?"

Well, Willie didn't know. It was cold all right, but there was a huge sky now of stars like wedding rings and all just thrown about against something as hard looking as an enamel basin. He half expected to hear them rattling. There was a great murmuring all over the ship that the talking men made, and the engines aching far below, but around that there was only the enormous single note of the sea. The green, green sea, darkening everywhere to black.

"England's difficulty is Ireland's opportunity. Did you never hear that, Willie?" said Jesse Kirwan.

"No, I never did, I don't think so."

"It wouldn't matter if England was fighting the French, the Germans, or the blessed Hottentots. Did you never hear of the French sailing into Killalla, Willie?"

"Oh, I did, maybe I did, yes, certainly. Well, years ago. In a history book."

"So, that's what you saw today, something like that. My father said it would happen. He sees a long way into things. And I should've paid better heed to him, I think."

"There's Irish lads, hundreds and hundreds of them, have lost their lives now fighting the Germans, Jesse."

Strange the grip of anger now when he said that, it seared along his throat, but he tried desperately not to let the anger escape. He was angry with this Corkman, but he thought the fella would find out soon enough his mistake. When he had a few bullets fired his way by the same Germans. And there was something about the man that you didn't want to be angry with him, at all costs. And anyhow, Willie thought a person should listen to another person first, and be sure of what was being said. Aside from that, the starlight was so crisp, so sad somehow, that his anger fell away. And on top of that, instead of a rough answer, that indeed Jesse Kirwan might have offered, all he said, after a neutral silence, was one very gently spoken sentence.

"Of course I know that, Willie," he said.

When it was time to get some kip and Willie went down into the light, he noticed that his uniform was badly stained with blood. It was the blood of that young man dying. Willie scrubbed his face at the basin provided and he tried a few scrubs at the cloth. There were instructions in his soldier's small-book for the cleaning of khaki. Yellow soap and a little ammonia in a solution of water was advised. But he had no yellow soap and he had no ammonia. He tried again in the morning but in the main he carried the young man's blood to Belgium on his uniform.

PART TWO

PART TWO

CHAPTER
EIGHT

Quick as a sleep and a shave he was duly back in Flanders just the same as he might have been with or without the events of the last days, which was enough to make his head whirl. Jesse Kirwan was sent on up to his own unit somewhere else, and Willie Dunne was sorry to see him go, but what could be done? Nothing.

The field flowers were just appearing; light rains washed and washed again the pleasing fields. In those parts the farmers seemed to have decided that they might prepare to sow a harvest. The little villages seemed queerly optimistic; perhaps the human hearts were infected with whatever infects the very birds of Belgium. The sun lay along objects with indifferent and democratic grace, gun-barrel or ploughshare. The war was like a huge dream at the edge of this waking landscape, something far off and near that might ruin the lives of children and old alike, catastrophe to turn a soul to dry dust. It was change so big in the offing that there seemed as if nothing could be done except to leave or continue. Even in Ypres it was said citizens were trying to persist, mourning every bomb that fell, every apple tree in every ruined garden, every brick of every finely constructed house, every speck of ash from the fires of habitual love. Nothing had changed just here where he found himself — utter change was just across the plains. Nothing had changed. But something had changed in Willie Dunne.

He found himself longing now for the solid words, the dependable thoughts, the plain and blunt expression, of Christy Moran, for his views on these curious matters, as he might long for the explications of a father. He had to talk to himself strictly when the panic rose in him, a panic that his sisters might be engulfed in some cataclysm beyond anyone's stopping.

He found his regiment in reserve not too far from a place called Hulluch and he was informed that the next day they were going up the line, which came as an unwelcome shock to him, considering what he had been through in his own home city.

But at least he found the sergeant-major his own sardonic self, and though Captain Pasley was dead, the new captain was that cheerful Cavan man, Sheridan, who had been through Sandhurst and everything but didn't look much more than nineteen himself. He was a tall, smiling sort of man, with a good hint of a Cavan accent, not one of those complete English types you found sometimes in the army with promising Irish names.

"Fucking miracle he got a commission," said Christy Moran. "They don't give fucking Catholics commissions in this fucking army. He must be of royal fucking blood or something, Willie. Were the Kings of fucking Tara fucking Sheridans?"

126

That night Willie Dunne held to what passed for barracks, a sort of low hut with a high bank of spring flowers raging just behind it. Way off in the distance clearly were heard high-explosive shells at their work, and he heard that big mortars had been brought up to Loos by the German artillerymen and extraordinary shells were being lobbed over, so it was something to look forward to the next day.

Although Willie might be hard put to describe to Christy Moran what happened in Dublin, it was harder nonetheless to get it out of his head. That that boy from Cork Jesse Kirwan should have been weeping was bad enough, but the young man dying had shocked him, shifted his very heart about, though he had seen a hundred deaths and more, and he was hoping that Christy Moran would have a cool perspective on the matter.

The curious part of it was that not many of the other Irish lads were talking about it. The news hadn't really filtered through, Willie supposed, and maybe it would be considered a little enough thing in the general mayhem of the war.

"The fuckers," was the sergeant-major's first judgement. "What the fuck are they doing, causing mayhem at home, when we're out here fucking risking our fucking lives for them?"

"I don't know, I don't. It seems to me a terrible thing. Just a bad, dark thing."

"And how does the thing stand now?"

"I don't know. They were holed up all over Dublin, and firing out at the soldiers, and us firing in at them, and the place I was, was a . . ."

And he couldn't really describe to the sergeant-major what Mount Street was like, he couldn't.

"Well, Jesus, they're going to get short shrift from the fucking mothers of Dublin, let me tell you, Willie, and what the fuck do they want anyway, to be Kings of Dublin or what?"

"I don't know."

"Fucking carry on of them. It will all blow over, mark my words. Anyway, Willie, — did you happen to get a bet on 'All Sorts', while you were there, like?" said the sergeant-major.

"Why, sarge?" said Willie.

"Because he's after winning the Grand National, the cunt."

"Did you back him, sarge?"

"I did not."

"Well, I didn't back him, but I know a fella that did," said Willie, happily.

"Well, that's good," said Christy Moran nobly. "At least some lucky bastard was thinking straight."

This day they were to go up to Hulluch and it was the Wednesday, but there was no day of the week holy at the war, even Easter week. News leaked through that the rebels were being shelled from gunboats on the Liffey and when Captain Sheridan announced this as the men were lined up four by four for the route march, most of the men, even the ones that came in from the

Volunteers, like Jesse Kirwan, and so might have taken pause at the news, and maybe dropped a tear, let out a cheer.

"You see, Willie," said the sergeant-major, just near by. "You see, Willie."

"All right, men," called the captain. "Come on then."

And they went on up to Hulluch.

It was evening-time now and they were in their new trenches. They had come up there in the darkness and they didn't really know how things were thereabouts, except of course there was a deal of firing and all the usual noises. The men were just talking as they always did, and they had had a decent enough supper, though scant. Willie was sitting in a corner of the trench where there was a tidy niche cut by some thoughtful person. It was a chance anyway to write to his father.

Belgium.
26 April 1916.

Dear Papa,

How are you getting on in the midst of all, are you all well and safe? I hope you will write and tell me. I saw the turmoil in Dublin for myself just as I was coming away. I hope very much you will be taking care and watching out. The men here are very scornful of the whole business. We have heard that the Huns put up a placard opposite the trenches of the Munsters. It said there was Fire and Ruin in Dublin and that the British were killing their wives and children back home. Well, the Munsters didn't think much of that, so they all sang "God Save the King", and last night I believe it was or the night before they crept over in the dark and got that placard. My sergeant-major said a lot of those fellas are out-and-out Volunteers and fervent Home Rulers and he would not have expected them to know the words of "God Save the King", let alone sing it to the Boche. I am praying that you and the girls are all right. What good times we had of it, when we were all small. Why I say that I don't know. There is not a man in Ireland that has served Ireland better than you. No one will ever know how much it has cost you. I am thinking of the ordinary days, going about the castle yards with you in the evenings. Mark my words, you have brought us through like a proper father. If Dolly had no mother, she had a father as good as any mother could have been, I do believe so. Please write first chance and tell me what has been going on.

Your loving son,
Willie.

After stand-to next morning and a daybreak like a row of sparkling dinner-knives, a strange slate-grey light mixed with sunlight that sneaked up through the ragged woods, Captain Sheridan read out a communication from headquarters to the effect that a gas attack was suspected imminently.

That was how they had put it anyhow, but the colonel came by later and put it more plainly. They were going to try to drive them out like rats, he said, and indeed the Welsh boys they had relieved last night told of hundreds of dying rats coming into their trench one day during their tour of duty, and it was sore suspected that some gas must have leaked from their canisters, wherever the Boche had them set up and ready. They came in, those rats, like fellas expecting to be helped, but the Cardiff lads that were there clubbed them to death as best they could with their rifle butts. So that was another kind of enemy.

The colonel was not Irish and it was remembered at headquarters that the Irish ran from the first attack at St Julian all those months ago. Willie and his companions had been issued long since with what were said to be the finest of gas masks. Yokes that went over your head, a kind of bag with a queer nose, and two big eye-holes. Like something the Irish Whiteboys might have donned when they crept out upon the countryside to burn hayricks and generally molest the landlords. They certainly gave a ghostly, menacing look to the men wearing them, but the wearer did not feel either ghostly or menacing. His cheeks got hotter and hotter and dirty sweat burned down into his eyes.

But the colonel stressed the need to stand firm, and he said he knew his lads would do so, and not be letting the terror get the better of them again. This word "again" did not appeal to his listeners. Everyone knew how many were lost at St Julian and even if some of the listeners were newer men and never had been there in that hellish time in the first place, no man relished a little bit of ironic talk just before what promised to be a nasty stretch.

To counter this, those that were inclined — and there were many, nearly all — went down on their knees with Father Buckley and had a quick pray. The sentries, of course, merely bowed their heads slightly, still keeping a weather eye on the mirrors that reflected the empty ground before them. Because they were in trenches which by necessity zigzagged every hundred feet or so, Father Buckley was invisible to everyone except where he himself was kneeling. But the twelve hundred men in the battalion nevertheless by some peculiar inner knowledge knelt or bowed their heads and a murmur of words rose up to the skies. Willie Dunne hoped God could hear them.

Father Buckley said the Our Father and a few Hail Marys and kept himself short. He didn't attempt a talk or warming homily because no one could hear him except the nearest twenty men.

Suddenly the enemy guns opened their filthy cursing mouths and belched forth a ruinous misery of shells. The men heard shrapnel searing about in every direction and the biggest bombs were being dropped it seemed into the support trenches a good way behind. But the men didn't drop a stitch of the Hail Mary they were halfway through knitting, one soothing word to the next.

Then mysteriously every man knew Father Buckley was done. Perhaps it was achieved by a seamless series of Chinese whispers, or Chinese winks and nods anyway. But it was a remarkable thing, Willie thought, a remarkable thing.

Of course, any fool knew it was bad news when the padre came right into the trenches. If they had been on proper orders they might have gathered in a field somewhere in the reserve lines and had a decent mass of it, and a sermon from his nibs.

It wasn't that he was unwelcome. He was well known because he showed his face everywhere, and though he was a bit strange and apart in some ways, the men liked him as they would perhaps a beloved aunt. If there was such a thing as a fearless womanish man, he was it. For he was gentle and spoke soft with a lettered accent.

There were round bits in his words where the men had sharp, and sharp where they had round, though indeed he didn't talk like a gentleman as such. It was whispered that he had been found in private weeping and yet he had been seen in a dozen battlefields tending to the dying with a dry eye and a murmuring word. A drink of rum he always refused, but he smoked woodbines with everyone and a woodbine was his calling card to a new man in. Religion as such he rarely discussed and sins or the like were not his constant song, though you could go to him for confession should you so have chosen and he would give you the stiffest penance he could within reason — within the reason of the war. He advised chastity all right, but only because a dose of the clap was a fearsome embarrassment to a young man.

Willie supposed Father Buckley was a man who had seen every type of wound the war could offer close up, because he had held every type of wounded man in his arms. He must have whispered last rites to headless men, and also to men with only a head left and the rest blown into a billion drops of air, he had surely felt the warm ballooning armfuls of entrails spill into his own lap, and strained not to lie to any dying man, to steady him and ready him for the off, like a flighty horse in the stalls before a race. Certainly he believed a man's soul would issue forth like a dove and fly up to its dove cot in the high realms of heaven. He told the men that their guardian angels had come back to them from childhood and were with them again, watching over them silently and lovingly. He had endured those that screamed in terror and those that screamed in self-pity, those that said generous last words — which might indeed be the memories that made him cry later — he had heard the sudden heart change that might rescue a man from the yawning pits of perdition. And indeed he had disappeared a few weeks back and it was said, also in whispers, that he had been given a week's furlough at home because his nerves were tottering. But you would have to expect that. A man, especially a priest, could not witness scenes like unto the end of the world, as if the armies of the West had joined battle with the armies of the East, in that wild apocalypse shown to poor St John, in his penal servitude under the Romans on the island of Patmos in that vanished world, and so on, without disturbing a few hairs on the head of his mental ease.

Be that as it may, Willie knew and everyone else knew without saying a word or exchanging a look that things would be of a harsh enough nature, because Father Buckley had elected to be with them.

The gas sirens went off suddenly and Willie nearly left the sanctuary of his pelt. O'Hara beside him jumped like a dog. He was trying to prevent it, but that cold, unfriendly terror flooded instantly into his brain. A sweat, incongruously chilly, formed in his hair under the helmet. Everyone struggled to don the wretched gas masks. Now if these were the finest masks in creation, they were a bloody muddle to get on, and there was always the fear you might be missing a little place where the poison might seep in. Captain Sheridan came up cursing from his dugout with Christy Moran, looking like storybook monsters. But they all looked like storybook monsters. The sergeant carried a canvas bag of trench weapons, more like the weapons of medieval times than anything else, sticks with nails in them, rough-cast things with iron knobs, and he was handing these out. Willie was given a thing like an Indian tomahawk, and he stuffed it into his webbing.

"All right, lads," said Captain Sheridan, but the words were darkened and muddled by the mask. He lifted it off viciously. "All right, lads, listen to me, look it, we can hold this now, we can. I want you to make sure you're well masked up, check each other's masks, lads. And just let the foul stuff go over. Don't take off your fucking masks for any reason. The gas'll fall in on us here and just sit for a long while. There may be a lousy attack following it. That's the important thing. And, lads, for the love of God, don't let the bastards get any further than this very spot in Belgium. You're to crucify the cunts, now, men, if you don't mind!"

And that was not a bad speech, thought Willie Dunne. It was a pity that the captain's voice trembled so. But you had to say something to fellas in this predicament. Three men up stood Quigley, who had come up only this very morning, arriving in with a few other lads. Quigley was a tall, gangly lad from the city. He had never seen a real trench in his life, let alone been expected to withstand some kind of assault that he could not fathom the nature of. He was having grave difficulty with the straps of his mask, and was muttering and staggering about. A big, clear, dark stain of piss showed now on his britches front.

And Willie was just glad he had his own mask on now and no one could see his eyes. The memory of the other time at St Julian was howling in his head. A hundred pictures returned to terrorize him. He shook his head in his misery. By God, O'Hara, whose leg touched his left leg, was trembling. His whole body was rattling. Suddenly Willie thought of what those fucking men were doing in Dublin and he cursed back at them, cursed them for their violent ignorance, he did. Captain Pasley's twisted form was illuminated there, it would seem, behind his eyes.

Through the silly murk of the eye-holes he looked at these twenty or so men in this stretch. The machine-gun crew were ready with their weapon to mount it on the parapet, three crouching men. Four men were assigned as bombers and had each a belt of Mills bombs. Better at least than the old beancans full of explosive they used to hobble together and fling at an ungrateful enemy. Maybe there was something

136

ridiculous in the scene. After all, every man crouched in the same direction, some head down now the German artillery had proper range on them and the shrapnel bombs were landing just feet in front of the parapet. They looked like the men at the back of any Irish country church on a Sunday kneeling on one knee in manly fashion, the women of the parishes ranged on the seats proper. But they were not talking of beasts and ewes now, it was not their God they were waiting for, but the long shadows of the friends of Death himself. There was no star of Bethlehem here, nor wise men nor kings, only poor Tommies of Irishmen, Joe Soaps of back streets and small lives. Heroic things had been suggested to them, and though they were not heroes as you might read about in old Greek stories, their hearts, such as they were, answered. No man could come out to the war without some thought of proper duty, some inkling of possible deeds to match the tales they heard as children. There were no fathers or mothers here now, no raggedy dresses, no ringing games, spires of familiar churches, no ancient stones set one upon the other, no St Patrick's Cathedral and no Christ Church. Only a furrow of excellent agricultural clay where they in their complete insignificance crouched. This was not a scene of bravery, but it seemed to Willie in his fear and horror that there was a truth in it nonetheless. It was the thing before a joke was fashioned about it, before an anecdote was conjured up to make it safe, before a proper story in the newspaper, before some fellow with the wits would make a history of it. In the bleakness of its birth there was an unsullied truth, this tiny event that might make a corpse of him and all his proper dreams.

The gas boiled in like a familiar ogre. With the same stately gracelessness it rolled to the edge of the parapet and then like the heads of a many-headed creature it toppled gently forward and sank down to join the waiting men. These excellent gas masks instantly lost their excellence for Private Quigley, who at any rate had failed to fit it on his crooked face. One size fitted all, but he had a wondrous cabbage head, and the straps would not lie down. Father Buckley rushed to help, and Quigley now was spluttering and coughing, and started to tear off the mask. Father Buckley was signalling wildly for him to do the bloody opposite. Now two other men at the other end of the trench were having trouble likewise and behind their masks were coughing and no doubt going as red as ripe apples in a good August.

The evil gas lay down in the trench like a bedspread, and as more gas came over, it filled the trench to the brim and passed on then in its ghostly hordes to the support lines and the reserve lines, ambitious for choice murders. Quigley had fallen down on the mucky ground and was writhing there like a python snake, the mask was off, and his wide eyes were black stones in a beetroot face. He was screaming between the choking. He was calling out and when he opened his mouth Willie could almost taste himself the awful gas that rushed gratefully in. And pity struck him. Yes, in the midst of all, pity struck him for the thousandth time, and he was almost grateful for the pity. Father Buckley

138

was in a paroxysm of helping and disquiet as if his own child were being horribly tormented. At least six lads now were entirely blinded and Captain Sheridan moved them roughly back to the parados side of the trench, and went from man to man remaining swiftly, to try to steady the group. Willie Dunne had just shat in his pants, he could not help it, no more than a man who was hanged could help the stiff pecker he showed to the mocking crowds.

"Oh Jesus," he said to himself, "oh Jesus, protect us."

He wished his father's lot could rush up now with batons drawn and dispel this horrible unruly gas, drive it off the page of the world.

"Papa, Papa," he said. Then he found a picture in his mind of the gates of his grandfather's house in Lathaleer, two big, fat, rounded pillars into the welcoming yard, with the mad hens going about the pack-stones, and his grandfather with his big white beard like a proper Wicklow man. "Grandpa, Grandpa," he whispered, "protect us."

Two of the machine-gun crew were still untouched and they scrambled their gun up onto the ground just in front of the trench and started firing into the gas. This was reassuring to the others.

Now, on top of the released gas, gas-shells were being lobbed at them, exploding with their own particular signature of hurting noise. The artillerymen behind them were also firing now, and they could hear their own happy shells going over as swift as young house-martins, you would think, and that was also a little heartening. There were so many shells in the air it was a wonder that they did not simply smash into each other. Then the machine-gun was heard no more. Something that they could not see had silenced it. One of the gunners slid back down into the trench still holding the canister of water he was using to cool the weapon, like a dying gardener or some such.

Then, equally abruptly, the firing of shells ceased on the Hun side, though their own guns continued, shell after shell, shell after shell. Then for some reason that stopped too. Even in the awkward masks, the men tried to glance at each other's eyes, to see what was happening. Pairs of frightened orbs stared out from the masks. No one knew. Quigley lay on the ground still as a sleeping tramp. This must be worse gas than the other stuff, Willie knew, if it could murder a man so quickly. The other afflicted men had the strange yellow froth pouring down from the mask itself, where a sort of bib folded onto the chest. They were staggering about so much that Father Buckley looked like a distracted mother hen, trying to tend to them. Maybe he was also trying to get them out of the way of the survivors. It was not a good thing to be facing God knew what with a poor bastard wriggling and thrashing in on top of you from behind.

Now there was that queer silence that was not a silence, because Willie could hear his own breathing like a water-pump, his heart pulsing and complaining in his breast from simple lack of air. All the world was close in and made of canvas; the level of distress in all his limbs was like a poison itself. Despite the masks now there was a stench everywhere, a stench in his mask, a stench

140

in his blood, his eyes felt like they were peeling away. Desperately he tried to keep looking upwards, up the steep wall of the trench. He got a thump in the back and he turned slightly and saw the sergeant-major passing roughly, gesturing for them to mount the fire-step. Christy Moran must have seen something above, for he had just popped his head up to see what had happened to that fucking machine-gun. What had he seen in the coiling mists?

A grey monster in a mask came leaping into their trench. He looked enormous. Whether he was or not Willie did not know, but he looked as big as a horse. He stood over Willie and all Willie could think of were Vikings, wild Vikings sacking an Irish town. It must have been a picture from a school book. He had never seen a German soldier before so close up. Once he saw three dejected German prisoners, poor maggots of men with heads bowed, being escorted to some prison camp through the reserve area. They had looked so sad and small no one even thought to mock them. They engendered silence to see them. But this man was not like them. He put his two hands on Willie's shoulders and for a moment Willie thought he was going to rip off the gas mask and instinctively he put his hands up to hold it on. For some reason, without himself actually registering it, he had got the funny tomahawk into his left hand and when he raised the hand the spike at the top of the short stick horribly drove into the underchin of the German. The man now clawed there himself and to Willie's surprise tore off the saving mask, which looked a very much more admirable design than

Willie's. Now Willie again almost on instinct struck at the man's face with the hatchet and it opened the cheek from the side of the mouth to the eye above. But such a wound was probably superfluous, because his own gas now assailed the huge man, his face not three inches from Willie's own, because the great soldier fell to his knees. He was roaring something in that German language.

There were three more of these soldiers now in the trench with them and, as if inspired by Willie's German, the Irish lads were making it their business to try to pull off the masks of the attackers. One Irish man got a knife driven hard into his belly and the German held him there like a lover, until Sergeant-Major Moran cut off the back of his head with a vile-looking mallet. Hands clawed at faces and necks. Captain Sheridan had been driven back against the wall of the trench and a soldier was beating him with his bare fist in the face through the mask, hitting again and again. This man was killed by one of the new recruits firing his rifle in terror into the man's back. The man fell backwards so heavily that his skull struck right into the back of Willie's head and Willie went out cold.

CHAPTER
NINE

When he awoke he saw nothing at first because his mask had pulled sideways and the eye-holes invited one of his ears to see out. In instant panic Willie tried to readjust it, thinking the gas would get him now for sure. But when he got the eye-holes right, he saw dimly Christy Moran sitting on the ground, like a drunkard in the small hours of a terrible binge, without his mask on. Christy Moran was sitting there and every few moments he was nodding to himself, as if he might be telling himself a story, and surprising himself with it.

Father Buckley was in his after-battle attitude, kneeling beside a dead man. The killed German who had loomed at Willie like a giant lay curled beside him, for all the world like a dead companion. The face was bruised and torn, the wound under the chin drying black. He was a little fellow like a whippet after all. Willie touched the man's arm and the dead soldier seemed all bone and sinew. He wanted to push the man away but somehow he did not. Quigley was just being borne away by the stretcher bearers, and miraculously he seemed to be still alive, though his lungs must be like some old gruelly hash.

Captain Sheridan was standing absolutely still and quiet, holding his gas mask tenderly in his right hand, his nice Cavan face like an elaborately decorated cushion, the bruises showing red and dark blue in a curiously symmetrical pattern. Then, as if these men were waiting for an unheard order, the captain bestirred himself and roused the sergeant-major and nodded to him and plunged down into the dugout, no doubt to try to phone back a message. He re-emerged immediately coughing and watery eyed, because the intimate gas liked to sink into such places. He dashed out a message in pencil in his notebook and Willie was told to run back to headquarters if he could find such a thing and deliver it. Willie Dunne was not a runner, but then who was a runner now?

He found the communication trench thick with the wounded, the maimed, men crying openly men shouting in pain, men sitting in dark stupors that heralded death. So Willie climbed up the parados and went that way over open ground. He hardly cared.

Then he looked back like Lot's poor wife to where the gas had come from. They could shoot him now easily. There were a few fallen soldiers in no-man's land, all of them seemingly Germans. Who shot them down Willie could not say. Because the ground sloped ever so slightly he could see also a good way up his own zigzagging trenches. There were heaps of men there also. Up the jammed communication trenches moved those eerie lines of blinded, miserable men, a hand on the shoulder of the man in front, a cursing, still-sighted man at the head of all, leading them away. Of the twelve

144

hundred, how many remained? How many letters would Captain Sheridan write tonight if his wounds allowed and all the other line officers with such mournful tasks? How many hearts stopped beating, how many souls to their allotted places, how many in the crowds now also clogging up the way under St Peter's gate, and did the saint wonder at these sudden hordes advancing on him with their Irish accents from the Four Green Fields to beseech the mercies of heaven?

The shit he had shat in his pants was hardening, making Willie Dunne's backside devilishly itchy.

It was Easter Thursday in that realm of myriad deaths.

Company headquarters was in what remained of an old barn. You wouldn't know something strange and dark had happened not much more than a mile away. The transport officers were shouting at the drivers just as they might anywhere at any time. The big munitions waggons were dragged forward by resplendent shires, as strong as engines, with huge, intelligent heads. They lifted their forelegs like dancers in a dance that had become stylized by repetition. They were almost ridiculously beautiful, like wonders in a story, and all about them ground on the columns of uniformed men.

Willie Dunne found the ruined barn nearly by instinct, thinking to himself, It must be this way, and eventually, mysteriously so it proved. The missing wall of the barn had been shored up roughly and there was a torn canvas awning for a roof. The three officers at their table, which looked like it must have been dragged out of an estaminet bar, were nevertheless neat enough. Their cheeks were shaven, although one of them had old-fashioned dundrearies, despite his years, which blossomed out at his ears. He had seen the major before, a Major Stokes, but the two other men were new to Willie. He came in and held out the scribbled note to them, covered in mud and blood as he was and certainly not shaven.

"What's this?" said Major Stokes.

"Message from D Company, sir."

"Who's the man down there?" asked one of the other officers.

"Captain Pasley — no, Sheridan, sir," said Willie.

"Oh, yes, Sheridan. Right, Sheridan."

"Bent as a cart-spring, Sheridan," said Major Stokes.

"What, sir?" said Willie.

"I wasn't talking to you, Private," he said.

Major Stokes read the note and Willie knew the information hurt him. He could see that clearly. The man's narrow face with a hundred pockmarks closed in on itself slightly. He put a hand to his forehead and tapped a finger there.

"That's another bunch of casualties," he said. "Christ Almighty." Then his face changed again. "What's wrong with you fucking Irish? Can't you take a bit of gas?"

"Excuse me, sir?" said Willie.

"Would you take it easy, Stokes, for the love of Mike. Can't you see he's been down there with them?"

"Now how would I know that?"

"He's covered in blood," said the officer. He looked like the sort of man you might see behind a bank counter, half his hair gone west, a soft grey pallor on his cheeks, which seemed to be squeezing his mouth like two puffballs.

"I tell you, you smell like hell, Private," said the major.

"Leave the poor bugger alone," said the bank-clerky captain.

Now the telephone was ringing and the third officer got his ear to it and listened, only grunting back replies.

"Would you stop interfering, Boston," said Major Stokes vaguely. "Can I not talk to this soldier without you heckling me?"

Willie Dunne felt only a numbness, a wateriness in his limbs. He was trying to read the man's face still, and not listen so much to the words. This was happening in front of him, but the death of the German man was happening still also. Now Willie started to tremble, not from any emotion he knew of, but his hands were rattling and he held on to his jacket to steady them.

"What's wrong with you fucking Irish?" said the Major again.

"I shat in my trousers, sir, that's the smell you're smelling."

"What?" said the major, enfiladed as it were by this honest remark.

"Shat in my trousers, sir."

"Why on earth did you do that, Private?" said Captain Boston.

"Terror, sir."

"Terror?" said the captain. "You say terror?"

"Why not, sir?"

"Well, you're an honest man, I suppose," said Captain Boston. "Yes indeed."

Major Stokes was just staring ahead now. There was a little table in the corner of the destroyed barn with a cut-glass bottle on it that Willie just happened to notice at that moment. Whiskey in it or the like, and three small red glasses beside it. It was like a fragment from another world adrift in these confusions. He wondered what went on here between the three, what they would talk about when he went off again. Major Stokes rustled the message in his hand, waved it about a bit.

"Fucking stinking war," he muttered.

The third soldier put the phone back on its box.

"What's the news from up there?" said Major Stokes.

"You can ring back to headquarters, if you like," said the man.

"To say what?"

"About two hundred dead Boche back there. Mostly in the trenches themselves. And they would appear to have finished up for today. No sign of any more of the buggers rushing over."

"That's excellent, that's very good, tip-top," said Captain Boston, and glancing at Willie.

"In the trenches?"

"Yes. Hand-to-hand stuff."

"Good at that sort of thing, the Irish," said Major Stokes, but it was difficult for Willie to know if it was meant as a compliment to the nation or what.

"Sheridan has a pretty miserable estimate of his casualties. Half his company, he says here. Wants his men relieved."

"I just got the total there of the battalion casualties," said the third officer.

"Well?" said the major mildly enough. "Whatever it is, I cannot relieve them."

"Eight hundred," said the third man succinctly.

"Out of twelve hundred men?" said Major Stokes.

"Yes."

"My good Lord," said Major Stokes.

The long pockmarked face stared into Willie's now. Hard to say if the man was really looking at him, though. He was definitely weeping, but not the weeping of a weeping person exactly — it was incongruous and peculiar weeping.

"How will the clearing stations deal with that?" said the major, and now he was trembling too, like Willie. Neither was trembling because he was afraid, or not just because he was, but because the world and the dealings of the world had set the pendulums of their hearts swinging, had set whatever they were swaying back and forth.

"They'll have to manage, David," said the third officer, who Willie now noticed was also a major.

"Poor fuckers, they will," said Major Stokes. "Poor lines of blind fucking men and worse traipsing about all over the football pitch."

"The what, sir?" said Willie Dunne.

"Go back to Sheridan, go back to Captain Sheridan, Private. Tell him I'll ring headquarters now and ask the general to do something about replacements. But he'll have to hold the fucking line till something is sorted. I'll send him a bunch of fucking coolies to bury his dead. And I'll send him a few fucking buckets of hot fucking stew or something. Isn't that what you Irish eat? And if the quartermaster can spare a tun or two of rum, he shall have that too."

"All right, sir," said Willie.

"And wash that fucking arse of yours, Private. This is the fucking army, you know. Not the fucking Dublin slums."

"Yes, sir."

"What's your name, Private — for the report?" said Captain Boston.

"Dunne, sir. William Dunne."

"Little Willie, yes?" said Major Stokes, in his misery.

"No, sir," said Willie.

"The fucking Kaiser's son, yes? Little Willie."

"I'm not, no, sir. Not the Kaiser's son at all, sir."

"Ah, fucking hell, come on. No one calls you Little Willie? A little lad like you, with the name of William. No?"

"No, sir."

"Ah, don't sound so fucking insulted. What's the matter with you? Little Irish midget with a shitty arse. Don't look at me like you're going to make a fucking complaint. Don't fucking look at me."

"Lay off him, Major, for Christ's sake," said the other major.

"Yes, yes. Very well, Private. Sorry about that."

"That's all right, sir."

And somehow he felt that it was all right. Given the new world that held sway over all things. And given that he himself, Willie Dunne, had had to kill a man. Anyway, you couldn't give an officer a box in the gob.

"Yes," said the major. "Of course it's all right."

Then Willie turned about and headed to go.

"Small William," said the major behind him. "Will that do it? That doesn't insult you? You don't mind that, surely?"

Willie risked going on without turning round or replying.

"Those fucking Irish," he heard muttered again behind him.

"They've had a hell of a day up there," he heard Captain Boston say.

He headed back through suffering and growing darkness to rejoin what was left of his company. With a scalded heart to guide him, and an affrighted soul, which, in these parts of the insulted earth, proved not bad lamps.

The dead were tidied away. Due to the cover of the gas and the failure of the machine-gunners to hold the hour, there were few enough mounds of grey-jacketed corpses up on no-man's land, and what there were their brothers in the far trenches showed no enthusiasm to come and bury.

Major Stokes was nearly as good as his word. Some dubious stuff did come up to them in a covered vat, and it may well have been stew of some sort, except it had been religiously boiled till every last thing gone into it had merged into a sticky brown.

A man brought up tenderly a little barrel of rum, which though evil in its general character was welcomed with the warmth of children by the men.

The promised Chinese labourers didn't appear and a detail from among the last four hundred men was drawn and all corpses, German and Irish, were carried back a ways and yet another little graveyard was instituted. There were no white picket fences, headstones, or the like. Just row after row of irregular beds, like a poor man's vegetable plot, and into these loamy beds were lain the vanished soldiers. If they were stiff, the living men broke a limb here and a limb there, with muttered apologies to the slain. They were clothed in dark army sacks, all stray things, wallets, pictures, letters carefully extracted from dusty pockets and bloodied places, and the commanding officers of all the units kept these scraps and flotsams with identifying discs and soldier's small-books and the like, eventually to be sent back to the mourning mothers and fathers in their counties. Many for the city of Dublin, parts of which were said to be still burning. Many to Kildare and Wicklow, Westmeath, little farms and labourers' cottages would find the dark postman at the door with a well-constructed package, brown paper over a box of thin floppy boards and good twine and a wax seal over all, like an inheritance. These would be opened, examined, reverently repackaged, and placed reverently in the safer niches of sad houses.

Willie Dunne sought out his German among the rows and heaps, and dug a hole for him first. He found in the man's pockets a little battered Bible, in German of course, funny, thick black lettering, and a little brown figure of a horse, which must be merely a keepsake. It was made of porcelain and did not seem the toy of a child, but nevertheless Willie thought it might have been handed to him quickly by his son or daughter at the door going away. He had a little leather fold, and when Willie opened it there were two little squares of gold leaf. He knew it was gold leaf because he had seen such things on the tables of the men who did the work on the castle chapel, gilding the shields and crests of the Lord-Lieutenants of Ireland that were erected above the congregation. Maybe his German thought it was a good sort of currency, or maybe he carried them as an emblem of his trade in peacetime. Who could know?

The sky glowered overhead. There was a new wind coming in from the west, and the freshening smells of rain were signalling in it. Nevertheless, the fields and woods about were washed by sunlight. Of course, his German had the expected photographs, a frowning woman with a heap of hair above her head, in a rough-looking dress. Her head looked too big for her body, and she could hardly compare to Gretta. The other photograph showed a line of children, seven of them in an obedient row, and Willie suddenly put the two pictures back and gathered all the small things together and put them aside for to give to Captain Sheridan. For Captain Sheridan had ordered even the possessions of the dead Germans to be retrieved and not pilfered. However, Willie on instinct pocketed the little horse.

Seven children like steps of stairs.

O'Hara was working about twenty yards off, whistling "The Mountains of Mourne."

It was a relief for Willie simply to dig, to keep whatever hole he was digging square to the angles. It was like digging a foundation for a house. He even found himself, as he would by instruction working for Dempsey throwing up stones in their allotted heaps, the bigger for filler stone for a wall, the rounded stones for cobbles, the pebbly ones for a mix of muck. But he knew it was ridiculous. And these stones would go back into each finished grave-hole as a sort of sore bed to lay the bodies on, but he did not think his German would mind, skinny though he was. Where the Mountains of Mourne sweep down to the sea. He thrust his spade in again, lifted a half load and tossed it out neatly onto the pile in the professional manner. Like a dancer. And the foundations of the wall of the city were garnished with all manner of precious stones. Where did that drift from? He thought it must be Sunday school in the castle chapel, where his father used to send him and the girls, though the minister's wife was a Protestant. And the twelve gates were twelve pearls. She was a nice woman called Daphne. He wondered what the state of his Dublin was now. He had heard of course that the artillery had been brought up the river and had shelled fucking Sackville Street with a will. Men who came over in the last days had brought news of shattered houses, standing naked to the sky with all their innards gone, showing their fireplaces to the world on the gable walls. It would almost make an apprentice builder weep to think of the deep work gone into the making of those houses. But men would come, he supposed, to build them up again. It was no more than the towns and cities of Belgium. Dublin and Ypres were all the one. And I saw heaven opened and behold a white horse and he that sat upon him was called Faithful and True. That was his favourite line in the whole Bible. And he didn't suppose it meant anything at all.

Funny how a person thought of one thing and then thought of another thing. And then another thing. And was the third thing brother at all to the first? He stopped a moment and leaned on his spade like a bad worker. That was Dempsey's voice in his ear. Little Mr Dempsey with his round face. The Duck Dempsey, he was called, because of his flat-footed walk and his funny arse. But Dempsey was the prophet of finishing on time and the poet of the mortar mix and the stone taken rightly out of twist. He knew the hardnesses of bricks and could easily tell without error where in the kiln an individual brick would have lain. A soft brick from the edge, a hard brick from the core of the stack. Hard bricks for outside work, soft for the weatherless interior of a house, to give a straight reveal, to give an arch to a niche for the range. Old Dempsey in his youth was a roofer and put the roofs onto barracks buildings which was why the soldiers of Ireland were not rained on. He was given the work of building the monuments for the Boer War in whatever places it was required to be

155

commemorated, and for this fine brickies were brought in from other firms, and no architect was happy till his roof had a dozen twists and turns, and it was Dempsey himself who laid the work out on the ground and nailed up those frames, dismantled them, and did the work then again from the walls. And he seventy years of age in the windy rain and the rainy wind. Dempsey and his fellows would build Dublin up again, Willie was sure.

"Would you get along with that, Dunne," yelled Christy Moran. "And don't be daydreaming like a lounger."

"Yes, Mr Dempsey, sir!" said Willie.

"Me who?" said Christy Moran.

After the digging was done he hauled his German into the hole, crossed the arms as best he could across the chest, breaking the arms at the shoulder and the elbow with a mallet. He knew Father Buckley would reach this grave and every grave in the course of his work and say a few words for him, the better to encourage his soul to rise up to heaven, but even so he said a Hail Mary himself in that sunlight smelling of rich rain.

And so in that manner they filled the holes with men and on the Sunday were taken out of the line and dragged themselves back to billets far behind the ugly terrain of death.

CHAPTER
TEN

The pigeons were walking on the glass roof, making a small tapping noise, and coo-coo-cooing. Of course, it was a miracle that a glass building had survived thus far. But it was an old building with an old job to do, to clean the crust and filth off the workers that used to create the slagheaps, and cut along the earth to harvest the anthracite lying innocently there.

There were twenty big white enamel baths in two rows. They stood on the floor of green flagstones with their regal curlicues and big, fat brass taps. All the water knew how to do was gush out at a tremendous rate, thick, ropy water with its twirling cloths of steam. The taps were left hot enough to put a red mark on your palm. Willie Dunne could not tell from where they piped this miraculous water.

He had stripped down as nature put him on the earth and his fellows likewise, Christy Moran in the bath next to his, O'Hara then, and Dermot Smith from Cavan, and the others. There were, of course, a good few men quite new, and Smith, a farm-labourer in former days in Kilnaleck, was one of them, and McNaughtan, a lofty spare fella with a strange face like a bag of dumplings, another.

They had all climbed into the water with eagerness, wincing at first as the scalding stuff touched their skin all weals and rashes and bites, and dancing from foot to foot, and McNaughtan was so burned he had to leap his feet out and perch himself on the sides of the bath. Soon enough they all got used to it and sank into the soapy world. Only their pale faces showed among the suds, because the baths were deep and wide. The water held them gently, warmed their inmost marrow, and if they had forgotten what it was to bathe, and some of them maybe never had a proper bath in their born days, they soon had it high on their list of sumptuous things to experience on God's earth. They would be devotees in their private minds of this immersion. The water touched them like a mother, soothing their backs and legs, and flowed around their genitals like the long hair of a lover.

"Jesus, that's better," said Christy Moran.

"Fucking hell," said McNaughtan.

"Holy Mother Church and all her saints," said Smith.

"For the love of Jesus and his Divine Mother and the Holy Ghost too into the bargain," said another slightly submerged voice. It might have been O'Hara getting into the game, but Willie's head had sunk below the level of the bath and he couldn't see anything except the walking pigeons.

"The Pope in the Vatican and the love of God, and Joey Lambert the handballer."

"Who?" said Christy Moran, laughing.

"And Patrick O'Brien the great Bulleter and John Johnson the boxer and your man the famous clog-dancer," said Willie.

"Oh yes, your man the famous clog-dancer definitely," said Christy Moran. "You mean Dan Leno, you fucker."

"And the Bohemian Girl and the Lass of Aughrim," said Private Smith.

"Oh yes, oh yes!" cried the men in unison more or less.

"Could someone go and fetch the Lass of Aughrim, please," said another contented voice. "There is room for her and more in here. In fact, I think I could fit the Bohemian Girl too at a pinch."

"Pinch is right," said Willie Dunne.

"Pinch is right!" said Smith.

"Who in the name of fuck is Pinch?" said McNaughtan.

"Pinch? Why Pinch is Bovril's brother," said Smith.

"Invigorator for businessmen," said McNaughtan, his baggy face chuckling.

"Exactly," said Smith. "A strengthening food for ladies."

"That's a fact, that's a fact," said Christy Moran, "the strongest stock for soups."

"Restorative for invalids!" shouted a man from down the line.

"Exactly!" shouted Smith in triumph.

"One thousand guineas will be paid if this statement can be refuted!" shouted the company sergeant-major, the water slopping out from his bath.

It was all nonsense, of course. Now they lay in perfect silence, a silence perfected by the show of bonhomie and common knowledge. The fact that they all knew what was written on any Bovril advertisement seemed to drive them deeper into contentment. If they had been young priests quoting the Bible they couldn't have felt a greater command of the things of the world.

"If the Huns were to go dropping a bomb on us here we would have a merry time of it picking the bits of glass out of each other," said Smith from the pit of his bath.

"I'm not picking nothing out of you, you bollocks," said McNaughtan. "You can pick out your own glass."

They, all of them, every man, broke into laughter. It was not that the joke was very funny; it was that the last week had been very dour of visage.

They laughed, and the pigeons seemed to quicken their steps above. The glass very naturally was speckled with green, mossy stuff, and though once it might have been possible to see up to the sky, no more was it so. They were in a slightly darkened underworld, and the steam had completed the job.

To amuse himself, Willie rearranged the baths in his head, and instead of two rows he put them in a continuous circle, like on an Irish tombstone from a thousand years ago, so that the men were like water disappearing down a plug. Then he put them all in a wandering row, so they were like a river of some one hundred and forty feet, he reckoned, with a salmon in each pool.

Now the great Lord of everything wielded His high fishing-rod — with the strength to fetch out a man, should the terrible hook in his mouth hold — and He cast across the waters of the baths, and he would catch and eat them all, Willie feared, one by one in the underworld.

"Sing the 'Half of Mary', why don't you?" said Christy Moran.

"That's kind of a religious song," said Willie Dunne. The "Half of Mary". He would not dream of correcting the sergeant-major. "And it's in Latin."

They were having a bit of a party; it was called a concert but there were no real entertainers. They had been given the little shed where these things took place, so they had a platform and four dozen chairs. Men who could find no place to sit were standing happily at the back, and most of them had found at least a bottle of beer.

Then a man got up with that sudden air and manner that seemed to characterize an Irishman's idea of a singing party. Everyone hushed immediately. No one needed to be urged to silence.

The man threw his head at an angle and put his hand to his face. It was very strange. Perhaps he was the sort of man who would usually have preferred to sing behind a door and not be seen by the company. Some of the best singers were behind-the-door singers, Willie in life had observed.

The soldier struck his first note and passionately gave a ballad from the days of the Crimea. It was very lonesome, tender, and bloody. There was a young girl in it, and a soldier, and a death. The listeners were stilled because in the song there was a melody that brought from their own memories coloured hints and living sparks of the past. The past was a valued thing but it was also dangerous to them in the toxic wastelands of the war. It needed a box of safety round it, and this small room for concerts was as good as they had found.

Each man to his own inward thinking, glimpses of the beloved faces left behind, shadows of arguments unfinished and regretted, the sense of youth not vanishing but being submerged in a killing sea from which no one might emerge, bathed in the acid blood of bomb or bullet.

Stretch of road loved and itemized, fold of field, loved turn of shoulder in a wife, her feet crossing the boards of a bedroom, her clothes thrown across a chair. The voice of a singing child, the sound of a child peeing in the pot, the tremendous affection of son or daughter, soft hair, big eyes, the struggle to find meat and cake. For single men the memories of their Grettas, foul words and good words, failed words of love and triumphant. How human nature fell ever short, but could be summoned to illumine the dark tracts of a life nonetheless. All the matter and difficulty of being alive in a place of peace and a place of war.

The man finished the song and there was another kind of silence, the silence of men whose heads were seeing old pictures and their minds were thinking old thoughts, and then there was tremendous applause. It

162

was the silence before the applause that had pleased the singer most.

"That is a beautiful song," said Christy Moran. "Fair play to you, Private."

Christy Moran himself longed to sing "The Minstrel Boy" but he was gripped by a kind of horror and unseating fear. He had sung that song for his wife many times and she had been kind enough not to complain of his croaky tones and that, oftentimes, he had forgotten the words and stumbled.

He wanted to sing it because he suddenly desired greatly to converse with his companions, to communicate to these men under his command his gratitude to them, and his love. It was not a thought that had come to him before. He wanted them to stand in place of his listening wife, with her sharp, long features and her ruined hand, lost in a miserable accident in their house. He wanted to tell them about his wife, obscurely desiring to, desiring, but terrified they might laugh at him, worse, laugh at her, for what had befallen her, a laughter that would be worse to him than bullets.

How guilty he felt when he thought he had come out to the war because he could not live with such trouble. The distress of his wife was worse to him than any charging Hun or gas attack. He could not look at the murky vista of such matters although he adored her in his heart, but adoration in the heart did not necessarily allow a life that he could bear.

He wished suddenly he could come down away from what he was to the men, and say these things, and sing the song that was most special to him.

"A beautiful song indeed," said Private O'Hara.

O'Hara was a bit of a musician, because his brother had a band in Sligo, called O'Hara's Orchestra, and sometimes he used to fill in for the piano player, who was consumptive. The sea air of Sligo was heavy with rain and moisture and that was good for neither houses nor people with a consumption. The rooms sweated with dew-like damp and the lungs of sufferers flared up, and blood was spat. The piano player was a giant of a man, he could walk to the top of Maeve's Cairn and place his stone on top of all the others with the best of them, as tradition bid him to, but those little insects had got into him, or whatever it was gave a man consumption, whatever it was loved the damp air and living inside a giant. So when the giant was indisposed and at home with his mother coughing his life out, Pete O'Hara sat in with the sheet music and banged out the tunes and the ballads with his brother, the dapperest man in County Sligo, with a straw hat as neat as a cake.

So O'Hara rose now like a prince coming into his kingdom, with a bit of sheet music being extracted from his army jacket, and, much to the friendly jealousy, the painful, friendly jealousy of Christy Moran, in that ordinary spot of Flanders, he placed the music on the piano and scanned it short-sightedly and sang a new song that they hadn't heard, although it was all the rage in the music halls of England. It was called "Roses of Picardy." It was a song written by a magician,

Willie thought, designed to slay the hearts of simple men:

> Roses are flowering in Picardy,
> But there's never a rose like you,
> And the roses will die with the summertime,
> And our roads may be far apart,
> But there's one rose that dies not in Picardy,
> 'Tis the rose that I keep in my heart!

sang wily Private O'Hara, as plain as he could, so the words would pierce home with proper violence to the composure of his mates. They had never heard the song before. Many at song's end were weeping openly.

"My God," said poor McNaughtan. He was mopping at his eyes with his sleeve like a bad actor. His big, doughy face was melting and as red as a red arse.

Smith looked at McNaughtan and then Smith patted McNaughtan on the shoulder. It was an extraordinary matter and one that Willie vowed in his heart to remember. How softened they were by the song. It was as if for those moments they felt queerly vindicated, all doubts and sorrows abating. That was O'Hara's strange work that Flanders night — in Picardy itself. There's one rose that dies not in Picardy.

There was a long silence then again in the room. Maybe there were sixty men there, all Irishmen of the battalion. The Royal Dublin Fusiliers. And many had seen hundreds killed, and many had killed; Willie himself had killed. Was the song a memory of what they were, or was it still possible they might be ordinary, loving, imperfect fellas again, in some other guise of peace?

"Well, Jesus," said Christy Moran, "I don't know if I can stand it, or if any of us can stand it, lads, but Willie Dunne, for fuck's sake and the love of God, would you give us your 'Half of Mary', please."

"Come on, Willie," said O'Hara, "and I'll cut the tune out on the piano, if you like."

"All right," said Willie. "But it's kind of religious."

"And in Latin, yeh, we know," said the sergeant-major. "But isn't the fucking mass in Latin? Sure we all know our bit of Latin, don't we, lads?"

"Yeh, come on, Willie, boy!" Smith shouted, maybe to shift himself out of his sentimental state.

So Willie started to sing the "Ave Maria". Well, it was the very selfsame song he had sung for the singing competition, when his father witnessed his undoing. But he had heard that twiddly bit between the verses now, and he knew he was ready for it.

"Aaaaaaveeee Mariiiiiiiiaa," he sang in the long drawn-out notes of Schubert, "gratia pleeenis."

It was true what his mother believed about him. He sang like an angel might sing if an angel were ever so foolish as to sing for mortal men. His voice was strange and high, but not a counter-tenor. It just seemed to put a knife into the air, the notes were so clear and strong. Like a true singer, he could sing soft with strength, and sing loud without hurting the ears. But the "Ave Maria" was all the same firm tone of things. The Latin itself allowed the men to keep the song from catching in the nets and snares of memories. It was all new and of the present. It seemed to be about their courage, and their solitariness, and the effort they made in desperation to form a bridge from one soul to another. And that these bridges were bridges of air. The word "Maria" they knew, because it was the name of the Mother of God. From mother's knee to now, they had been inculcated with all the promises and warnings of their Catholic faith. Few had gone further than the teachings of school, and their faith was bare in its bones but strong for all that. They thought of heaven as the next stop without question. They knew it was so because their mothers, their fathers and their priests had told them so.

Willie crossed the gap between the verses with a leap, without a hitch. O'Hara didn't even notice. If that bloody judge could have heard him now! First prize with a fucking ribbon to prove it.

Ave Maria, gratia plenis, full of grace, and many of the men caught that it was just the Hail Mary all dressed over in another lingo, the prayer of their childhoods and their country, the prayer of their inmost minds, that could not be sundered, that could not be violated, that could not be rendered meaningless even by slaughter, the core inviolable, the flame unquenchable.

And Willie sang, and maybe in truth he was an amateur, his breathing O'Hara noted was jagged and awkward, but the admiration of his dead mother was in it — indeed, as Willie's mind now leaped to think, to remember, the tone of a child in a room in Dalkey singing to his mother, after the birth of his sister Dolly that killed her, his father sitting sternly back in the scullery and going out for a sudden walk into the dark, God knew where, and Willie aged eleven sneaking in to see her, a thing he had forgotten till this moment of singing, to be with her, and him singing that song to her, with the pennies on her eyes, and the midwife cleaning the baby in the front parlour, and no one there in the bedroom, only the distant heave of the Dalkey sea, and his song, "Ave Maria, full of grace, the Lord is with thee," and his mother's face not listening and listening, and similarly now he sang for these ruined men, these doomed listeners, these wretched fools of men come out to fight a war without a country to their name, the slaves of England and the kings of nothing — in Christy Moran's secret, bitter words.

CHAPTER
ELEVEN

Royal Dublin Fusiliers,
Belgium.
3 May 1916.

Dear Papa,

Thank you for writing back, Papa. I am very glad
everyone is safe, very much so. It is a great relief. The
Dublin Metropolitan Police taken off the streets! It was
terrible to read about the Countess Markievicz shooting
the unarmed recruit at Stephen's Green. I am sad to think
of Sackville Street blown to nothing. The men here have
the papers going round and we all try to have a read of
them, especially now we are back in the reserve lines,
thank God. Maybe at home some of the lads might be
getting into trouble with you and your men! Here I have
to say they make fine soldiers. Nothing is too hard for
them, they will dig all hours, and you would not think
city boys would be able for a hard march, but they are
masters. They are wonderful lads. They say it is from
walking everywhere in Dublin, down to the Shelly Banks
in the summer to swim. They have been through a lot
just recently. They are really wonderful men. I am to

169

leave this aside for a while and I will add to this tomorrow before it goes with the other post.

"They're shooting those buggers in Dublin," said O'Hara, scanning a newspaper. It was funny in the Irish papers to see the advertisements for saddles, for soap, for wigs, for shotguns, for poultry, for furniture polish, scullery maids, footmen, apples, and all the paraphernalia of that eternal Irish life. New things were casualty lists, men who would not be coming home to saddles, soap, wigs et cetera, ever again.

"What's that?" said Private Quigley, the miracle man, who went off gassed rightly to an English hospital but who had arrived back as right as rain. He was playing a game of cards with Joe Kielty, one of the gentlest and nicest men that ever lived, as far as Willie was concerned, who would do anything for you if it was in his way to do it. He was the best builder of revetments in the company, he had a knack for it, and no wooden revetment put in by Joe Kielty ever fell down on a man unless it was a bomb that did it. Those Mayo men were sweet as nuts. And even when he had lost his cousin Joe McNulty in the first gas attack, he took it with a great solemnity that did him credit. But Willie saw him in the graveyard alone by Joe McNulty's grave, saying things that no one could hear. He was a small man too, like Willie, with a plate of black hair it looked like on his crown, and he was a man who had been out in all weather since he was a little boy, working beside his father on a few windy acres in Mayo between the lakes of Callow.

So now Joe looked up from his cards when Quigley spoke. They stuck together maybe because they were both miracle men, since Joe Kielty took the same blast of smoke that his cousin did, and yet his lungs thought nothing of it, which was very strange, and rare. They were pals now in that army fashion.

"Shooting them," said O'Hara, matter of fact, but not matter of fact. "Court-martialled the lot of them, all the leaders that signed that bit of unholy paper, and dozens and dozens more. They're all to be shot by the military and they've made a start now yesterday morning with three of them. They'd be the high-ups, I suppose."

"Well, good enough for them," said Quigley. "I was worried the Mam would be caught in the crossfire. She's a terrible one for going out when it doesn't suit her."

"We were all worried," said Willie, with feeling.

"Did they have officers then and all the rest?" said Quigley, more lightly.

"Bedad and they did," said O'Hara. "And platoons apparently and companies and I don't know if they had regiments but."

"Sure, Pete, there was only a few of them," said Quigley, "you can't make a regiment out of a handful."

"No, no, rightly, but battalions they had, for sure. Well, I mean, they were all Irish Volunteers, that broke away from Redmond, and then the other lot with them, the Citizen Army it's called, that James Connolly used to drill. I mean, Jaysus, there used to be Volunteers in Sligo marching with hurleys and bits of uniforms their mothers stitched up for them. They didn't look too menacing. The little scuts in Sligo used to jeer them.

171

But there's three of them shot anyhow. About a hundred of them killed in the fighting itself, and about two hundred of our soldiers and some policemen, too."

"Jesus Christ," said Willie Dunne.

"Yeh, Willie," said O'Hara. "A few of your father's lads done in, and some Royal Irish Constabulary men and the like. Dozens of ordinary Tommies mown down, mown down I was reading, at Mount Street Bridge. Just like here. Advancing shoulder to shoulder and mown down like, like what's-it? Stalks of them yokes."

Somehow Willie didn't want to say anything, to describe what he had seen and done at that very Mount Street. He didn't know why exactly. It was as if he wished he had never been through there, seen those things. It was foul enough where he was betimes without having to think back to other foul things — confusing, awful things. He was sure he had told O'Hara all about it, but maybe not. It must have run out of O'Hara's head anyhow, what with all the goings on. It was a wonder they had thoughts at all still in their heads. Brains poached and scrambled by noise, terror and foul deaths.

"Wheat," said Joe Kielty.

"Yeh, Joe, wheat," said O'Hara. "Thank you, Mr Kielty. Anyhows, they shot the first three in Kilmainham. Firing squad, short straw, blindfolds and all. And I tell you, the fella writing here is delighted. Nothing could suit him better you would think. But he's right, I suppose he is." He paused a moment. "That's the funny thing."

No one said a word for a while. Joe Kielty and the Miraculous Quigley attended to their cards again.

"I think the Mam's mind is gone entirely, that's what it is," muttered Quigley. "You can't keep her in the house."

Willie looked out through the billet window at the vague terrain of fields and hedges. The hedges were growing up wild and there was no one hereabouts now to give them a hair-do.

"Pearse, Clarke and McDonagh," said O'Hara almost to himself. "Fancy."

After a very long time Joe Kielty said, in his mild Mayo voice: "I hope three will be enough for them, Pete."

"Not a bit of it," said O'Hara.

It was in the canteen later that day and it was just O'Hara and Willie on their own.

"The queer thing is," said O'Hara, "the queer thing is, they were hoping the fucking Germans would help them."

"Who, Pete?" said Willie.

"The fucking rebels, Willie."

"Oh yeh, I know," said Willie. "I know. Sure it was written on their piece of paper. Gallant allies in Europe, it said, wasn't it?"

"So that means, like it or lump it, we're the fucking enemy. I mean, we're the fucking enemy of the fucking rebels!"

"That's it, more or less. That's how I understand it anyhow," said Willie.

"You see, I think that's very queer indeed," said Pete.

"It is, very," said Willie.

"I mean, whatever way you turn it, I would like to believe, I would like to anyhow, that what we're doing

173

out here has a reason, to push the Hun back and all that, even if it doesn't have a reason."

"I know," said Willie. But he didn't completely know.

"So, what can we call that?"

"I don't know, Pete."

"So where does it leave us?"

It was the very same question Jesse Kirwan had asked. Willie hadn't known the answer then. He thought he knew the answer now.

"Sitting here, Pete, is where," he said.

"Like eejits." And then Pete O'Hara said nothing for a little while. "But I wish they hadn't shot those fellas all the same." It was almost a whisper.

"I wish they hadn't too, Pete," said Willie, surprised at this change, "to tell you the truth. So what does that make us?"

"Even bigger eejits!"

4 May.

It is a little while later, Papa. We got the news now about the three leaders shot. Some of the men think it is a good thing. Myself, I cannot say what I think hardly. How I wish I were at home now and was able to talk these matters over with you. I wish they had not seen fit to shoot them. It doesn't feel right somehow. I don't know why. What does John Redmond say about it? When I came through Dublin I saw a young lad killed in a doorway, a rebel he was, and I felt pity for him. He was no older than myself. I wish they had not seen fit to shoot the three leaders. It is the thought of it all happening at home in Dublin too,

174

where nothing bad should happen, that has got me unhappy. By heavens, Papa, I hope you are not angry with this letter. I am proud to wear this uniform and I am doubly proud of the Royal Dublin Fusiliers. Please give my love to Maud and Annie and tell Dolly I saw a blackbird, or maybe it was a crow, yesterday, building its nest in a chimney. A chimney all up in the air and on its own! That was all there was left of the house, and still and all faithfully he was collecting twigs and bits of string and whatnot, to make a nest for his wife. I wish I had not come through Dublin the way I did, and just was in Flanders all the while.

Your loving son,
Willie.

Darling Gretta, thank you for your kind and interesting postcard showing poor Sackville Street in ruins — who would ever have thought — thinking of you — here's one they make here of poor Ypres — old Wipers as we like to say — the Cloth Tower etc. — With all my love — kisses — Willie.

He nearly had no room for the last few words, which put him in a panic, but he squeezed them in and hoped they were clear.

That night in his narrow bed he fell into a sleep with dreams that had the blessed clarity of childhood dreams.

They were billeted in the remnant of a small factory that was used to make the industrial suits that now-vanished men had worn to their dark work, three layers of linen stitched together against the flares and eruptions of a former steelworks close by. Their beds were ranged in a long, narrow anteroom of some kind, and in the next room the men had peered in at a strange sight, a hundred and more thin paper patterns, hanging up in rows, the shapes of the very workers themselves, jackets and trousers, through which unknown company a mild breeze moved from the broken window, lifting and nudging the shapes, like the very shadows of living persons.

The army had not cleared them out. Perhaps in their silence they were too voluble of past lives and other days.

In this makeshift place Willie Dunne discovered a peace of sorts. Yes, the wild guns struck their great notes in the distance like the bells of a horrific city. Hearts asleep in the shires of England close upon the sea must have heard them too. But he fell down between the boards of memory and sleep like a penny in an old floor. He lay there in the dust of nowhere, sunken and alone.

The dream in which he found himself was nearly too clear to be a proper dream. He was back in trenches somewhere, looking out across the shell-ploughed between-land without a mirror, with his naked eyes. His soft head peered out, he could see it himself, poking up like a turnip, as plain as day for a sniper. But he could not extract it, it was stuck there. Very near, absurdly so, was a German soldier in his own trench, fiddling about with a little box. Into the box the soldier was putting grain, seeds perhaps of the hapless grasses. He left the box on the parapet and ducked down. A wide, hot, yellow sunlight flooded the world; a heavy, dark grey lid of rain sat on the far horizon. The breeze rustled through the small woodlands, and in the trees hung the paper bodies of lost men, the patterns of their expended souls. Wood pigeons made their familiar call, sixteen wooden notes that Willie had often counted in the woods of Kiltegan and Kelsha as a boy. Co-co-co, coco, co-co-co-coco, co-co-co-coco, co. And always, Willie, and always, Willie, and always, Willie, all. That's what he used to think they were saying, when he was seven in the realms of his grandfather, White Meg himself, the onetime steward of those woods. Now the wood pigeons called in these Belgian woods, imagined though they might be, and dreamed. A sweat appeared on his sleeping form, seeped into his long-johns. The lice moiled in his armpits, despite the boon of the baths. But he didn't feel them. He was watching now in the dream. A pigeon landed fussily near the box of the German soldier, walked along the parapet plumply and poked its head into the box. When it could not reach all the grain, it darted right in, and just as it did, up popped the German, blocking the exit of the pigeon with a hand, and grabbing the box. Willie Dunne nearly cheered. He certainly made a noise of some kind, because the soldier stopped instantly. The long face turned and looked intently across no-man's land, right into Willie's stuck face.

Willie knew it was his German, the lad he had killed. He wanted to call out to him, to tell him he had kept the little horse for him. The soldier drew the pigeon out from the trap and held it in both hands. Isn't he going to kill and eat it? thought Willie. Pigeon was not to be sneezed at, and if he let it boil for a couple of hours in his mess tin or whatever he might use, he would not regret the effort. One shake of the head would break the weak neck, quicker than a chicken even.

Willie longed for the man to do it. He could taste the dark meat of the pigeon, hints in it of woodland and secret weather. Kill and eat, kill and eat.

But his German just lifted his arms to the threatening sky and opened his hands, and the bird rose up like a silly angel, like a grey rag.

Always, Willie, and always, Willie, and always, Willie, all.

The pigeon and all his fellow pigeons called in the wood. It was a cacophony. And the arms of his German remained aloft, as if he had forgotten them, and the face of his German remained fixed on his, and the rainy light sat in the face, replacing the long wash of sun.

CHAPTER
TWELVE

That strange week the roads leading in and out of the reserve districts became burdened in their ditches and banks by flowers. Willie and his company suffered the inexplicable indignities of fatigues. Trenches were dug that never would be used, they were marched from spot to spot like madmen, they were given long lectures about their feet, how to avoid trench foot, how to boil vegetables in their mess tins, though none of them had seen a true vegetable for a long while, the deep lore of saluting and the nervous rituals of sentry duty. A hundred things they knew already, and if they did not know them by now, they thought they did not need to know them.

Meanwhile, the roadsides burgeoned up and grew almost noisy with memory-laden colours. The arrogant sun had touched them and the casual rain had done the rest, leaving these million marks of respect on the neglected edges of fields and paths and roads. Even in fields, where most likely some calamity had stolen away the tillers, great weaves and plethoras of field flowers appeared, army after army of yellow heads, golden heads and blue, red and burning green. It was like a sudden paradise. Birds fiercely sought those sites on which they would bestow their efforts all the summer, the heroic house-martins and swallows come back from whatever Portugals and Africas they knew, to rest their faith again in Flanders, and the safety of Flanders. Willie wondered what houses knew them all the winter, what families and children had regarded them as their own. Or did they live out in wild marshes and desolate woodlands away from troubled men and women and their young? Now they had returned and of course they did not ask for news of war; they patched their muddy nests under the eaves with spittle mixed with clay and fired round in the evening air like old arrowheads without their sticks. And he thought of the many unseen beasts seeking each other out in the underwood, and the tadpoles making a crowd of rusty commas in every narrowing pool.

And in from Ireland trickled the names, every day two or three, of the executed, sending some Dublin men into sore dances of worry in their minds, thinking Armageddon would descend on their unprotected homes. Men got dizzy, the faces of their six-year-olds, and seven, and all that chance and precious cargo of their children, tormenting them, calling to them to return home. And they could not.

The executed men were cursed, and praised, and doubted, and despised, and held to account, and blackened, and wondered at, and mourned, all in a confusion complicated infinitely by the site of war.

But perhaps Armageddon lay not so far away as Ireland.

180

The beds of the young men of England were empty, they had come out to the war. And the goosedown covers, the plain starched sheets, the feather pillows of a thousand Ulster farm-houses had no young men now to dream in them. The cities and the towns of the Irish North sent their vivid sons. The old, lousy warrens of Dublin. Of course, the two sets of sons liked to trade insults with each other when they passed by chance on the road, or fetched up in billets near each other. The Ulstermen thought the southern boys were all suspect, Home Rulers and worse, and suggested as much in forceful phrases. At any rate, geat armies were massing everywhere, great divisions, so that a single man was only one flickering light in a wide sky of millions. There must be movement on the front, all were agreed. The French boys were drowning in the caverns of Verdun, drowning in their own blood. Millions must push back millions. The Kaiser sent his myriad boys, the King of England his. Great troops of women followed, to bandage, bolster and bury. And all of England, and all old empires, British, Austro-Hungarian, Prussian, the empires of halfpenny lives and the hungry, sad kings and commoners all party to the same haze, strained for news, and the mountains stood away and a thousand widows wore their black ribbons in Ireland on their arms, and were treated kindly in the main, with whispered sympathy and whatever was left of wise words. Because the box of wise words was emptying.

"You mean they tied Private Kirwan to a gun-wheel," said Willie, "and left him out in the open for a month?"

181

"Now, that is how we properly understand a Field Punishment number one. It is only for two hours a day and it is only three days in a row. I say only, though I understand the shame of it," said Father Buckley. "But, Willie, that's all done and he is facing far worse than that now."

It was late evening and Father Buckley had come to the billet to find Willie Dunne and have a private word. He had asked Willie how his father was and Willie had said his father was well. He had asked Willie then if he remembered a private called Jesse Kirwan from Cork City and Willie had to think only a moment and the little man came back into his mind, from the awful doings in Dublin. And Father Buckley said that Private Kirwan was locked up and waiting for a court martial and that Father Buckley had been to talk to him at the request of the CO. And that he asked Private Kirwan if there was anyone who knew him and could speak for his character. And Private Kirwan had given Willie Dunne's name.

"But I only knew him a day or so," said Willie Dunne. "That one day mainly. And what has he done, Father?"

Usually you heard of a fella arrested for talking bad to an officer, or shirking. Or the military police might find an eejit wandered into some forbidden part of a town or a village, or doing any number of foolish things the army didn't like, such as not saluting an officer or the wrong thing uttered in the wrong place. For no matter what mayhem was afoot in the ruined fields of the Lord, the army was deeply attached to its regulations, always allowing for the fact that the staff officers didn't see battles, didn't understand what happened in battles, and probably didn't want to. It was line officers only that knew the drear paintings and the atrocious music of the front line.

But just now and then a man was arrested for something pretty dark and there were bad deeds done in the back towns, there were girls done in and murdered by rummy men, there were twisting, turning parts of men that the war maybe brought to the fore. It was often said that the Chinese fellas in the labour corps would slit your throat as soon as look at you, and that they ran little sidelines of opium all through the service, and that that was how they survived the shocking tasks given them. And you heard odd whispers of murders, and even dark acts of carnage on prisoners. Hearts turned black like the hearts of slaughtered cows, the bright blood congealing into a night-time character. So maybe this Jesse Kirwan had become one of that dread number, but all the same Willie Dunne would be surprised if it was so — though he only knew him the day or so.

Father Buckley's face looked as haggard, deeply haggard, as an old, old man's. If there was ever freshness there it was now historical. Yet Willie didn't think the man was too much past forty, which was old enough for a soldier — but then, he was not a soldier. His hair under his hat looked like old wire, tangled up, and useless.

"His charge is disobedience, Willie. There is something deeply amiss with him. He has refused,

Willie, refused to go on. And got his Field Punishment for that. Then he would not do as he was bid, even by his sergeant, and declared he would not be a slave. His friends had to quell him and tie him forcibly to the wheel. Then he would cry out and caterwaul, and shout out at the passing soldiery. And even when he was not tied, but required to swill out his billet and empty the pots —"

"I am sure he did not like that!" said Willie Dunne.

"No, and he did it all with a grudge and a moan, and I was told that he spoke on certain unwise topics to the fellows in his company, liberty and freedom and the like, and rebels, and he spoke I am told a double Dutch of such matters on his own in the dark, as if his wits were astray. He has stopped dead and will not obey an order, any order. He gave rank abuse I am told to his commanding officer, a young fellow from the rich vales of County Dublin that probably never heard a proper curse in his life till now. Now he will not eat, he will not say an earthly word to anyone. I spoke to him for an hour in his cell, a little room they have him in, beside of all things an old abattoir, and he never said a thing, until I asked him if he knew anyone that would speak for him, and he said, just those three words, Private William Dunne, and by a miracle, a miracle, Willie, of course I knew you, in all the armies of the King."

"Well, it might have been another Willie Dunne he meant," said Willie, "because I knew him only the day."

"They'll court martial him now in a little while," said Father Buckley, "and I don't know what will happen to him, only I wouldn't like to think, in that they are

184

making examples of fellows now in wartime, and there have been those two men shot you know among the Irish divisions for desertion, and I can tell you, Willie, they were fine men, I knew them both, and one of them was out here a year and came through flames, literally flames, at Hooge, and had his whole company just seared away by the flame-throwers. And the other man left three children and I can't bear to think about that, those three little chaps, and all the death around us already."

"I know, Father, but I don't know why he said my name. Why didn't he give the name of his sergeant or the other lads in his platoon, or someone close to him?"

"Well, because, Willie, he has bitten his sergeant's head off more or less, and I don't know but that the other boys have despaired of him. Will you come and talk to him anyhow? Captain Sheridan said it will be all right."

"I don't know, sir. Did you ask my sergeant? Did you speak to him?"

"I didn't speak to him, but I could speak to him. Do you want me to?"

Willie Dunne didn't know what he wanted.

"They might shoot him, Willie, and even at the very least they will give him a prison sentence, and that is a very terrible thing."

Willie passed only the once a man chained to a gun, a stricken-looking Tommy like a ruined Christ. But you turned your face away from such atrocious shame.

"Look it, Willie," said Father Buckley, "I can well understand, being the chief superintendent's son, you would be reluctant to do a thing like this, when a man is on a charge. But quite frankly now, I need to know what's amiss with him, if I am to help him at all. You do not need to speak for him in court if you do not wish."

Willie still said nothing. He was flummoxed.

"I don't expect a man to be a saint out here, do you, man dear? Willie, now and then we know, and you have seen it, there is a touch of hell out here. And my occupation in the matter of war is to bring a man, any man, to a safe place, if I can, where his soul might flourish, and I do not think God expects us all now to be earthly saints."

The chief superintendent's son. It was certainly not that that held him back. Why, his father would be the first man to urge him to the task! No, it was that — well, he had no words for it, but the truth was he was weary in his spirit. It was emptying out and thinning and he felt less than ever he did. There was a section of him so tired and yet he was fit enough in his bones and sinews. He ate his grub with a will. He could dig in the ground three hours without a stop. But he was afrighted in the place of — wherever that essential business indeed so prized by his father resided, but Willie did not know the word exactly. Because what he really wanted was to marry his Gretta and row with his sisters and build buildings for Dempsey. He did not want to be visiting snaky-looking Corkmen in their cells. And he would not do it. And yet, and yet, Father Buckley had used a phrase that Willie knew well from his childhood, when the old steward his grandfather used to address him so, even as a boy of five or six — man dear.

"I suppose I am appealing to your compassion, Willie," said Father Buckley.

"I am sorry to make such a trouble over it," said Willie. "It is not me after all is in the lock-up."

"Then you will come and talk to him?"

But Willie could not say he would or would not. He fell silent now too, but not as silent, no doubt, as Jesse Kirwan. He was trying to remember what Jesse Kirwan had said about himself. He could not remember a thing. But the narrow face and the funny broken nose, and him weeping in Mount Street, that eerily returned. He did have a temper on him, certainly leaping at Willie's throat like he had. But Willie also sorely wondered what in the world was the matter with him that he refused to obey orders? Orders were not such a great thing in the upshot. It was a way for things to go forward, to advance. Perhaps that was not the fitting word.

Father Buckley held Willie's left arm a moment in a gesture of friendship and equality and then let the arm go and nodded at Willie. He had a mouth, Willie saw, of long yellow teeth. The teeth, top and bottom, glimmered in the light of the oil-lamps like two tiny brass fenders. The serious, wounded eyes were as black as a caught trout's.

The weary priest was smiling at the weary soldier. So Willie knew he had said yes without saying anything.

At last army clashed against army but it was not for them this time to be involved.

It was the Ulstermen of the 36th Division who went over 1st July.

Terrible brave news came down to them, the men of the 16th in cosy billets. There'd been two thousand fellas killed and dying of wounds, and another two or even three that were wounded. Some mad battalions reached the enemy trenches, but had no further men coming up to back them. The guns and counter-attacks ate them.

But O'Hara looked at Willie Dunne and he looked at Dermot Smith and Smith looked at Kielty. It was a strange time. They knew what two thousand corpses looked like, that was a fact.

There were villages in Ulster would have no men in them now. They would never come back to guide the plough and curse the Pope on a Sunday, more was the pity.

It had been a dark ruckus and the news of it confounded their hearts. There was odd love there for the brave Ulstermen; what could a man do against that love? Nothing at all, only add to it by thinking and weeping privately. Maybe there were some there, many, that didn't give a tuppenny damn about the fucking Ulstermen, or anything else in these changed and muddied days of the war. Maybe so.

That very day 3rd July of the savage news, Willie went with Father Buckley to the rear of the rear lines where Jesse Kirwan was held captive, a kind of underworld of an underworld.

Yet the fields there were bright enough, and the French farmers were hoping to take a harvest anyhow at the end of the summer, if the war would only progress the other way Germany-wards. The poplars along the white roads rattled their merry leaves; there were geese standing in the wet margins like swollen ducks.

Jesse Kirwan was being held in the privy of a working abattoir. Willie and the priest passed through the big concrete hall where there were dozens of bullocks standing in pens. Willie saw a bullock led through some iron railings, goaded with a metal stick to make it stumble forward properly. A fine, handsome fellow felled it with a stun hammer, driving a good blow to the temple. The bullock knelt like a praying animal and fell dead like an actor, without a speech, only a truncated yowl, horribly like a dog.

Willie never heard such a sound from a bullock in his born days. Then the cleavermen moved in, the beast had a hook attached to its leg muscles, it was hoisted up, and the cleavers sliced it in two. There was a Niagara Falls of curtainy blood, it drenched the yellow coats of the men, it poured out over their heads. You would think they might hang the animal first and bleed it for the good of the blood, but there was a sense of ugly haste. Battalions, divisions indeed, to be fed.

The head was sliced off expertly, the heavy front legs, the enormous rear legs, the little ruined bollocks, the tail, there were insides ripped out and down, there were parcellers to gather the different bits, thrown into big tin carts like imperial prams, and wheeled away all busy-like.

Why they were holding Jessie Kirwan in such a place Willie did not know. But how many things did Willie Dunne know? Not many, these times, he thought.

Perhaps it was not a privy, strictly speaking, or was a privy in its civilian days. Certainly there was a metal plate saying "Hommes" above the door, but when he went in with Father Buckley there was no sign of pissers or places to shit. There was a soldier though, on a chair like one of those folding chairs you would be given at a concert in the park — or one of those green tuppenny chairs in St Stephen's Green, for which the keepers would gather the coins in the sleepy weeks of summer, among the geraniums and the nasturtiums in their rich, black beds. The soldier rose smartly when Father Buckley appeared, a regimental newspaper falling from his lap. He saluted the priest accurately, trimming his arm and timing his hand perfectly.

"I'll go on through and talk to him," said Father Buckley. "See how he fares. You wait here, Private, with the corporal."

"All right, sir," said Willie, and stood where he was like a pony.

Father Buckley waited for the corporal to turn the key in a small metal door, ducked his tall figure down, and disappeared through. The corporal looked at Willie in a neutral way.

"I've only the one chair," he said, in an Irish accent.

"Oh," said Willie, and shook his head, as if to say, No matter.

"Yeh. He's not a bad fella — you know, his nibs inside there. Quiet, shy sort. Someone should have a word in his ear. If he'll act the white man now, well, they'll surely spare him."

"Have you talked to him yourself, sir?" said Willie.

"Oh, I'm forbidden talking to prisoners. That's not allowed."

"Oh," said Willie.

"They don't want you to be, to be swayed, talked round into something you might regret, because, well, this is as near to death row as bedamned. Where you from?"

"Second battalion, RDF."

"No, where in Ireland?"

"Oh, Dublin, sir, Wicklow. You know. Dublin mostly."

"Yeh, well, that's good, isn't it?"

But Willie didn't know any more if it was good or not. He supposed it was.

"Yeh, well," he said.

"I'm told he got upset when they started shooting those fuckers in Dublin," said the corporal. "But I wouldn't get upset."

"No?"

"No. Fucking jubilant, me. Bastards. I never spoke to him but the once. He was begging me to tell him what was going on. This would have been that first time they had him here, around May it was. And he's been in the clink since, I believe. Or Field Punishment. And back again now. Worse this time it'll be. Major Stokes, a bit of a bollocks really. Wouldn't think twice about shooting an Irishman anyhow. Says we're all fucking rebels. Me, that never crossed the fucking road in the wrong place."

"Where's Major Stokes in this, sir?" said Willie. He remembered the man well enough. A kind of crazy man at the end of his tether, right enough.

"Chairman, what's the what'sa, of the court martial. The main man and all that. Yeh, so your man there, he was begging me, begging me, back in May, and you know, I can't say anything, mustn't speak, but one evening — all right, I felt sorry for him, it was the middle of the month by then, and maybe I was a little, just a little tad upset myself, like all the lads, at the news from home, but fuck him, there's a war on here, so I just stand there, in the darkness, and I say the names, and the dates, you know, 8 May, Kent, Mallin, Colbert, Heuston, and so on, and so on — Yeh, and how did I remember them, well, I don't know, burned into the fucking brain, and I said all the names and the dates, and he just stands there looking at me, like I fucking shot them myself. And I could have been court martialled myself for that, so don't say anything about it, Private."

"I won't, sir."

"Fucking business. We're getting shot to hell by the Hun, aren't we, boy, and this boyo in here's all tied up in his own stupid guts, bellyaching, making a holy show of himself. It's his mother and father I think about. What'll it be for them if they shoot the stupid bollocks?"

"I don't know."

"No more does he himself," he said, then spins on a sixpence: "But a nice lad."

192

Then Father Buckley poked out his sleek head and beckoned Willie. He nodded to Willie and patted him on the shoulder and nodded again, as was his way, and stepped out into the anteroom to let Willie go through.

The little lock-up was dark enough, with only a sprinkle of light in a corner, from a small window. Maybe that was why they chose it as a clink, because there was no way out that Willie could see, except past the philosopher at the door outside. Somehow or other he felt he was going to talk to a man he knew all his life, which was a strange thing, since he met him only the once.

In the corner on a narrow cot lay Jesse Kirwan, with his wheat-coloured hair. The uniform on his small form was surprisingly neat, as if the little man hadn't moved about much. He didn't look like a rebel anyhow, or a person that had refused to obey an order. He looked like a small stone figure carved long ago by a not especially gifted carver. There was a metal cup of water on a stool at his head. There was a bowl with some decent-smelling stew in it and a spoon in the bowl, but the food hadn't been touched.

There was even a nice hunk of black bread that Willie would quite like to try. But he went over to the cot and stood there looking down.

His eyes grew more used to the murk and he could see Jesse Kirwan's face a little better. The pallor of the skin was quite yellow and damp, and Willie frowned to see that.

"Are you all right? Are you getting on all right?" he said.

After a full half-minute, Jesse Kirwan turned his head a bit and squinted up at him.

"Hello, yourself," he said. "That's Willie Dunne, isn't it? Because the old eyesight isn't the best."

"Yeh, it's me."

"My old mate from the streets of Dublin."

"Well."

"No, I just wanted to see you before — well, of course, they're going to have to shoot me. But I don't know, we had a right day of it in Dublin."

"Father Buckley asked me to see you to tell you not to be disobeying and to be contrite and the like, so they won't have to shoot you."

"No, but they do have to shoot me. I want them to."

"Why in the name of Jesus do you want them to do that?"

"It'll be all the same, Willie. They'll just put 'Died of Wounds' or 'Killed in Action' on my sheet and send that home with my uniform."

"Why do you want them to do that?"

"Because an Irishman can't fight this war now. Not after those lads being executed. No, indeed."

"And what about your father and mother?"

"They would understand me, if I could explain it to them, which of course I cannot."

"What's the use in dying, when no one will know why, or anything?"

"Ah, yes, it's a private matter, between me and my guardian angel. See? But look it, that's all decided. I just wanted to see you again, so someone will know what happened, and why."

"Do you want me to get in touch with your father?"

"No, no, nothing like that, Willie. Definitely not. Just so that someone knows, just that, is why I asked to see you. One living person. Well, they asked me if someone would speak for me, and I don't know a soul out here that knows me well enough to do that. But somehow or other your face and name swam into view I hope you don't mind, Willie?"

"I don't know what you want."

"I don't want anything."

"Why did you come out to the war, Jesse, if you felt like this?"

"I thought it was a good thing. It seemed like a good thing. But it's not a good thing now. I'm not making a big thing of it. The army just thinks I'm a mystery. That suits me. I know I can't get out any other way. I signed up for the duration. But I won't serve in the uniform that lads wore when they shot those others lads. I can't. I'm not eating so I can shrink, and not be touching the cloth of this uniform, you know? I am trying to disappear, I suppose."

Now Jesse started to shake. It might have been just because he was weak in his body, but it looked like plain fear. Willie was fearful of that fear, if it was fear. The little man continued to tremble. Maybe he was even sobbing a little.

"I don't know what to say to you," said Willie.

"You see, what it is, Willie, I want a witness to my plight, but not a witness that will say a word about it, and I know you can do that."

"Do you want me to speak at the court martial, give a character thingamabob?"

"It won't do me any good. I don't mind if you're to be there. So you can witness, you know. But they will shoot me. It's just army regulations. One thing leads to another thing."

"Well, I won't be there unless I'm to say something. But what will I say?"

"Say you saw me crying in the streets of Dublin. Did you think I was afraid? I wasn't afraid. I was thinking, They've ruined everything. Now we won't have a country at all. Now everything you and me and the others were trying to do is useless. And maybe I could have dried my tears then and got on with it. But then they started shooting those poor men, and that was a filthy business. Why did you volunteer, Willie?"

"I don't know."

"Ah, well."

"Because I never reached six feet."

"What's that, Willie?"

"The reason."

"You're a strange one, Willie."

"I know."

"Keep all this under your hat and if they let you into the court martial, well and good."

"All right."

"All right?" said Jesse Kirwan

"All right," said Willie Dunne, and even started to go. But something kept him; he didn't know what it was. A dread of moving forward into the next moment, a dread of history and a dread of the future. And the coin of — what? — strange friendship maybe, spinning in between, in this bleak room.

"Look it, Willie," said Jesse Kirwan. "Millions of lads have died out here. Maybe millions more will yet. Heaps and heaps of us. I will acknowledge my mistake, Willie Dunne. I thought it would be a good thing to follow John Redmond's words. I thought for my mother's sake, her gentle soul, for the sake of my own children, I might go out and fight for to save Europe so that we might have the Home Rule in Ireland in the upshot. I came out to fight for a country that doesn't exist, and now, Willie, mark my words, it never will. Don't think I am not gobsmacked by that news. I know you don't think like me. I don't know what has brought you out here. Maybe you think that Ireland is just fine as she is and you are fighting for that. Well, Willie boy, that's an Ireland that maybe did exist two years ago as you set out, but I doubt if it will much longer."

"Can't you just eat your maconochie like the rest of us, Jesse, and to hell with Ireland and this Ireland and that Ireland? You'd give a saint a headache with that talk, man dear. Didn't you have the winner of the Grand National? That's what we should be talking about."

"Did I, did I? I never even thought to look. Lord Jesus, I hope I still have the docket."

"That's the right sort of talk. That other talk of yours is lousy talk."

"I know, I know. You're a gentleman to put up with it. And I got the habit from my father. Such a self-torturing, complicated, mad-thinking man you

197

never met. Better he had been an accordion player and handed me down an accordion. Don't you know? But it had to be this song, this rigmarole, this torment of talk of freedom. I knew it would do for me in the end!"

"Come on, Jesse, say the good word and when we meet again you can talk as much nonsense about Ireland as you please. Come on now."

But Jesse Kirwan only turned a weary smile on him, and raised up a shaky hand. And took Willie's right hand in his, and shook it very nicely.

"All right," said Willie, "then, I brought you this."

And he fetched into one of his pockets and brought out the little Bible that Maud had got for him.

"I've taken out the letters I had in it and a photograph."

"I have a Bible, Willie," said Jesse, but he took it right enough.

"Yeh, well, there's one without my piss stains on it."

Then Willie Dunne came out again to the curious priest and the curious sentry. But he didn't say anything to them. He felt like there were lice in his blood; his arms were uncomfortable. He had wanted for a moment to embrace Jesse Kirwan like you might a child, but he hadn't, and so his arms were aching.

Father Buckley walked him back to billets. The ordinary business of war proceeded around them; they were bringing up lorry-loads of munitions in a great and endless snake. Some cavalry regiment was billeted back here and there were a thousand horses or so all saddled up and ready, in two seemingly infinite lines in a broad field. They were beautiful, like beasts out of fables. There were peaceful enough woods far over to the right with tall black trunks and an air of simplicity and the force of a storybook.

"He knows that Jesus loves him, he said to me," said Father Buckley. "His mother is a great believer, he told me. A convert, as a matter of fact. What did he say to you, Willie? Do we have any chance of saving him?"

Willie stopped on the gravelly road. Some fellas only recently had cast the gravel over it, to counteract the unseasonal rain. The Engineers it might be, or the Chinese coolies. But the July sun was piercing and heroic now. It was like a music in itself. A prayer.

Anyway, Willie looked at Father Buckley. Of course, now he was under a sort of promise to say nothing. To be a queer sort of witness that witnessed and said nothing. For what?

Willie had a sudden desire to be drinking, to be happily whoring, to be doing anything but this, walking along with this morose padre, with his serious and rather ugly face. He didn't understand Jesse Kirwan. He had met him only the once, more or less. Why should he pay him any heed in the upshot? There had been thousands of deaths just in the last days over by the ruinous river. Two thousand Irishmen of the 36th alone. He thought Jesse Kirwan was all twisted up in a rope of his own making; he knew he was. He had made a trap for himself in the wood of his own heart. He was the snare, the rabbit, and the hunter all in one.

"Why doesn't he just buckle down to the job and see it through and go home then and think his thoughts as he likes?" said Willie.

"I wish he would. It's not the time for that, maybe. People of all sorts are having notions. Maybe it's a time for notions, Willie. When death is all around. Well, we can pray for him. God is good."

Willie shook his head and they moved on together.

CHAPTER
THIRTEEN

In August, just as the weather worsened, Jesse Kirwan was executed. It wasn't that Major Stokes showed special vindictiveness. In fact, as chairman of the field general court martial, he spoke with a measure of grace and mercy. But they were all bound in the bounds of army law. Father Buckley did his best to speak of his character. Willie Dunne, as it happened, was not allowed to speak, nor was even called to attend, because he was not an officer and therefore had no force for such an occasion. Father Buckley in the presence of the judges felt awkward and clumsy, out of his element. He had grown used to the company of the private soldiers. Nevertheless, he said what he knew candidly. He couldn't help wondering in his private mind whether it wouldn't have been better to get the Anglican padre to speak, though Major Stokes treated him with utmost courtesy. But the prisoner himself seemed entirely unrepentant, and though he was able to sit in his chair in the room appointed, he was obviously very sick and weak. There was nothing Major Stokes could do. The whole of the world was at war and both the conscripted and voluntary soldiers were bound to do their duty before the horrendous challenge that faced them. It was liberty herself that was imperilled. Major Stokes said all these things with a grave and florid face. He reminded the court that in the first year of the war six hundred French soldiers were shot for cowardice. His Majesty by comparison had been lenient. But the war was coming into a new phase of emergency, and discipline was now as precious as life itself.

By tradition a man was killed at dawn in that moment between darkness and growing light. Twelve of his fellows were chosen from his own battalion as an example to them. But Jesse had had only a chance to touch but lightly on his fellow soldiers. They did not know him, because he had changed his mind so swiftly and had had no time to be an ordinary soldier among them, pissing and shitting and joking with the rest.

When he was brought out to stand against the pole, they had to tie him, because he had no strength at all after his long fast. He was as thin as a greyhound.

It was rather cold that morning and the men could smell the rain burgeoning in the west.

Someone pinned a piece of white cloth on his breast over the heart, like a military decoration. Or as if his heart were partaking in some weird act of surrender. Certainly he was a man of uncomplicated faith and straight reasoning, but his heart was pierced by a bullet from one of the gathered party.

They lifted their cold rifles and when Major Stokes dropped his officer's stick, they killed Jesse Kirwan.

The birds began to sing in the stand of trees behind the fallen body. It was as if he never had been. It was as if there never had been a proper reason for a life, as if

202

all stories and pictures were a lie and a nonsense. It was as if blood were ashes and the song of a life was only the painful extension of a baby's cry. How his mother had loved him and rejoiced in his coming and fed him were hardly known. He seemed in that moment to leave no echo in the world.

Willie Dunne was given permission to join the detail to dig a hole for him in the earth. The truth was, that earth would be disturbed four or five times in the coming years. Jesse Kirwan would be blown out of his resting-place and scattered across the bombed earth, blown and scattered again, till every morsel of him was entirely atomized and defunct.

As Willie dug, he could not help thinking of the uniform removed from the body, and sent back to the father and the mother, and how they might puzzle over the bloodied hole. How the father and the mother might hold the uniform without their son in it, and wonder about a thousand things.

Father Buckley of course attended. He was voluble in his grief. When the slight body was lain down to rest and the earth thrown back in and over with the glistening spades, he expatiated to Willie. He could not help it, Willie thought. He told him things that were no good for Willie to know. It hurt him to know them, as if Jesse Kirwan were being brought closer and closer to him, like a brother. He wanted to stop his blessed ears against the information.

But Father Buckley wanted to slow down this awful speeded-up death. Maybe he wanted to sing the praises of a soul as it started to fly up towards heaven, and all so unexpectedly. Jesse must have said a few things right enough to the priest in the dark of the lock-up; small, useless things.

That Jesse's mother, Fanny Kirwan, was a little woman from Sherkin Island on the coast of Cork. Her own people being millenarians from Manchester, who had come to Sherkin to await the New Jerusalem. But in the end the sect had dwindled and there was no one left among them for Fanny Kirwan to marry. She had gone away to Cork City with Patrick Kirwan, a lithographer, and a Catholic, Jesse's dada himself, never to return again, causing hurt to herself and to her own father. It was the rule of her sect that no one could marry outside the chosen families, and if they did, loved as they might be, they must go and never return. And she chose that, because she had been so intent to have her children. Losing her place in the New Jerusalem and by the hearth of her family, to have her children. And she had had a child, said Father Buckley, and they had just lain him in the ground.

Well, it sounded like a fable to Willie Dunne, a fable, not a truthful account. It made him want to shoot the bloody priest, listening to it, and the doleful voice it was spoken with. Willie didn't want the story hanging from his heart for the rest of his days, for the love of God.

The story hung from his heart for the rest of his days.

That night in the blowing darkness Willie Dunne sneaked away to the grave and sang "Ave Maria" to Jesse Kirwan's vanished shade. It was the edge of a storm. As it was a song he sang often to his father, he couldn't help but think of his father now.

Poor Jesse. He hardly knew him, but he felt brotherly about the matter. He sang both verses of the hymn. The moon was quite playful among the August clouds. As Willie Dunne was no fool, he knew that he couldn't be the same Willie Dunne he had been before this happened.

"That's very fucking sad," said O'Hara, lying on his bed.

Willie was thinking, Yes, it was.

"It's fucking terrible what they can shoot you for out here," said O'Hara. He was keeping his voice very low. He was lying on one side so his lampy face was opposite Willie's own, in the August dark. Far off in the distance they could hear a continuous ruckus of big guns, which had woken them both up. It must be still five o'clock. Maybe the bombardment was further up the line where the French were, who were fond of a four-thirty bombardment. But it could be anywhere.

"How do you mean?" said Willie.

"I mean disobedience, shooting a man for that. I mean. There's much worse."

"How so?"

"Well, you came in in '15, didn't you, Willie? But there were RDF men in earlier, the old hands. Well, we were stationed out in India when the war broke out, and had to be shipped back here. You may have heard of what we went through in the first weeks. A lot of us were killed. It was terrible days."

"I heard that. A lot of the old hands were killed."

"Yeh, that's right, Willie. Fellas that were in the army because, well, fuck it, Willie, there wasn't much else for them to be doing. But a lad like your man there, your pal, shot yesterday, now he was a volunteer, right and proper, you might say. Now a fella volunteers and you'd think they'd treat a man like that different. You know? Would you go shooting a man that volunteered to help you, if he suddenly decided he didn't want to help any more? Hah? No. You would not. Anyway, I was saying, it was in the early days of the war and —"

Then he stopped. Willie was listening but O'Hara stopped.

"What?" said Willie.

"Ah well, maybe I shouldn't be telling you. Maybe it doesn't reflect very good on me, either. Come to think of it. You see, your man there being shot makes me think what I could have been shot for, and proper order maybe, and better deserved."

"Why, Pete?"

"Well, in those days the war was a little more open, just a little more, you know, moving about. You could lie down at the edge of a field and see the fucking Hun across the wheat or whatever, and engage like that. It was the fucking guns and the armies swinging round about that fucking made these fucking trenches from north to south of the fucking world. But in those times it was different. And you might be in a place that the Germans were in a few days before and vice versa. And the soldiers were old hands and that, rough lads and had seen grim old times out in India; we were always dying out there of dysentery and malaria and the like. We were like fucking stuck pigs out there from the heat and the fevers. It was nicer in fucking Belgium! Anyway, my little crowd was sent in to be checking out this little village, little place like a little Irish fucking village, and in we went, scared as rabbits, but, you know, willing enough, for the sake of the grub and the rum ration, you know? Well, Willie, of course there wasn't a soul left in there. That was the time when Jerry went fucking through, he killed everything, he drove everything in front of him, and what he didn't kill he ate, and worse. And worse is what I'm getting to. Now you heard of the nuns being, you know, done over, you know, and you heard of babies being, yeh? — and now I never saw such things, but we came into this little place like I say, and there was nothing there, a few people lying around dead, a few dogs even I remember, but in the middle of the village was a small building, it might even have been a chapel, but it was just rough and ready, I don't know. Me and the lads went in and there was a woman, a girl, tied up there. Well, she was tied belly down onto a kind of a yoke that might usually hold a saddle or something, and she was lashed to that, and her skirts were all up at the back, big dark blue skirts she had, and her poor bum all exposed, and I swear as red as a beetroot the whole fucking vista of it. Now the first thing we did was we hurried over to her, you know, thinking to untie her. And I was the first to get round the front of her, where her face was, and Jesus Christ, it was a horrible thing to see, although we had come through a battle by then and had seen men slaughtered rightly. Someone had cut out her tongue and you could see the blessed thing lying in the straw, like a what's-it, a baby mouse, you know, all hairless and bloody, and into her forehead someone had cut the word 'd-e-u-t-s-c-h', which means, Willie, German, and one of the lads said, 'Hold on, Pete,' he said to me, 'is that written on her head because she's after going off with the Boche, or is that written there because she betrayed her own people, or what's it written there for?' And I said, 'It's there because they're after raping, after violating the poor woman, and now we should cut her down loose and help her.' But this lad said, 'Well, now, Pete, we don't know that,' but the young lieutenant that was with us comes in then, and he said, 'Help that woman and we'll report back.' So right, Willie, we cut her down and of course she's, you know, wonky in the head, she can't speak, she's in terrible pain, she's weeping and making a horrible moaning sound you make when you don't have a tongue. It was just fucking horrible. And this lad said, 'What'll we do, sir? Sure we can't bring her back with us,' and the lieutenant said, 'Of course we can.' Now the lieutenant in question was about nineteen years old, I do not lie, and if he ever saw a woman naked, let alone without a tongue, I am willing to hand over the million pounds you bet me. Well, bugger me, we head back through the village, helping the girl along, well, and she's kicking and sort of groaning like that, and won't be easily helped, and the blood starts to pour again from her broken mouth, and we make our way across a stubbly field the way we came, and just as we get out into the middle of the field, some fucking joker in the woods over to the right of us opens up with a machine-gun, and down goes the lieutenant because in those days the officers still wore their officers' uniforms, like eejits, but what did we know about that, and down goes a few of the other lads, and I don't know, but we haul ourselves over with that mad girl and heave ourselves and her into the ditch along the field-path, like burning dogs. And this lad I was talking about gets such a scare, he hits the woman in the face with his fist and calls her an ugly German bitch, but she couldn't have been, out there in the middle of Belgium, but he was frightened, you know, and had that little mad thing in the head you get out here. Then we wait. Not a sound from the woods, not a squeak. We wait about ten minutes. A — what do you call it? — an airplane goes over, and that was a rare sight in those days, and it gave us another fright, and it had those funny markings on the wings, so we knew it wasn't one of our lads, RFC. But you'd never hear a shot from an airplane then, or a bomb dropped, they were just for looking, but looking seemed bad enough, and we were thinking there'd be all sorts of bits of the Boche army coming after us then, and we were half a mile at the least from where we wanted to be. So this little bastard gets a hold of the woman and he lifts her skirts and doesn't he start to hump her himself, right there in the ditch, I mean, the daftest thing you would ever see."

"What did you do, Pete?"

"That's the thing, you see. I didn't do anything. I helped to hold down her shoulders. Jesus Christ. And I don't know why to this day."

O'Hara looked shriven now and contrite. That was plain. But Willie Dunne was no priest. The sound of the guns in the distance was very like the sound of the great waves down on the Great South Wall in the depths of winter when they came marching and crashing against the Half-Moon Swimming Club that was once the barracks of soldiers when soldiers wore red coats. Willie lay as still as a suspected mouse in the corner of a room. He looked at O'Hara's face in the speckled moonlight. He must be twenty-three or four, Willie thought, an old man by some standards, a young man by others.

He had never heard a story so terrible. He had seen terrible things. He had buried Jesse Kirwan. He had been witness to that and the death of Captain Pasley. But now he had heard a story and all he could see in his mind's eye was Gretta; Gretta in that dark blue skirt, and that stupid, vicious lad getting a hold of her in a ditch like a dog. Without knowing what he was doing, he sat up abruptly on the bed and reached towards O'Hara and landed a serious punch right into his face. The face stared back astonished. Before O'Hara could speak again, he pummelled another closed fist into the shocked features. The lip was split by the blow and immediately started to bleed dark blood in the darkness. But O'Hara didn't say a word; all that could be heard were the faraway guns like wild, otherworldly horses ploughing through stony earth.

"You black cunt," said Willie Dunne.

"Will you keep the voice low," hissed O'Hara. "Do you want to have me lynched?"

"You deserve it, you bastard."

"I only told you the fucking story because your mate was fucking killed!"

"What in the name of Jaysus are you talking about? You think I want to hear your foul fucking story? In the darkness?"

"And you'd've done different, of course, the fucking policeman's son!"

It was tricky to have a conversation like this and keep your voice down and not wake another soul. Why Willie felt duty bound indeed to keep his voice down was a mystery to him, or would be if he considered it.

"You just fucking tell me that's not true, Pete; you just tell me that's not true."

"Don't be fucking self-righteous, brother, you fucker. Didn't you fucking come with me with those whores just weeks past? Hah? You think you're so holy?"

"It's not holy, it's not holy, you're talking about murder!"

"We didn't fucking murder her. We brought her back to the captain. It was the lieutenant was murdered, and the lads were murdered. And it's fucking murdered we've been ever since. And who gives a fuck about us, Willie? No one. Doesn't matter to them if we live or we die, there's always another stupid bastard to take our place."

"And what happened to her, Pete?"

"Who?"

"That Belgian woman, Pete, that you — just like the sainted Germans did, just like all those stories we were told, Pete, what they did to the women."

"Don't be so holier than thou, Willie. You'd've done the same."

"What happened to her, what happened to her?"

O'Hara said nothing for a moment.

"All right, all right." But he didn't seem able to say it for another few moments yet. Then he nodded his punched face. "She died of what had happened to her. She was bleeding all those hours. She was not treated right. She was fucking torn to pieces, wasn't she? And she died. And we tried to save her."

"You think so?"

"It's just a story, Willie, a story of the war."

"You can keep your story, Pete. You can keep it."

And Willie lay back trembling on his bed. The guns were silent now. He imagined the French troops climbing out of their trenches and heading off across the unwholesome ground. There had been hundreds, thousands of the people from all these ravaged districts killed no doubt, women like that woman, and old men and their women, and the children of Belgium, all swallowed up in the mouth of the war. And if O'Hara and his pal did that at the start of the war, what would he be able to do now? What would Willie be capable of himself? Were they not mirrors of each other, mirror after mirror, in bed after bed, in billet after billet, in battalion after battalion, in regiment after regiment, in division after division, all across this ruined place? What of such hearts and souls? Could the soul hold good, could the heart? Was O'Hara a child thrown among blood and broken souls? Was O'Hara his brother too, if Jesse Kirwan was? Was the family of mankind in all of itself the enemy? Was there no friendly army left upon the unkind earth?

CHAPTER
FOURTEEN

But everything, no matter what, no matter how vexing, ruinous, or cheering, could be brought into battle, with the rest of a soldier's pack. It had to be; grief and horror could not be left behind. They folded to nothing and were carried like boulders.

They went, the lot of them, marching two by two, along that fierce road, with every step moving away from that makeshift paradise of the rear camp. No more the birds in the morning and the filthy work at fatigues, hacking and digging, and parades on the parade ground and those "fucking eternal press-ups", as Christy Moran tenderly referred to them, especially "that fucking fancy one", when you raised yourself on your arms and then lifted a leg "like a fucking ballet dancer", first the left and then the right.

"Just exactly when", he asked the men rhetorically, "have ye found it useful in the fucking trenches to be able to lift your left leg backwards till your bollocks falls off?"

But it was all in the manuals, and a sergeant-major must be faithful to such things, like an agnostic priest. And God knows, when reason and mercy had fled out of the world, there was nothing like a manual. And it was a wonder to Willie all the same that the officers did seem to have a passion for those exactitudes, and he saw Captain Sheridan every day in his temporary office producing a thousand sheets of written paper, the Cavan hand patiently scratching across, line after line. And the runners came in and ran off, or he was yapping away on the telephone when the lines were good.

They knew, everyone, that the darkest year of the war was being endured all along the line from Portugal to the sea. But especially all around the River Somme, Death had been smiling his contented smile. There were days when the newspapers had three thick columns of men's names in tiny type, special red-letter days a person might say, the red being the life-blood of thousands.

It was not just the Ulstermen of the 36th, not for a moment. It was Scottish Highlanders (some of them hailing oddly from Canada, Willie noted), black Africans, great clumps of Chinese workers incinerated while they worked, Australians and New Zealanders, in violent teems of youngsters faithfully plodding across acres to receive machine-gun bullets in their eyes, their brains, their cheeks, their breasts, their legs, their stomachs, their ears, their throats, their backs (more rare, unless the Boche came in behind them), the small of the back, the small of the knee, the small of the heart. There was no town or village on the anatomy of the human body — if the body could be considered a country — that had not tried the experiment of a bullet entering there.

Just now they heard queer good news, that sections of their own regiment had gained an objective against the doomy fusillades, and the mind-exploding explosions of shrapnel. They had gone through certain slaughter to take at last the flattened village called Guillemont, only days past, though they lost some hundreds of Dublin lads, and hundreds more gashed by bullets, faceless, armless, screaming in the hospitals. Perhaps no man could speak of victory when the bodies of his mates were visible and tormented in his dreams, and he was following after to the same sites of hurt and death.

And they had been at it, the Allied forces, since February of the year when the ground began to dry, uselessly, astonishingly striving. Guillemont itself had been assailed at least three times already and whatever poor men they were — of the nations come innocently to war — had been hard driven back with bayonet and desperate ferocity, or added to the filthy ground.

But this recent death-laden victory was what brought Willie Dunne and his mates back towards the line, in the words of Captain Sheridan, "to consolidate the victory and attempt to follow on to Guinchy", another mysterious and villagerless village. In the words of Christy Moran, "to thump the bastards back to Berlin".

They came into a region of the dead. It was the strangest thing. The only spot Father Buckley could find for his little service before battle was a segment of a field that had been fought over some days before. The few hundred of Willie's battalion stopped there in the darkness. Ahead it was as if some vast fairground were afoot, with wondrous rides turning and turning in the night, with some regal fireworks thrown in to delight the crowd. The noise of the bombardment at that distance, however, was not festive — the bombs thudded deep, one after the other, like a giant punching a stomach. They laid down their arms and their packs and looked about them. The whole area was strewn with killed men, and by their tags and bits they knew they were Irishmen. Some lay like fallen automatons, as if for a while on the ground they had tried to keep stepping along, in the slow dance of the attack. Machine-gun bullets had done their awful work, tearing into faces and bloodying the soiled uniforms.

But Father Buckley had to have somewhere to speak to them. He handed candles to a few men and these were lit so that there was some suggestion of a place of worship.

"I want to speak to you all equally," said Father Buckley. "Many of you are new in the line and may find these experiences demanding. I want to assure you that Our Lord God is with you and watching over you. You are part of a division of astonishing men. I have observed the extraordinary piety among you men. Your sincere faith and your devotion to Our Lady in particular. You are fighting a holy war, not only in defence of the Catholic peoples of Belgium, but to attain a sure and incontestable certificate for the freedom of Ireland and her existence as a separate, proud and loyal nation. What unites us all is that certainty that God, who sincerely celebrates the

217

goodness of every man, wishes only the best for you. That you will flourish as soldiers and as men. He understands your fears and wonders at your courage. And know, men, that wherever you will go, I will follow, and insofar as it lies in my powers to do, I will be there at your side in your hour of need, not just as a simple priest from the county of Kildare, but as God's shadow on this earth, and I will whisper in your ear all that you need to hear. So, my good friends, fear nothing, for the good God flies by your side and breathes into your hearts untouchable joy and love."

The candles shook and trembled as men breathed out, as though in the very act of trying to hear every word of the priest, they had held their living breath, as though in some strange fashion they were content to die a moment while they strained their ears.

It was indeed as if even the dead were listening and he was speaking also to the dead. It was all too clear and true that those other battalions of the 16th used to take Guillemont had been divided into three parts, like Caesar's Gaul: the wounded who had filled every field hospital and were now clogging up drear Trônes Wood with their cries and pain; the living, exhausted and shattered; and the dead, who were here.

Father Buckley asked the Mother of God again to protect the men. The slight, stooped priest with the ugly face made soft and young in the moonlight and the rising and falling glares of explosions, recited the Hail Mary: "Ave Maria, gratia plenis . . ." The men strained to catch the words, though they knew them perfectly since earliest childhood. There was no Sunday indifference of men at the back of a country church here. Willie Dunne joined his hands together with the rest and felt the sudden balm of the priest's prayer. The idea of a mother blazed out to him clear and new, as if he had never heard the word before, or knew there was such a thing. He thought of his own dead mother in her days of ordinary strength and, as if for the first time, wondered at the vagaries and mere chances of a life. "In the midst of life we are in death," said Father Buckley — this had a miserable truth where they stood, listening in those moments mostly with the ears of sons.

There were things he allowed himself to be thinking, he realized, and things he had grown to forbid himself. He stared about him at the other faces: O'Hara over there with his secret, Christy Moran on one knee like a countryman though he was from Kingstown, Joe Kielty's gentle face showing nothing but a sort of dreaming attention. Joe looked as relaxed as a sleeping baby. Willie had no words to tell what he was feeling in response to Father Buckley's words. He wondered suddenly and definitely for the first time in his life what words might be. Sounds and sense certainly, but something else also, a kind of natural music that explained a man's heart or heartlessness, words as tempered as steel, as soft as air. He felt his sore head clear and his back lighten and his legs strengthen. It was as strange to him as the sight of death. He hoped the words would work on the dead and be a balm to them also.

Meanwhile, the explosions up ahead seemed to be tearing at the stars themselves, sorely extinguishing them, ripping those buttons of timid light.

The approach trench was a reeking culvert with a foul carpet of crushed dead. Willie could feel the pulverized flesh still in the destroyed uniforms sucking at his boots. These were the bodies of creatures gone beyond their own humanity into a severe state that had no place in human doings and the human world. They might be rotting animals thrown out at the back of a slaughterhouse, ready for the pits, urgently so. What lives and names and loves he was walking on he could not know any more; these flattened forms did not leak the whistle tunes and meanings of humanity any more.

There were bombs falling everywhere now in an industrial generosity. Sadly these were their own bombs, fired out some miles back by their own artillery, whose gauges and sights were so worn by use that the missiles went either too short or too far — in this case, as they stumbled along under the cargo of their packs, too short. Willie tried to half close his eyes as he passed now over fresh bodies, the exterminated forms of his own mates. He didn't want to see men he knew mangled like this for nothing. He wished he were a horse on the road with his leather blinkers doing good service.

Now they rose up in the violent moonlight and entered bizarrely a huge field of high corn, the frail stems brushing gently against their faces, and because Willie was a small man, he had to grip the coat of

Sergeant-Major Moran in front or he would be lost, set adrift to wander for ever in this unexpected crop. The absurd bombs followed them religiously into the field, smashing all about the darkness, the stench of cordite and other chemicals obliterating the old dry smell of the corn. Willie heard men cry out, he stumbled through little sites of disaster, he could not help but see through his squinting eyes here and there a ruined face, or underfoot stumble on the wet branch of an arm or a leg. How easily men were dismembered; how quickly their parts were unstitched. What this war needed, Willie thought, was men made of steel, who could march on through chaos so that when they were blown into a thousand pieces there were no mourners for them at home and no extremity of pain. He passed poor Quigley, no longer miraculous but with his arm sheared off at the shoulder, so there was only a bloody boil of flesh there. His face had been lifted by the blast and torn half way off, so that his awful jawbone was bare with bare yellow teeth.

They came to a series of barbed-wire lines, and here there were older bodies heaped, in places three deep and more, men of Ireland also in a hundred terrible attitudes. Willie knew the gaps they had left in the division would be filled. More men from old Dublin and surrounds brought out on the crowded boats and along the rail-lines and bussed over puzzling country and inserted into trenches and then on into these local and myriad infernos. The thought somehow panicked him further, as if he were responsible for everything, for the dead men and the men soon to die. He wanted the dead to be alive again and the living men to go back home. There was one battle in this war but the armies were changing all the time, like a tube emptying at the top and filling at the bottom, so that no one man, he thought, knew what was afoot and no one man could feel he had done anything but piss his trousers in terror. For now Willie had the cold fingers of terror at his measly throat, he was starting to gabble, to pray not to God as it happened but to Gretta: Dear Gretta of the beautiful arse, preserve me, rescue me. He was chopping as best he could at the wire, as they all were, this cat's cradle of death they must get through as quick as nifty rabbits.

"What's that you're saying?" said a voice behind; it was Joe Kielty.

"Oh, forgive me, Joe," he said, hacking on at the wire with the clumsy cutters, "I don't know what I'm gassing on about."

"Don't worry," said Joe Kielty, who after all was twenty-five years old and no spring chicken or chicken of any nature, "we'll be all right, I am sure of it."

"I'm glad to hear that, Joe. I was urgently requiring to hear that."

And when he said that in his best cheerful manner, O'Hara looked over.

"That's it, Willie, you keep our spirits up."

"I will, Pete, I will, if I can."

And there was no trace of the horror he had felt at Pete's story.

"What's this fucking crop anyhow?" said Christy Moran.

"I don't know, Sarge," said Joe Kielty, "you don't see it in Mayo."

"Isn't it rocks you grow there?" said the sergeant-major gently.

"It is, aye, it is," said Joe Kielty. "But they're our rocks. We like them."

"It's wheat," said a voice.

"It's not wheat anyhow," said Joe Kielty, "begging your pardon."

"Is it beet?" said another.

"Would you go and jump with your beet," said a Wicklow voice, pleasantly scoffing. And even Willie himself had seen piles of sugar beet on roadsides in September in that Wicklow. "That's in the ground like a turnip."

"For the love of God, who cares what it is?"

"Well, I don't know, damn me, can you eat it?" said another.

"Little specks of yellow shite at the top of these rough stalks? I don't think so, my lad."

"If you can't eat it, fuck it."

"Fuck it yourself," said O'Hara, and they all had the grace to laugh at the worst joke in Flanders. It was as good as a little sermon.

They came then to a place so loud, so bleak, so bare, that human eyes had difficulty in seeing it, in seeing what it was. Technically — that was, according to Captain Sheridan — they were moving up to the captured German lines, and were then to pass through Guillemont itself and get into trenches beyond for the kick-off. But to get across to the first line of trenches they had to cross a field of some twenty acres. This looked to Willie like it had been the very heart of the battle, either this battle or some other battle. The warriors were still there, all killed, every one. It was like a giant quilt of grey and khaki, like the acres had been ploughed vigorously but then sown with the giant seeds of corpses. There was a legion of British soldiers there, mingled astonishingly with the Boche. Grey jacket and khaki jacket, a thousand helmets scattered like mushrooms, a thousand packs mostly still attached to backs like horrible humps, and wounds, and wounds, such as . . . Willie moved forward with O'Hara and Joe Kielty, following after Christy Moran and Captain Sheridan. Captain Sheridan kept banging his stick on his leg and had not even drawn his revolver.

"Come on, lads," he kept saying. "We'll be all right. Come on, come on, lads."

Death was a muddle of sorts, things thrown in their way to make them stumble and fall. It was hard and hard again to make any path through the humbled souls. The quick rats maybe had had their way with eyes and lips; the sightless sockets peered at the living soldiers, the lipless teeth all seemed to have just cracked some mighty jokes. They were seriously grinning. Hundreds more were face down, and turned on their sides, as if not interested in such awful mirth, showing the gashes where missing arms and legs had been, their breasts torn away, and hundreds and hundreds of floating hands, and legs, and big heavy puddles of guts and offal, all mixed through the loam and sharded

224

vegetation. And as solid as the ruined flesh was the smell, a stench of a million rotted pheasants, that settled on their tongues like a liquid. O'Hara was just retching as he went, spewing down the front of his tunic, and many others likewise. There was nothing they could do, only follow each other to the other side. In the corner of his eye Willie caught a glimpse of Father Buckley, taking up the rear of the battalion, far back at the edge of the slaughtered troops. He quickly looked away. He didn't like the way Father Buckley stared about him. Too many souls without prayers to speed them, too many, too many.

They passed through Guillemont two by two and it was a queer thing to think that this was a site of victory. There was nothing there. The sappers were labouring to flatten sections of ground so that the machinery and supplies and trucks could be brought up. There was a long road being strengthened and repaired by about two thousand Chinese. Someone, either their own guns or the Boche, had the range of all these enterprises, and there were myriad bombs falling on everything, like a wild scene in a play without meaning or purpose, only mere spectacle. It had a filthy fascination, to see the coolies digging and hacking as if ignoring their peril. What could they do? The bombs fell among them and there were distant screams and then the ranks of the diggers closed, and on as before. Well, they were fucking heroes, all right, thought Willie Dunne. It was the very picture of strange courage, weird indifference.

When they reached the assigned jumping-off trenches, by some miracle there were vats of steaming stew. How they got up there no one could tell, but they were not complaining. Captain Sheridan shepherded his section into the new trenches, and very beautiful trenches they were, to Willie anyhow. They were the very peak of German workmanship, with revetments properly palisaded and the mud packed back with trimmed branches, and there was even drainage at their feet, the duck boards laid down over concrete and a culvert carrying off water beneath. Willie peeked into a dugout, fifteen steps down, and there was a light burning there, like a further miracle, and he saw the edge of a table and some papers neatly there. There was no sign of the Hun that had lived in these trenches for months and months past, no corpses at all, so someone had been in to clear them. They all shook their heads at the oddness of it all, and gladly tucked into the wonderful stew. The best of lamb it tasted like! Willie was drooling, he couldn't help it. The juice of the stew was better than water, better than rum even, it slaked and perished the thirst. They felt like kings at the feast.

A dozen worn men in muddy uniforms cupping with sore fingers the rough tins of their food.

Captain Sheridan smiling to himself.

All Christy Moran could offer to this moment of general relief was one incongruous word: "Bastards!"

But whom he referred to no one could tell. All of wretched humanity, maybe.

And then they were allowed sleep if they could. Well, on this occasion they slept like hunting dogs. Christy

Moran often referred to it later as "the Good Kip we had before Guinchy".

Captain Sheridan occupied a dugout and wrote sheet after sheet. Health of the men reports, supply-sheet reports, operational replies, assessments, a letter to his wife in Cavan Town, four letters to the families of dead men, a request for the home address of Private Quigley to divisional headquarters, a report on the state of the trench, a request to the quartermaster for provisions and supplies, more soap for the men's feet in particular.

While he was finishing all this an order came up with a runner that they were to get into position at 0400 hours and follow the bombardment at 0445 hours, their objective being the east of Guinchy village to be reached by 1530 hours if possible on the dot for the purpose of liaison with, et cetera.

"Of course," he muttered to himself. "We are not digging in here. What was I thinking? It was that blessed stew."

By four o'clock they were indeed wakened and in their positions. The trench was longer than usual and so they had an unusual sense of their own company and some of the other companies of the battalion. It was a sense of numbers that was not unwelcome.

Willie Dunne, like the rest, leaned against the parapet with his gun and his pack. It suddenly occurred to him that this would be the first time he engaged in a proper attack. It was not a mightily entertaining thought. It was still very dark across the lands ahead, although every few minutes went up from the Boche lines a starry shell that lit the ground extravagantly in front. There were a few new lads now, a fella called Johnson, and three lads that seemed to be all from around Gardiner Street in Dublin, whose names Willie hadn't been able to garner. They looked like kids really. They had come straight into this and it would be their first understanding of the war, and as Willie himself didn't understand what was going to happen, he pitied them. Yes, he pitied them. What should he feel, he wondered, for himself? By Christ, didn't the blasted piss thrum in his bladder again; he was nearly bursting. As he leaned against the finely wattled side of the trench, gripping a beautiful German assault ladder, he tried to keep a grip on that bladder, he did. Suddenly the artillery went off in a vast line of explosions somewhere, a distant enough sound, and then very quickly the passage of the big-calibre missiles passing overhead and making tremendous noise about a quarter-mile back across the fields. They must have suspected something coming and were trying to get the range of the British guns, hopefully now marshalled on that cleared ground in Guillemont, or somewhere advantageous and efficient. Oh, he prayed now, did Willie Dunne, advantageous and efficient. Good Lord of the advantageous and the efficient, I pray to you, I pray to you, give me courage, oh Lord, let me not die today but return home safely in Your own good time to Gretta, dear Lord, protect me. The noise was beyond the scope of any other noise he had heard. O'Hara whispered to him between blasts, "New ordnance, Willie — big stuff, hah?" and Willie did not doubt his intuition for a minute. Maybe these were the new mortar bombs they had heard of, the barrels for them as big as sewers, huge ruddy things like armoured beasts unheard of in creation. The piss burst straight out and drenched his trouser legs.

"You pissy cunt," said O'Hara kindly, and gave him a dig with an elbow.

"Holy Jesus," said Willie Dunne.

Now the Boche guns found good range on what used to be after all their own trench and the ground ahead was given a horrible pulverizing. Surely no man could be expected to leap out there with his own jolly human skin and walk through such a torrent? No, no, it must be their own guns, because the barrage started to go forward along the fields in a wild display, creating suddenly a thousand thousand holes in the muck that would be miserable to walk across.

"Arra, fuck it," said O'Hara. "Arra, fuck it."

Willie glanced left at Joe Kielty. Joe Kielty looked back at him, serenely, and gave him a friendly wink, and a nod. He wasn't in the gun detail that day because he had scalded his hand. Such a strange soul was Joe Kielty. He even gave Willie a pat on the back, and then before anyone could do anything else — piss, cry, panic or die — Captain Sheridan gave the company his order, and Christy Moran gave his lads the same like an echo, and up the ladders with them.

Before Willie lay suddenly the open ground. Away to the east was the sunrise, cold, pink and clear. There seemed to be woods everywhere on the horizon, but not a tree near by, only this bare, exploding vista. He gripped his gun in two places and hauled himself forward. Captain Sheridan, in his best Sheridan manner, looked fearless, waving them on with his stick, still not bothering to draw a revolver, shouting something at them that no one could hear. He went on ahead of them about twenty yards, they walked solemnly after him, keeping in line as they had been trained, even the new lads doing fine, despite the shell-holes. Their own barrage was just ahead of the captain, about fifty yards, and they knew they must try to keep after it and not be left behind, because then, by God, they would be out in the open and would find out quick what state of disorder or order the Boche were in. But the barrage ran on ahead of them and ahead of Captain Sheridan and not even a bunch of whippets could have followed it, not even a bunch of whippets.

But they went on unimpeded. The barrage had done wonders for the enemy wire and they found it quite easy to pass through, and suddenly a wonderful feeling rose in Willie's breast. He suddenly felt fierce and true and young. It was something close to a feeling of love. It was love. He had strength in his legs despite his burden. He could see now as in a dream Joe Kielty on one side and O'Hara on the other, admirably pushing forward. The whole line was going on, a whole line of Irishmen, he thought, yes, yes, it was magnificent.

Their barrage disappeared into a tumbled copse far ahead and almost immediately machine-guns opened up across the dim way. Captain Sheridan was shot and went down like a statue. Everyone saw it clearly. In one raking stream two of the new boys of Gardiner Street were removed from the line; one was left screaming behind, but no one could stop to help him, it was forbidden. Willie glanced back and saw line after line of his battalion coming after, and dozens and dozens falling under the weird and angry fire. A detail carrying their own machine-gun went down in a bloody heap. Then a splash of dark blood crossed his face, because now there were mortar bombs being dropped among them, and someone had been blown to nothing. Yet at his side still moved, thank God, his blessed companions, Joe Kielty and Pete O'Hara. Willie hardly knew it, but he was crying, crying strange tears. He moved ever onward. They passed Captain Sheridan still alive, sitting on his bottom like a six-month-old child, looking entirely stunned, his whole left arm full, it looked like, of bullet wounds, and just on his chest there was another hole from which rich red blood was pouring. Mrs Sheridan, Mrs Sheridan, Mrs Sheridan, were the odd words that leaped into Willie's throat. On, on they went, they walked, they stumbled.

There must have been a measure of chaos in the order of the lines because Willie could hear clearly Christy Moran's bitter voice caterwauling at people to keep up and close up. Everyone could somehow sense what the machine-guns were doing, as if they were all the one body, and as men fell, they all fell for a moment, fell and rose up again, miraculously pacing. Then it seemed like a second before they reached the ground below the enemy trenches, and Willie saw a bombing party go ahead a little and start lobbing their Mills bombs and there were wild explosions then and maybe by the grace of luck they got the machine-gun but, whatever it was, they were able to keep going and then in another whisper of a second they were at the trench itself and it was like a mad version of training but nonetheless they plunged down into the trench and the first thing Willie felt was a man's hands at his throat, at his throat like a crazy dream, what was happening to him, and Joe Kielty, gentle Joe Kielty, had a murderous-looking yoke in his hand, a sort of rounded hammer, and he struck at Willie's assailant, and then he smashed the hammer or whatever it was into another man and there were shots and mayhem and then the Germans came round from the next part of the trench and they had their hands high and they were shouting like monkeys, "Kamerad, Kamerad!" or such like and though the remaining boy from Gardiner Street did fire into them, he realized his mistake and was soon rounding them up into a clump, and what the fuck was happening then Willie didn't know, but it seemed like a hot, dark, thirsty dream, the whole thing, and he wondered that the heat didn't dry the piss on his trousers.

Then they were told by Christy Moran to group up and hold the fucking trench because the cunts would be back for a counter-attack in a moment, the fucking bollocking lot of them, the bastards. And he looked very wild, and frightened even, his face as white as the shining moon, thin as a dead man's, but oddly enough, when he approached the prisoners, he wasn't violent towards them, but gentle enough, and told them to sit on their arses and be good.

The thirst in Willie's throat was beyond all his experience. He lay there panting all day, panting. The counter-attack never came that day anyhow. Nothing came, no water, no food. The captured Germans were led back across to Guillemont. Maybe they were given some supper, Willie thought. What about the buggering Irish?

Were they heroes or eejits or what? Hour after hour he lay panting, they all did. Towards evening another battalion of the 16th came up and relieved them, and they were sent on their merry way, with Christy Moran in charge now, because Sheridan was wounded and the two lieutenants who had been leading the companies beside them were killed.

Wearily, hungrily, thirstily, they slogged back. They passed men they knew and men they didn't know, all freshly killed along the way. They were like paint marks painted on the fields. Willie could see where the machine-guns had raked in an arc, with a sickle shape of the fallen for their reward. It was a wonder, a wonder that they had not all been killed. He didn't know how they had come through. He had prayed and prayed to his good God and somehow it had sufficed.

They got back near the other trench and the wicked truth was that Captain Sheridan had died and they were putting him on a stretcher. Willie and the others seemed to be pulled towards that stretcher, they followed it through the labyrinth of the jump-off trenches, and all the way into Guillemont. And as they passed along, other members of their battalion watched them go, and even raised a cheer, for these lads who had come through, with their leader slain. Because the news travelled back fast that Guinchy had been taken, that men of the 16th were walking through Guinchy, although it was only a stretch of flattened ground with some light white patches where bricks and mortar of houses had been long since pulverized. So they were heroes of Guinchy after a fashion, Willie Dunne and his mates. But they were ghosts in their hearts. They didn't even look at the men who cheered them, or honoured them, or whatever it was that was happening. Because they knew, because the fellas in question were not there beside them, that at least four men of their platoon were gone, and maybe two-thirds of the company, and maybe half the battalion was dead, and another third terribly wounded. Poor Quigley was gone. The field hospital couldn't manage the deluge of grief and distress. The world was distressed into a thousand pieces. Captain Sheridan was a lolling corpse. And their heads were all screaming, screaming inside, the heads of those heroes of Guinchy.

PART THREE

CHAPTER
FIFTEEN

There was a letter waiting for him from his sister Maud, which was unusual, as Maud was no letter-writer so far, though she had sent a few good parcels:

Dublin Castle.
September 1916.

Dear Willie,

I hope you are well I hope this letter finds you. Dolly and Annie and me send our love. But Papa is annoyed at you Willie. Your letter of recent date he says was not good he is angry Willie. What is it you said to him maybe you can write again and put his mind at rest. He says you must not be asking him about Redmond he wants you to write to him Willie. I hope you are well we send our love and please find a flat daisy from Dolly in the folds of this letter she found it in the castle yard. It is as good as heather she says. All for now Willie.

Your fond sister,
Maud.

He racked his brains then for what might have offended his father, but truth to tell it didn't take much racking.

They had been brought back again into quite a pleasant district and it was so far from the lines that even the artillery could not be heard and only the airplanes speeding along overhead, which was a gay enough sight in itself, kept the war close.

Even writing his last letter he had had a funny feeling in his water that he was getting at things he shouldn't be trying to get at in the company of his father, as it were, but since, as a child and a boy and a young man, he had always been quite open and at ease with him, and praised and nurtured well enough by him, he had thought he might follow his mind as always and speak it. But all the same he had had an inkling of the little rat of unease creeping about, a few words too far that might unsettle an old-fashioned mind like his father's. And now he was a long long way off and he feared it would be too tricky to put it all right by mere letters, especially as he wasn't quite sure what had caused offence, though he had a fair idea. But Maud would never have written if it wasn't a serious matter, because Maud wrote only for births, deaths and marriages, which were what she considered letters were for, being absolutely against gossip and mere news.

Nevertheless, the distance between the site of war and the site of home was a long one and widening. Not the ordinary pragmatic miles between, but some other, more mysterious measure of distance. Icons could be cold things in an army bed, no matter how bright, no matter how burnished. So it was in dreams that his father weighed most heavily; in dreams lay Gretta.

The great spectacle of those days was not a battle but a fight. Not a fight belonging to a battle as such, because now the foul winter was coming in with fearsome frosts and the locking of the land. They pitied the battalions still up the line, with all of the winter ahead to freeze their bones in and try to keep their feet from turning black with frostbite. Boys, with poor food at home and only in those times a few months of hurried training, could freeze in a few hours of that, like poor folk found in the yards of tenements when the temper of the weather snapped in Dublin and brought down a great cloth of murderous snow. So it was along the lines, Willie feared and knew, with French, Irish, English and German alike suffering in the raw ditches of that world.

The fight in question was the closing bout of the great inter-regimental boxing match and, as fate would have it, two Irish lads were posted to face each other, one a Belfast man called William Beatty and the other a tall, bleak-faced hero called Miko Cuddy. The fact that the first was in the 36th and the second in the 16th was strongly noted, and before Guillemont and Guinchy it was billed as a clash of enemies, but after the battles, since some battalions of the Northerners had taken part, this seemed less true, and it was billed as the "Battle of the Micks". But the clash of divisions still gave the proceedings a certain tasty salting. Even God, said Father Buckley, could make up an Irish story like the best of them.

The fight was held in the divisional hall, a decent, big building where Father Buckley was wont to say his masses, and lectures were given in the arts of foot hygiene and the driving in of the bayonet to kill or to wound, distances, how to know where you were in an attack and read the map references correctly, and all such things important but always less interesting than a boxing match.

The hall could boast of four great gasoliers that had been attached to the beams of the ceiling, and that cast down four tents of murky light. The carpenters were drawn from the battalions and a beautiful arena was constructed, with panelled sides and even some Gothic detailing on the uprights, which strictly was not necessary. But everyone felt the passion and rightness and the poetry of the contest. There was nothing about it that anyone objected to. It was, in Father Buckley's odd term, "unobjectionable". By which he meant it wasn't an engagement in the field of death and therefore no one would get killed by machine-gun or shrapnel bomb, and an hour or two of good excitement would be had by the men watching and well deserved. Father Buckley had buried so many men after Guinchy and heard so many death-bed confessions and spoken the rites of the dead to so many that every minute and a half his whole body went into a strange tremble, like a chilly dog, so slight it would not be noticed only that a man might see the soutane minutely wavering. He was a warm man now who could not get warm. About three dozen men had had to be packed off to London on the trains because with them the trembling was ten times more afflicting. Willie had seen lads sitting on the ground and their arms flailing and their heads shooting here and there out of control, and sane as saints but for that, rendering them useless to war and probably to themselves but that they might be cured.

Willie Dunne himself was deep in the pleasure of the times. He was longing to see the fighters come out and he was longing to see them tear into each other with that vicious elegance. Never in his life had he seen a boxing bout, never in his life had he thought of such matters. And now he, in the days leading up to it, was as anxious and oddly happy as the rest, and edgy, and talking with Christy Moran about it, and O'Hara. Beyond these impulses swung the heavy and bloodied blades of terror, but within, for the moment . . . O'Hara himself unwisely opened a little book on the outcome, but because the odds were so short for both men he quickly closed it again, because he saw that he would lose a fortune in the fractions.

Everyone went to the fight because a fight without death — in all likelihood, though indeed it was a bare-knuckle contest — seemed to a man's mind like a bird singing in a verdant wood.

They came in after their grub in great noisy droves and filled the hall speckled with its curious light. Because of the position of the gasoliers, there was little enough light on the ring itself — why a square yoke like that was called a ring was a mystery to Willie Dunne.

He sat down with his own platoon, or the remnant of it, on small wooden chairs with metal backs, that creaked under their arses but held. There were fifty rows of chairs encircling, or perhaps en-squaring, the ring. They tried to leave a little ditch of a gap by which the combatants themselves could enter. The sergeant-majors of the companies did their best, but they knew the nature of the evening. The line officers were content to sit among their men, as they had grown accustomed to doing in the trenches. But the staff officers had a section to themselves right up against the ring, and they sat down there in all their braided glory, having elected to wear their evening dress uniforms. These were creatures rarely seen who nevertheless designed and planned the battles, if did not fight the actual buggering things (said Christy Moran, without evident bitterness).

The gathered faces were plundered by the gaslights, like an audience at a strange theatre where only males were allowed to enter. A person might have suspected a risqué show was about to start, but of course it wasn't so. The rickety doors opened at the top of the hall and the two warriors emerged together, or at least at a discreet distance of a few feet, and came down towards the ring. Whatever Ulstermen were in among the Southerners roared in a mighty bellowing, because William Beatty walked down first, and when Miko Cuddy came stepping grimly along, up went the cheers and caterwauls of the Southerners.

The boxers were both big men but Beatty was a giant.

"Holy mother of Jesus," said O'Hara, "that's never a man, that's a bullock."

Willie Dunne laughed joyously.

"That's a fucking bullock," said O'Hara. "I swear to the good Jesus."

"Poor Cuddy's a midget beside that fella," said Joe Kielty, "and I stood beside Miko Cuddy in Westport one time, and all I could see was his waistcoat buttons."

"Westport, Joe, did you see him in Westport?" said Willie Dunne.

"Didn't he fight his whole way along the western seaboard three or four time," said Joe Kielty, the gentlest man along that seaboard. "He's from Crossmolina."

"Three or four times?" said Willie Dunne.

"Ah, yes, Willie, ah yes, Willie," said Joe Kielty.

But the boxers were very polite, and as the referee examined their hands for possible shards of tin or glass, and saw that the bandages over their knuckles were tight and clean, and were not soaked in oil or vinegar, one to wipe on their own face after the bell, or the other to give a wound a bit of a sparkle all unbeknownst, as the referee saw to these essential but tedious matters, the two boxers stood opposite each other without hostility, "in the best Irish tradition", as Father Buckley pointed out to no one in particular, and when all was ready they shook hands — at least, they knocked knuckles against knuckles in a friendly fashion. Then someone rang a bell. It seemed to Willie that it was the colonel himself, who only some days ago had ridden down to them on his fine black horse and praised their actions at Guinchy, who must have banged the bell, because the noise came from just behind that regal person. Then there was a slight pause and every man in the hall erupted into a wild cheer, and then they fell into the deepest dark silence, and suddenly the four lamps were heard guttering in the smoky air. The pause went on, it seemed to Willie, for a whole minute, and then William Beatty gave a little frisky dance, and lunged forward wonderfully, and gave poor Miko Cuddy such a blow to the head that Willie was sure it would have to fall off, if such a thing were possible. His ear took that blow and he must have heard music all right. Then William Beatty, as if in an ecstasy of good manners and glory, stood back on his heels, and let down his arms, and shook them, as if they might be hurting him a little, and Miko Cuddy leaned and flung such an uppercut at his chin that the hundreds of assembled men gasped as with one breath. No human person could take such a blow and not see blooming stars.

William Beatty stepped back three or four steps, as if indeed he might be counting the galaxies with his eyes open, but then he stepped forward again to Cuddy, and the two circled each other on light feet, and began an exchange of murderous blows, every one to the head if they could. And Willie Dunne could not only hear the odd thud of fist against cheekbone, which had a noise all its own, and sounded excruciatingly sore, but see the sweat break from the men's heads in little fountains, and all under the weird gloom of the hall. Then some invisible person rang the bell and the two fighters

244

slumped away from each other and staggered over a little to their corners, where regimental sergeant-majors from both divisions were dressed in khaki vests and trousers and had bowls of water for their charges and, from what everyone could hear, very severe advice.

But the crowd was deeply pleased. It was evenly matched and, what was more, there was a measure of quite good-natured banter between the different sectors of the audience. Certain political names were mentioned, and other political names were thrown back. The recent trouble in Dublin was indeed mentioned in the tones of Derry and Belfast. And the likely allegiances, religion and backgrounds of both sides were referred to, but not in a way to cause the ultimate difficulty of a furore beyond the furore in the ring, which was curious to Father Buckley, and well noted. For in his heart Father Buckley was a Redmondite — not so much John Redmond, who was the actual leader of the Irish Party, but his brother Willie, who was just a Member of Parliament, and who was with the division at the front and indeed an "old man" like the priest. Father Buckley was reading just yesterday a speech of Willie Redmond in the House of Commons, where he had expressed the pious hope again that the fact of Nationalist and Unionist Irish soldiers fighting side by side might some day foment a greater understanding of each other and bring Ireland in spite of the recent rebellion to a place of balance, peace and mutual nationhood . . . Now the bell went again and it seemed Miko Cuddy was in a fever to finish the fight, no doubt at the prompting of his seconds — the very same name as the men in an old-fashioned duel, Father Buckley noted — who had probably measured the big Ulsterman with mental measuring tape and had fearfully taken in the long reach and the thick muscle of the arms. So Miko Cuddy came forth like a veritable whirligig, like a windmill on the flat white plain of the ring, whirling, whirling his arms, and before he could do much damage, William Beatty came at him like a ballet dancer, side-stepping and jigging and bouncing and finessing every punch, like a man inspired by the very poetry and possibility of movement, and curled in another punch to the very same ear he had caught in the first moment of the fight, and Willie Dunne swore afterwards that he seemed to feel that very punch himself on his own ear, and O'Hara did point out that in his excitement he had indeed landed a gentle box there, but only a shadow of the real thing.

Miko Cuddy stood there a few moments staring at William Beatty. He didn't seem to be thinking very deep thoughts. His ear had swelled between bells, and now with the new blow it was as large as an orange, a very flat, raw blood-orange. William Beatty's chin was profusely bleeding, so maybe one of those whirling punches had caught him after all; it was difficult to say in the gloom. But Miko Cuddy regarded William Beatty. Father Buckley doubted he was thinking of the peacemaking words of any Willie Redmond, or thinking of anything much. There was going to be a great deal of throbbing pain in that head shortly, but not just yet, because Miko Cuddy's legs folded under him and he

246

went down to the canvas — strictly speaking, the side of armament boxes fixed end to end with devious under-screwing — in a flounder of sweat and blood, and a little divvying up of dust.

The referee was a Nigerian from the African Labour Corps who nevertheless had been a licensed referee in civil life. He was an elegant man in a beautiful set of referee's clothing, quite American and impressive, and his features were set in an unsmiling and philosophical grimace. He slowly began his count on Miko Cuddy. The Southerners in the hall at first sat back in dismay and heard the murderous numerals climb to six, to seven. Then they got to their feet like an audience offering an ovation to some great musician and they bellowed and screamed at Miko Cuddy to rise again, and by the love of God and the grace of things in general, he did. He came up in his well-nigh stupor like a god rising from the ground of an old story, and he raised his fists again and simultaneously the hearts of his supporters. And William Beatty, though he shook his head, sending the blood through the strange air, rested on the flat of his boxing boots — strictly speaking, a better class of trench boot — and seemed to await illumination. Then the bell rang again, like a sea-bell rescuing a wandering ship, and Miko Cuddy gratefully sought his corner and lurched down onto his mercifully stoutly constructed stool.

Now there was a different pandemonium in the hall. Perhaps now there was an element of accusation, and over in the corner was a brief mêlée of soldiers, broken up quickly by some watchful NCOs. Pungent remarks were made. "Rebel cunts" was one, and "Ulster bollockses" another. But generally it was only excitement, and a sort of horror-struck happiness.

The bell was struck again and Miko Cuddy lost no time this time in going over to the centre of the ring and swinging a punch at William Beatty. Perhaps he intended it to land somewhere on a welcoming jaw, perhaps he merely hoped to hit something, anything, on the Ulsterman to even up the account of pain. But he went back as he swung on a little pool of his own blood just as treacherous as grease and laid himself out on the floor. William Beatty leaned over and helped him up. An extraordinary shout went up in the hall; no one had ever seen such a weird and even foolish spectacle. William Beatty stood back for two seconds, then lunged forward, and received a blow to his own chin from Cuddy, which sent a thin umbrella of blood out into the air of the ringside, and it fell in a diaphanous curtain across the gathered staff officers, making them stir in their chairs. But they barely flinched all the same, for it wasn't the blood of their own death as such, and to give them their due, they were as enthusiastic as the rest to pursue the fight with their eyes.

There were four more rounds then of traded blows and each man had the measure of the other. Admiration rose up in the watchers and no one could be entirely partisan now. It was a fight of equals, and these equals were drifting slowly into that haze of weariness and living intent, where ebbs of energy were being called on to throw heavy, costly punches, and

248

make feints and darts on legs as tired as Irish histories themselves. Smoke, sweat, blood and dim lights mingled, and the faces of the gathered hundreds were open with shouting and desire, and the fists continued to find face and breast and shoulder. Blood gathered on the torsos of the boxers; it welled up under the skin in dark black patches like frostbite itself that the soldiers had seen for themselves out in the trenches. The blood fell out of noses, it dripped from broken ears, splashed down from small wounds and gashes and made a bib of blood on Miko Cuddy's chest. And all the way through was that odd crunching noise, as if the very bones themselves were being mulched. A miracle that tomorrow, Willie thought, these men would surely be walking about with swollen and bruised faces, and one of them no doubt smiling and talking about the fight. Or would they be buried six feet under in the Flanders earth? By God, they might well be if this went on much longer.

Now they were trading blows like very reluctant traders. At what wattage their brains were working, Willie couldn't guess. He was sitting now quite still in his seat, following the general urge of the crowd. No one was shouting now, an odd peace had descended. It was as if this spectacle of fighting had calmed those soldiers, put some introspective spell over them, as the two big Irishmen struggled to continue the fight. And when at last Miko Cuddy against all the odds caught poor William Beatty a glancing blow but nevertheless of a cudgel-like ferocity, on the left temple of his broken head, down went the giant foe, and yet up came the

249

voices of the crowd, almost in a tuneful roar, like a choir, an awful, simple and beautiful note of deep-throated approbation, and Miko Cuddy of Crossmolina, County Mayo, was the hero of hundreds for a day.

Another night, the officers got up for the grateful men a performance of "The Rising of the Moon", an Irish play for an Irish regiment. One of the line officers played the Policeman, and Major Stokes the Rebel — he was standing in more or less for poor Captain Sheridan. The major's Irish accent was brutal. It was strange to see his florid face heaving through the lines. But, even though many were the King's men — all of them were, to some degree, seeing as they were sitting there in his uniforms — still and all, everyone wanted the Rebel to go free, and felt duly relieved at the end when he did. Maybe true enough the play was set a hundred years ago. But still and all.

The entertainment the following month was a sort of dance, with music from fellas on a little stage, but only a sort of dance because there were no women to be dancing with, although they thought the nurses might be allowed to come in to them, that was their dream. But it turned out Major Stokes had said that he wasn't going to let a lot of poor nurses in with a crowd of Irish lunatics. It was a night intended to delight the whole battalion anyhow, and although there were fewer men in the battalion despite new additions and recruits, and many of the new lads themselves were not Irish, there was just enough Irish lamb in the stew to make the old flavour hold true.

Still and all it was clear to those who had eyes to see that a great number of the men that had come into the 16th Division in '15 were no more. There were few enough like Willie Dunne, and it was strange for him looking about.

"I think the old Somme has taken the most of us away," said Joe Kielty as he surveyed the mass of men. "I know few of these faces, Willie."

There was a very lonesome note in Joe Kielty's voice, like he was almost in fear of what he was saying. But there was little enough Willie could say in comfort.

Anyhow, the little band struck up, a piano player and a horn player and a drummer, and they got a good lick of music going, and then the lack of women was sorely felt. What were they supposed to do? They all stood in a great herd and watched the musicians, but it was very jaunty, good American music they were playing, and most of the men were young and wanted to dance a little and forget the war. So a few here and there jokingly waltzed with one another, and that seemed to catch on, and there was great laughter then, and fellas bowing down to each other like courtiers or good-mannered men, and other lads to roars of approval and mockery doing a curtsy and allowing themselves to be led in the dance like real ladies. And by heavens when the engines got going, the leaders truly danced the lead off their boots, and swung them round, and there was hooting and howling, and young, light lads were nearly bounced into the rafters. Willie

Dunne was danced like a chicken, and it was O'Hara dancing him, all six feet of O'Hara, and he heaved Willie along in such a manner that Willie retrospectively was quite glad he had not been born a woman and certainly not O'Hara's girlfriend, because he would have been killed by now by such dancing.

The air seemed all blue and green and yellow, and twisting around like a typhoon, it was the dizziness of it. Joe Kielty, that dapper Mayo man with flat feet, passed as fleet as a girl, smiling regally. He was swung into Willie's path, and they nearly collided. And then colliding was all the rage, and there was a pleasant mayhem, lads steering other lads into danger.

Towards the end of the night, when everyone was nearly spent, the piano player, who unlike his fellow musicians, was from Galway, played a beautiful reel, and Joe Kielty, who it turned out was the champion of the combined districts of Charlestown and Foxford, got himself up on a table, and did a dance. He stood as still as a stone for a few moments, in his khaki uniform marked by damp, and let the music in the doors of his ears, arms strictly by his sides in the approved manner. Then suddenly like an electric charge the music went into his very boots, and away went his feet like amazing hammers, striking the table lightly and at great speed, but the whole upper body not stirring at all, and the head held highish, and the eyes set stern ahead. It was the most wonderful thing to see, thought Willie, especially in the surprising body of Joe Kielty, who betrayed in his person or his character normally nothing of this genius. It was a wonder the table itself withstood it, as it certainly was bolstered in no fashion against dances. The rest of the soldiers, in particular the Irish soldiers, but soon the Scots and the Welsh and the English also, raised up their hands in approbation, and Joe Kielty danced for them all. They raised their hands in approbation, and he thundered and danced.

Afterwards they were back in barracks and Willie Dunne couldn't help slipping over to Joe.

"That was great dancing, Joe," he said, gleaming.

"Not so bad!" said Joe Kielty, smiling bright as a meteor.

"Jesus, Joe," said Willie, "that was something to see."

"Ah, sure," said Joe Kielty, embarrassed but delighted.

Then Willie Dunne swung there a little on the neighbouring bunk. He didn't really know what to say further, he had shot his bolt.

"What brought you into the army, Joe?" said Willie.

"Ah, the usual," said Joe. "I'll tell you what it was, Willie. I was walking along by the river in Ballina minding my own business. My father had sent me in to see about the purchase of some bolts for the barn doors. And a girleen came along and in her hand like a bunch of flowers she had a fist of white feathers, and she crosses over the road to me smiling and hands me one. Now I didn't know what that was, and my mother kept bees back in Cuillonachtan and I thought she was an itinerant selling feathers, because, you see, Willie, you use a goose-wing for the bees, to be brushing a rogue hive into the carrier box, and I know it wasn't a full wing or the like, but. So I asked her, I said, 'Are you selling these or what?' and she said, 'No.' 'Is it something for the bees?' I said. 'No,' she said, 'something for the war. I'm to give you that feather so you will be feeling bad about not going and go on out with yourself to the war.' And I said, 'Go way. I never heard the like of that.' 'Oh yes,' she said, 'what do you think, will you go?' And do you know, she was so pretty and nice and all that, and I felt so awkward about it, I said, 'Yes, yes.' And of course I mightn't have gone out at all, but just bought the bolts and gone home to my mother and father, but you know, when you say you will do a thing to a person, you like to go and do it."

"And that's how you came to join up? I can hardly believe it," said Willie with the tone of a child.

"That's the gospel truth now, Willie, and didn't my cousin Joe McNulty come in with me for the company," said Joe, and threw his head back in pleasing laughter, not ironical or anything like that, just amused himself by the daftness of it all, considering how he had found the war to be, and all that.

Willie went back merrily enough to his own niche, neatly removed his uniform, neatly folded it, neatly folded himself into bed. The billet he supposed folded itself into the dark field, the field into the sky, the sky folded itself like a letter of savagely written stars into the armpit of the great God, if such a person there was, and God folded Himself into — what did God do in the night-time? He would not have known the answer as a child and as a man he did not know.

254

"And it is a stupid question anyhow," he muttered to himself. All about him grew the busy, curious sound of his fellows falling into sleep. Their farts mingled with the startling smell of their feet and their folding and unfolding lungs breathed out like engines, the soft exhalations condensing on the cold window-glass.

And he thought these easy thoughts, and then quite abruptly his brain was rinsed by a queer pain, all the words in his brain were swamped by a black ink and obliterated, he dug himself as deep as he could into the shallow mattress, his teeth chattering, and wept.

The war would never be over. He had come out for poor Belgium and to protect his three sisters. He would always be there. The tally-sticks of deaths would be cut from the saplings for ever more. The generals would count the dead men and mark their victories and defeats and send out more men, more men. For ever more.

The hedgehogs were hidden in the leaves of the woods. The owls were in the sycamores and the ash-trees. And one more altered soul inside that winter in Flanders.

CHAPTER
SIXTEEN

All too soon, they were back in the line, although it was
one of the so-called quiet sectors. He hardly even
noticed his birthday going by, though by some marks to
be twenty might be a great thing. Maud didn't forget
him, though, and sent him a tin of cocoa. He ate the
dark powder from the tin with his fingers without
bothering to think of adding water. But the year died
away and a new one came in fearfully enough. It didn't
look like there were too many fellas volunteering at
home, only "a few soft-headed creatures", said Christy
Moran sardonically. Willie's company was patched up
all right with new men — but very few of them were
Irish now.

The new leader of his platoon was from London,
called Second-Lieutenant Biggs. Joe Kielty's machine-
gun detail had four new "jokers" — again Christy
Moran's affectionate phrase — from all corners of
England. They didn't seem to mind too much that they
were in a so-called Irish division, and in a regiment by
the name of the Royal Dublin Fusiliers, even if not a
soul among them had been to Dublin in their lives. One
of the lads was from Worcester — "I never was even in
Birmingham," he admitted, "till the day I went to see

the recruiting sergeant there with my brother John." But they didn't seem so different to Kielty, or O'Hara, or Dunne — just young lads with the similar misconceptions, similar dreams of all young lads, war or no war.

None of the new-minted soldiers had seen the front line before, and the queer stagnation and all-whitening cold must have been a shock, Willie thought.

In Willie's platoon now there was also a young sprat called Weekes, and he was a Londoner too.

"There was seven of us," he said. "We were called the days of the Weekes."

So that was a good joke to start with. Timmy Weekes's father, the father of all the days, was a gardener to one of the big houses in Hampstead, and also kept the yard for the rector of St John's.

"He knew his bulbs. He knew all the names on the headstones too," said Timmy Weekes. But his father had been killed at Gallipoli, first day.

"When I was a little boy he brought me to see the grave of a little chap like me, Joseph Lange, that died aged seven, in 1672," said Timmy Weekes. "And John Keats the poet is buried there and that was a thing started me reading books and I never stopped since."

Willie Dunne tried to keep back as much as he could from these newcomers, in his heart, not because they were English, but because, as a rule, if not a golden rule, raw men were usually killed first. He was wanting sorely to keep back from that. But you couldn't shun a man called Weekes when he had six brothers and sisters and could make a nice joke out of it.

Christy Moran did his best for them and made sure they could fire their rifles and tried to illustrate by imitation the different sounds that the different shells made. He told them about the principal types of gas and drilled them for the gas mask till they were blue in the face. Father Buckley knew from their small-books they were Anglicans but he made it his business to get chatting with them.

"The padre's not a bad sort," said Timmy Weekes.

"Ah, he's grand, yes," said Joe Kielty.

"I suppose he knows I'm a pagan?" said Timmy Weekes.

"Ah, we're all pagans here," said Joe Kielty.

"That's all right then and dixie."

Timmy Weekes turned out to be a great reader, right enough. Normally it would be the regimental paper going round for reading matter, novels picked up in stations on the way out, penny dreadfuls and other stories of the Wild West — the Wild West of America, that was, but was it as wild as this west? Not by half.

But now Dostoevsky started to circulate among the platoon, folded as it was in the folds of winter. The Idiot it was. He had Leaves of Grass by Walt Whitman and that became a sure-fire favourite, almost every man liked that, in particular Joe Kielty, who thought Walt Whitman had the soul of a farmer, more or less. He said people in Cuillonachtan were always talking like that, or nearly — similar sentiments anyhow, or senniments, as he called them. Walt Whitman was a favourite certainly. But the book they all couldn't get enough of was the Dostoevsky. It wasn't about them at all, it was about the bloody Russians, but somehow it was about them. They devoured the book like it was beef or sugar. They were all Dostoevsky's men now.

Willie Dunne was glad of them too; he started to relish a couple of hours secreted somewhere in a handy niche. He could disappear down into that tumbling world of Russia. He thought he might like to meet some of those real Russians who were fighting the Hun on the Eastern Front. They sounded, though, like they were twice as big as an Irishman, that was his impression — bulky, philosophical gents. He didn't know if he admired the Idiot or not. He didn't know if the Idiot was an idiot or a saint, or both.

The little library of books that Timmy Weekes had brought out under his armpit became grimier and grimier and more and more universally desired.

By contrast, Biggs was silent and efficient. It was hard for Christy Moran to be on his third captain — or, in this case, second-lieutenant, but third leader anyhow.

"He's all right," said Christy Moran. "I was getting used to Captain Sheridan, God rest him. I suppose a man might miss Captain Pasley the most."

"Do you think, Sarge?" said Willie Dunne, almost grateful to hear the words.

"Even though he was a fool not to run that time. An eejit."

Yes, thought Willie. He was a fool. Because if he had run he might still be with them. What did he gain, with his lungful of gas? It was no heroic death in the mournful upshot. But then, Captain Pasley maybe wouldn't have claimed it was. If he was an idiot, he was a holy idiot, for certain.

"What was it like in your father's time, at the Crimea?" said Willie Dunne, as he contemplated in his mind the sore list of names of the men he had seen killed. "Was it all the same as this?"

"The same as this. Smaller, maybe. Trenches just the same under Sebastopol, the arses freezed off them, Irish fellas frozen upright in them. The dead in their hundreds, horrible little battles. Army life, Willie. But, don't we get our grub? Well, most of the time."

"Yes, Sarge."

Of course, the sergeant-major was joking. No grub on earth, no pungent pheasants, the sweetest of puddings, no custard of Maud's, no particle of food of the fervent earth, could be set against the great, dark list of sundered names. The graves of vanished souls strewn across the broken woods and farms. Suddenly he wanted to say to his sergeant-major, that it was all an ugly, vicious, bullying trick, it didn't fucking matter if it was a Plumer or a Gough, good general or bad, everything ended always in the ghastly tally of wrenching deaths. His head was heavy now, sore as a boxer's, he wanted to have the matter explained to him, he wanted God Himself to come down to where they were talking there, and tell them what could be set against the numberless deaths, to stop their minds inwardly weeping, like cottages without roofs in a filthy rain.

"King and country, Willie, King and country."

"Do you think so, Sarge?"

"And I do like fuck," said Christy Moran.

* * *

It wasn't that they had never seen a winter like it, just that they were sorry to have to stand out in it. Many of the days the trench was just a white ditch of snow, the frost was in cahoots with the very clay, everything was frozen and slimy in the same moment, you could burn your fingers if you laid them carelessly on a gun so cold indeed it could not possibly have fired. They had welcomed the new year of 1917 the way soldiers do but now they heartily cursed it. Their hair frosted over so that they all looked like aged men. What could they do many days but stand on the duck boards like cattle in the mist, puffing out the dense flowers of breath? Men stood so still it was as if they had tuned themselves down into a near-lifeless state, like fish in a winter pond. The wind blew and hit their faces like hammers.

Then a day of sunlight would come and crack the landscape open like the shell of a huge egg and they could hear the trees in the woods making noises like gunshot. Here and there along the supply trenches, men found birds that had collapsed, small black deaths in the snow. They didn't pray any more for salvation, forgiveness or rescue, just that the tea would be hot when it reached them. And yet they must have been the philosophers of that weather, because when they could get a word in or out edgewise, it was oftentimes a bitter joke, as if to try to give a little heat to another man, any way they could.

Now and then along the line shells blasted over and sometimes it so happened that one would land among the helpless sentinels, and streaks and splashes of red would appear on the whiteness, and rawness, and cries. In the nights little details might go over and try to nab a few prisoners, or the Germans would come over and try to nab a few of them. Even snipers cursed the general whiteness for sniperish reasons.

Letters were at a premium then but nothing was coming in for Willie Dunne. He wrote back faithfully to Maud and wrote to his father with chilled, stiff fingers. He wrote to Gretta every fortnight and tried to remember her face as he did so, and talk truly to her. He tried to rub the sticks of mere existence together and keep a sense of the future alive but it was very hard. If it had been proved to him beyond a doubt that his previous life was only something in a novel by Dostoevsky, he might have been tempted to believe it. Or maybe a penny dreadful, or a book with only white pages in it. He was living in a landscape that was only a white page and in the frost it was difficult to make a mark on that whiteness, it was hard to make his presence felt; maybe, he thought, his heart was shrinking in the terrible cold. Certainly his poor pecker was a pea; it had retreated as far as his stomach, he thought, the last warm part of him left. There were thousands and thousands like him, he knew, standing stunned in the darkening and brightening snows and frosts, the day coming and the night following, week in, week out. It was difficult for his head to love and think of the future when he could not feel his feet.

"By the good fuck," said Christy Moran, "this is some war."

Then something miraculous occurred. The lice in Willie's clothes began to stir again, and one morning the music of the cold, with its piercing little notes, seemed to pass away. The greens and browns seeped back into the world. The fogs were blown away by little breezes and he saw the tower of Ypres crisp and clear in the distance. Men seemed more chummy again and it seemed to everyone that they had come through something impossible because it had been so simple and unvarying. That something was winter. The new something was just spring. But if he had been the first man in the first spring he could not have worshipped its coming more.

Then they all had to uproot themselves again and Private Weekes packed his bundle of books and they hauled themselves away through the ruckus and the din of the roads.

They were shown with great amplitude what was expected of them now. They were brought to an enclosure of some acres and in those acres was a vast model of the landscape they were to attack over and it was an astonishing thing that human hands had done. It was not exactly the place they had lurked in all winter in miniature, but another similar terrain, all the country under a little village called Wytschaete, which meant, said Father Buckley, the White Village. Which was a beautiful name in that formerly white country, with formerly a white sky and a white earth. The Hun, said Biggs, had held it now for three years, and it would be the privilege of the 16th and the 36th to win it back

263

for the poor Belgians. As Willie Dunne gazed over it and heard his instructions delivered in a serious monotone by Second-Lieutenant Biggs, he wished heartily that they had placed authentic models of them all, in their hooded and whitened misery, in the tiny trenches, just for the sake of decoration, like a kind of Nativity scene. But he knew it was a foolish thought.

It was a strange sight too to see the brigade drummers, banging the shining drums, all marching forward in a furious line — bang bang bang bang, kaboom kaboom — and the hands whirling and the shining boots going forward, all meant to be a picture of the intended barrages that would creep along the real earth, with real men following. Those drumming men representing the bursting shells.

General Plumer sat up on his beautiful grey horse. It wasn't often a man saw a general.

Biggs thought the general was a good and clever man. When he said that, he blushed.

"He's not the fucking worst of them," muttered Christy Moran.

Then two letters arrived tied together but with different dates on them, as welcome as boxes of gold.

dear Willi come home soon I love you best of all. do not forget the choclat I love you school is funny. love Dolly xoxoxoxoxo

The other was a postcard from Annie. It showed the beach at Strandhill in Sligo. It was a summer scene, of course, in the photograph they had used for the postcard. Willie peered and peered at the men on the beach in their trousers and shirts and straw hats, and at the ladies in their nice dresses, and the children holding their hands, and all of them looking out over the waves, and one resplendent motorcar on the esplanade, and a jaunting car also. A soldier could cry looking at such things, he thought, only because they were so ordinary and living. He must remember to show it to Pete O'Hara, when he had hoarded it to himself for a while, and got the good off of it.

> *Dear Willy,* [wrote Annie in her schoolroom blueink writing] *Heres where we had the holiday in October, we were nearly blown away by the storms. But it was lovely and Papa was in great form and we had big teas at the hotel, and Dolly loved everything especially the train (just like you years ago). Your loving sister, Annie.*

And that was all. But he read them both over and over again.

They had all gone down there on holiday without him. But what else could they do?

Still nothing from Gretta in all those weeks.

They knew they would be moving again shortly, so Father Buckley set up his canvas hut as was his wont on those occasions, and all the men of the battalion that wanted to queued in a long line for the confessions. And Father Buckley sat in one side on a little stool with a cushion that had a picture embroidered on it of a woman in a cornfield, not that that was important in any way, and he put a jug of water at his feet because he said sins were thirsty work. He didn't mean it particularly as a jest, but it was the sort of agreeable and encouraging thing he would say, so the men would feel freer about bringing their sins to him.

The spring had taken the countryside well in charge and small blue birds seemed to be everywhere, gathering wisps of grass and scraps of things for their nests. In that part of the camp there was a corner full of snowdrops. There were so many men waiting patiently that Willie thought it looked more like the whole brigade rather than just their own battalion, especially as he supposed these were just the Catholics. Even so, at the very far limit of the line everyone could hear the muttering from the canvas hut, although they couldn't make out the words, thankfully. But every so often they heard Father Buckley's voice rise a little, even shout just a tad, which was amusing to the waiting soldiers, and they nodded to each other, as if to say, Oh yes, we thought so, we know what he's been up to. Of course, it had to be what a person might call a field confession, short and sweet, and how could Father Buckley give out a penance beyond saying so many Our Fathers and

Hail Marys, given they were stuck in the middle of Flanders?

Nevertheless, Willie, and maybe many others, felt oppressed by the task. He wanted to tell the priest about the poor fallen lassie he had slept with — if he had actually slept with her; he thought he must have, for a few minutes — back in Amiens. He felt if he could say it out loud, and it was by no means the first time he had gone to confession since it happened, Father Buckley might see it in his heart to forgive him, or in God's heart, and he could put it behind him. Because he thought it was a deeply wrong thing to do, not only for his own sake, but for Gretta's. And it troubled him; it troubled him time and again.

When his turn came he let the other man out and climbed into the little space. There was a canvas-bottomed stool there and a strange green light seeping through the thin partitions. A leery slit was where he was supposed to speak, and he knew Father Buckley was in there because he could see the features of the priest dimly floating, but not looking in at him at all.

He confessed then to a few sins, pulling his wick a few times when he had got a chance alone, which wasn't very often. And often he didn't feel like it. But nevertheless, there were the few times.

"I don't think we'll make much fuss about that," said Father Buckley.

Then Willie mentioned the girl at Amiens and how it troubled him when he put it against the thought of his girlfriend at home.

"Is that you, Willie?" said Father Buckley.

"It is, Father."

"I wouldn't make much of a fuss about that, either, Willie. Just try to keep away from the girls next time, Willie. And I hope the old hosepipe isn't stinging?"

"No, Father."

"You were lucky so, Willie."

"I know, Father. Thank you, Father."

"Is there anything else, Willie?"

"No, Father."

But he supposed there was something in his tone that Father Buckley was used to noticing in the tones of soldiers.

"What, Willie?"

"Well, there's an awful long line back, Father, waiting."

"Never mind those lads, Willie. They won't mind waiting a few secs. What's on your mind?"

"Well, anyway, it isn't a sin as such, Father. Well, maybe it is. I'm worried about my father, Father."

"Who is your father, Willie? Is he the chief superintendent, yes?"

"He is. I wrote him a letter a while back and my sister wrote to me and said my father was angry with me about the letter, the letter I sent him, you know?"

"What was in the letter?"

"I don't know. I was upset about that time coming through Dublin with Jesse Kirwan, Father, you know? And I just described all that, how it seemed to me, but I must've said something that, you know, not annoyed him, but."

"Upset him?"

"Yes."

"What, Willie, though?"

"About the thing there. I saw this young lad in a doorway, Father, just like myself. One of the rebels. I looked at him and he looked at me. He was killed then. That's all. It's very fucking confusing, Father. Excuse me."

"Yes, it is."

"So for a while there I didn't know what was what. And when Jesse Kirwan was shot, Father. What can a fella say about that? And the reason he gave me. I still don't know what he meant. I don't know anything at all these days. So I just eat my grub and do what I'm told, but, Father, what for, what for, I don't know."

"Did you ever hear of a man called Willie Redmond, Willie?"

"Yes, Father. He's the brother of your man."

"That's it. Well, now, Willie, I'll try to explain it. He said we were fighting for Ireland, through another. You see? Fighting for Ireland, through another."

"What does it mean, Father?"

"That all this terrible war you've seen with your own eyes is for Ireland, that by fighting for all the poor people of Belgium in the army of the King, you are fighting at end of day for Ireland, to bring Home Rule and all the rest, to gather the ravelled ends of Ireland together, the Northerners and the Southerners, the 36th and the 16th, and that it is all a good and precious thing. That's what Willie Redmond said in the House of Commons. He's an MP, Willie, and he's out here with us fighting for what he believes is a wonderful cause. For Ireland, Willie."

"I don't think my father would like the sound of that, either, Father."

"What about you, Willie?"

"It nearly makes me cry to tell you the truth, Father. And a man shouldn't be crying out here."

"You can know your own mind and your father can know his."

"But my father and me always had the one mind on things. That's the trouble, I think — I don't even know. I'm confused, Father."

"Well, God bless your confusion, Willie. There's many a man out here only to be sending the few shillings home, and that's no crime neither."

"No, Father. Well, thank you, Father."

"Say ten Hail Marys for that girl, Willie. Are you due any leave at all, Willie?"

"I don't think so, Father."

"Well, God bless you, Willie. Send in the next man. Good luck tomorrow."

CHAPTER
SEVENTEEN

Biggs was a bit of a mystery to them, with his face the colour of pastry. They could not tell how the coming battle affected him, but they certainly each and all of them peered in at that face to try to decipher the measure of his confidence.

Christy Moran was in a high good mood and regaled them with stories of his drinking days. As always when the sergeant-major was at his ease — if that was what it was — he wandered quickly from topic to topic, and didn't seem to know himself whither his thoughts might blow him.

At any rate, they were led into trenches at about midnight. A gentle rain had fallen and done the little duty of fixing the summer dust. It was early June of the year and even under starlight the heat was like a ridiculous coat. The thoughtful general had had water laid in everywhere, and the sappers told them that new roads had been put in as far up as the forward trenches, so that after the battle everything could be ferried up quickly. That was unusual.

The guns had been firing for three weeks on the trot. The pilots of the airplanes thought a lot of good work had been done. Wytschaete was up on the Messines ridge so they didn't fly as far as that, because the Germans were like fowlers up there. Nevertheless, it was reported that all the ground in front was utterly bombed. The huge howitzers had been labouring at the great fields of barbed wire. Despite the ambiguous Second-Lieutenant Biggs, Willie Dunne was impressed. He was terrified but impressed.

They were given two water bottles that night and the second they found was full of tea. That was an Irish touch all right. Their boys at the kettles and the big pots far behind at the field kitchens hadn't let them down. A big stew came up after them and a double ration of rum. It wasn't the war they knew.

The guns had stopped a good few hours and the land about had returned to itself. It was like a new country, a fresh place. The summer rain had loosed the smells of everything, the new grass that was boldly coming up everywhere like a crazy green beard, the briefly drenched woods all about. There were even nightingales in the woods that any man could hear for himself and wonder at.

"What's that bird going on?" said Willie Dunne.

"Fucking nightingale," said Christy Moran.

They were warmly bidden to show no lights, so no one could have a smoke. They sat there or lounged there in the silent, murky conduits. They talked in low voices. All the equipment was up and Joe Kielty and Timmy Weekes were now the machine-gun operators, so they had four men to carry the huge ammunition boxes. They had to shoulder the Lewis gun themselves, but, compared to the bullet belts, that was a doddle

272

really. It stood to reason that carrying the boxes would be like fetching lead along the way.

They were only waiting there like that when all of a sudden the guns opened up behind them. There had been a whole week spent digging them in and putting the camouflage tarpaulins over them. There were said to be about two thousand guns all told and what was more all fit to fire. The artillery liked to fire two-thirds of them at a time and let the other third cool off. So in the darkness there was a roof of shells above them. For once in their lives, Willie thought, they seemed to have the range, and he could see the shells exploding in the distance along the lower part of the ridge. It was like bright red blood and yellow sweets, the colours. The noise gathered all together and made into one noise was like a terrific wailing of all the damned that had ever been stuffed down into hell. If you stopped a sound like that, you would still hear it for about three minutes after.

The ladders were already in place. Everything was bizarrely in place. They had enough iron rations about them to meet emergencies. Even their uniforms were clean because they had been told to brush them down religiously as if they were new recruits, as some of them were. They had used the special smelly stuff to rub off stains. All this had been done. It was as if the world had been made anew. The fact was, said Christy Moran, there was a real fucking general in charge. A fella that had fought battles before. They should make him a field marshal, he said.

Even Biggs started to look like a good thing. He had all his maps and order papers in order. He did look even more like a pull of pastry, but his voice stayed calm and the men were grateful for small mercies. Christy Moran in particular didn't have to tell him what to do.

"You know why I came into the army?" said Christy Moran.

"Why, Sarge?" said Joe Kielty genuinely interested, considering his own entry had been quite accidental.

"Well, why would you think? King and country? Bad debts? To escape a murder charge? Did it for a wager? Lost my fucking way and found myself in barracks? No, none of those things. None of the fucking reasons that brought you bastards in," he added affectionately.

"Why then, Sarge?" said Joe Kielty.

"Because the missus burned her hand off."

There was a silence then.

"She what?" said Pete O'Hara, feeling a little uneasy.

"We were the both of us drinking one night. Both of us half-seas-over when we went to bed. The missus likes to smoke this little pipe for herself. So we wake up in the small hours and the bed is blazing away on her side. And she's too drunk to stir. So I pull her away. Hasn't the fucking pipe set the bed alight, and she out to the dickens and didn't even feel it. It was her right hand. So there went her work right there. Seamstress at the Kingstown Asylum. Gone. So I had to do something. So I joined up, seeing as they were looking for men. And she's glad of the separation allowance, let me tell you. There you are now."

274

"That's a fucking desperate story, Sarge," said O'Hara, who felt quite green now.

"There you are now," said Christy Moran, very satisfied with the response. There had been no laughter anyhow. Laughter would have killed him. Christy Moran, R.I.P., died of laughter. "That's what got me in."

"Your poor missus and her hand?" said Joe Kielty. "Jesus, the poor woman."

"Poor woman is right," said Pete O'Hara.

What a strange flood of relief washed over Christy Moran's thinking head. He didn't know why hardly. It was ridiculous to feel relief with such a ruckus around them.

"You think so?" he said.

"Well, certainly, Sarge," said Joe.

A person might have thought that Christy Moran would then have proceeded to tell the men how he felt about them, since that maybe had been the point of the story. But such was his sense of victory, it overwhelmed him, he said no more, he forgot to say what had long hidden in his mind. But it hardly mattered, in essence, they knew well his mind. They knew it well, without him having to say a word.

The guns went on wailing and caterwauling. There were ferocious blows and bangs and thumps. The sergeant-major, for reasons of his own, was whistling "The Minstrel Boy" now low under his breath, which was a curious fact, since he never whistled. Willie could see in his mind's eye the gunners work their guns, the way they were so used to it, and knew all the movements, like in a Saturday dance. Like they were waltzing or something with those metal guns. Then, after three hot, fierce hours, they fell away again, and their noise rang in everyone's ears, and then a wilder, rarer thing happened.

"Wild and rare", Christy Moran called it later.

But for the moment Biggs looked at his watch and told them all to kneel or lie on the ground. They had been told that the sappers were going to try to blow some mines underneath the ridge. But they had been digging since 1915 and it was 1917 now and no one really knew what would happen when an attempt was made to blow them. It was funny, they had been told all that but no one could imagine what that would look like, so they had presumed in the main that there would be some little fiddly explosions in the distance, which might or might not help them in their enterprise.

In three places in front of them far ahead the fields opened up. Huge brown mountains came up from that ground. They looked to Willie as big as Lugnaquilla itself. The brown shot up towards the stars and seemed to hover there. A hundred rainbows fanned out from the top and sour-looking yellow light flung itself at the dark enamel of the heavens. The puddle at Willie's feet shrugged and a miniature storm at sea was created there. Then the whole warm night of Flanders was thrown in their faces, fierce zephyrs tore along the trenches like a brief tropical storm, and the earth they were now hugging and half-praying into shuddered. A mighty whap-whap-whap sound tore past, heading in violent haste they thought all the way to old Blighty.

Then, behind them, a long, long line of machine-guns opened up, sending a lacework, a veritable solid cloak of bullets towards the ridge. And Biggs was urging them to go, and they were up the ladders and off, Willie scrambling like the rest, so astonished on that occasion he forgot to piss his pants.

Joe Kielty and Timmy Weekes were making fine progress with the gun on their shoulders. It looked to Willie like a good half-hour's walking lay ahead and he knew from experience that if they were opened up on now they were entirely finished. The ridge looked down on them, and even in the wild dark, if the Hun could recover and get their guns going, by morning there would be fewer men to go back to Wicklow, Dublin and Mayo when the war was over. Just moments after the mines went up, the Boche had sent up coloured lights, to signal along their own front that an attack was in train, so there were some still up there. The heat was as bad as a mud, and as terror grew to be out in the open, a big, heavy sweat drenched them from inside, so they were like big feet sloshing about in big stockings. Pete O'Hara and Smith and McNaughtan kept pace and all to the left of them stretched the other men of the battalion. But the whole division was engaged, and this was the leading wave. To their right they knew the men of the Ulster 36th would be pushing along just like them, no different. But it was a gigantic army moving over this ground, a horde of terrified men moving for all they knew into the nasty arms of Death. And any second they expected to feel bullets tear into them, or shrapnel do some evil damage to their too-soft bodies. The fumes of the explosions also met them, and Pete O'Hara finally gave up trying to hold down his ration of stew, and started to vomit forth into the brittle and violent darkness. Men could be seen falling not from wounds but from that terrible nausea.

It was like running through colours, that was all Willie could think. Stumbling more like. Filthy browns and then sudden flaring colours, yellows again and reds and even weird, wild greens, and heavy, hard acres of blackness, and swords and God-high spears of whiteness like lightning.

Biggs walked ahead of them, turning every moment to shout them on. It was intensely strange.

Before they expected it, they were nose up against the slopes of the ridge. There was a bomb crater just below as big as a lake, as round as an ornamental lake. So they hurried around the rim of that as best they could, finding themselves divided and separated from the main line. The great battery of machine-guns far behind was firing remorselessly into the high ground, like some manner of creeping barrage. Then, maybe fearing there would be British soldiers coming up amid that hail, it stopped. Immediately somewhere to the right a machine-gun opened up, firing queerly over their heads.

"Fucking bastards," said Christy Moran. "Come on, you stupid cunts, we're going to put a fucking sock in that."

And gladly they would have followed him, but that he seemed to have shed all heaviness and weariness and was scrambling along like an animal well used to that slope. He had a Mills bomb miraculously in one hand and was hauling his rifle with the other.

"I tell you, you fucking cunts, if you don't keep up, I'll fucking shoot yiz."

But they were trying to keep up, they were trying. Now Willie saw the odd sight of two German soldiers standing by a concrete shelter. They looked in a very bad way, and were swaying and moaning like drunk men. The whole pillbox was cracked in two right along its middle, and there was smoke and stench everywhere, and that one machine-gun firing out through a ravaged slit, as if a child were directing it. Christy Moran did what he had to do to the Mills bomb to prime it and threw it through the damaged air so that it banged against the concrete and fell into the gaping crack. There was what sounded like a muffled gasp inside the building and then nothing. Flames suddenly tore out through the crack. Then Christy Moran started screaming at the enemy soldiers and ran at them with his bayonet fixed just in the learned manner, and before Willie's amazed eyes he ran the bayonet into the stomach of the first man, drew it out with another wild scream, and rammed it again into the other, catching him somewhere in the upper ribs, because Christy cursed loudly as he tried to draw it back out. The soldier fell and Christy stood on the man's chest and heaved out his weapon again.

"Bastards, bastards," he muttered, clear as day, snarling like a giant dog.

Biggs was jubilant. There was nothing wrong with Biggs that blossoming morning. The light was marching up fast from the eastern woodlands. He was shouting now.

"All right, lads, we've reached our line. We're on the blue here. Well done, lads. The other boys will be coming through us. Don't get in their way."

And even as he spoke the second wave of the brigade was clambering up and going through. Jesus, Willie thought, if it had always been like this, he might have been a soldier in the first place.

"Who are you lads?"

"We're the Dublins."

"Go on, the Faughs, go on, the Faughs."

"Good luck, lads, good luck."

It was very sweet talk, very sweet and easy. Never mind the tugging cacophony all about, the bleak ripping of the shrapnel shells overhead, from God knew what direction, Willie couldn't tell.

Jesus, they might go all the way this time, blast the poor Hun off this ridge entirely and drive them down into the plain behind. Let loose the horses and witness a thousand riders stream across open ground. That would be a sight, manes flying.

Then, quick as a curse, the sappers were up behind them with rolls of wire and all sorts and they were already making everything as it should be and had to be.

"Where's Moran, Private?" said Second-Lieutenant Biggs. "Where's your sergeant-major?"

"He was just ahead with Joe Kielty and another few men," said Willie. "Just ahead there."

"I'll follow them up. They've gone on too far. I'll go up the rise there and see if I can see them. Hold on to this lot here, Private."

"Right, sir," said Willie Dunne, astounded. He had never been asked to do anything like that. Of course, he was the most experienced man there, though Private Smith was maybe older. He didn't relish it for a minute.

An hour went by and Willie wondered if they should be pulling back. Or even going on. The place was filling with sections of other battalions. He didn't know what to do. There were gangs and gangs of German prisoners being moved down to the starting trenches and beyond, gangs of them, trainloads. But anyhow, wonderful amounts of water came up to them and the fetchers seemed to think it was destined for them as well as the rest. They were like men in the dry desert, sucking at the necks of those bottles. It was a thirst like the thirst of babies, the first thirst, that you almost couldn't satisfy.

Then Christy Moran came back down. He was very quiet. Joe Kielty, Timmy Weekes and the other four were with him as right as rain. It was hard to tell if they had used the machine-gun; it didn't look like it. How they had carried the blasted thing up that slope and down like a stray sheep was beyond Willie. Those machine-gunners were grown a queer bunch all right.

Willie was suddenly exhausted.

"How is everything up there, Sarge?" he said.

"Fucking great," said Christy Moran. "We walked right into that fucking village. Where were you cunts?"

"We weren't meant to go on. Biggs said so. He went up to fetch you back."

"Is that what it was? We saw him. A great big fucking yoke came down and landed on him. I don't even know what it was. There was just these fucking stars bursting out of him. It must have been a flare of a thing. Killed the poor bugger."

"Jesus," said Willie Dunne.

"All the fucking lads up there. You should see the place. It's just a flat fucking few acres with little spots of white dust on it where the fucking houses were. And those devious Ulster lads from the 36th milling about and calling us wonderful fucking Paddies, that's what they said, and shaking our hands. And Australians and all kinds of mad bastards. And hundreds and hundreds of fucking Boche surrendering and shouting out that fucking Kamerad thing they do, and you couldn't blame them. What a fucking to-do. You wouldn't see it in Dublin on a Saturday night in the fucking summer, Willie. We're after winning this one. Isn't that a fucking how-are-you for the books?"

It was true they went about for the weeks after in a different state of mind. They were all quite buoyed up. The general was pleased, though they didn't see him. It all seemed a right job of work well done. Of course, it was sad about Biggs, on his first job too. But they gave him some kind of posthumous medal. There were a good few medals flying about. Even Christy Moran got a medal and it was noted down in his soldier's small-book. Major Stokes pinned it on him at a little ceremony. For valour in the field. For putting holes in Germans, Christy said. They liked that sort of thing, he said. If he got another, he said, he and Willie could play toss-the-medal, he said. Winner takes all.

Christy said much, much later it was a pity they didn't leave it at that, them that knew about these things, as if.

Then Willie was away off for a day on a bayoneting course, and he came back to find Christy in a right good state.

"You'll never fucking believe it, Willie," he said.

"What, sir?" said Willie.

"The King was here," said Christy.

"What king?"

"The fucking King of England."

"No, not here, sir."

"He was, the beggar. King George himself. Came up in a nice big car, got out, and was over chatting. Chatted about everything under the sun. The flaming King of buggering England."

"But, Sarge, you hate the King of buggering England, you often said so," said Willie, a bit disappointed himself he had been away. Just for the curiosity of it.

"Ah, well," said Christy Moran.

"What do you mean, 'ah well', Sarge?"

"Ah, well," said Christy Moran. Then he said nothing for a few moments. He was thinking, Willie supposed. There was a happy, faraway look on the sergeant-major's face. It was very odd. "He was very polite," said Christy Moran, as if that explained everything. "It kind of suits an Irishman to curse the King of England, all things considered. But he spoke to us, man to man. It wasn't like an officer even. Like he was one of us. Like he was a fella like ourselves. Yeh. Said we were brave men to be bearing up so. Said he knew just how fucking hard it was for us out here."

"He didn't go cursing?"

"No, he didn't, Willie, he didn't. That's just me. He wanted to know if we were tired of the fucking maconochie. Well! He said he knew we would carry the day in the end, because God was on our side and our cause was just. That's what he said."

"What did you say?"

"I said to say thanks to the missus for the Christmas boxes she sent out to us last year."

"For the love of Jesus, Sarge. And what did he say?"

"He said he would."

Christy Moran hummed some tune then tunelessly.

"A gentleman, a gentleman," said Christy Moran.

It was only the next month when they were on the move again and by the grace of the good Lord if they weren't being shifted down near Ypres again.

"I've spent longer in Ypres than I have in bloody Ireland," said Christy Moran. "They'll have to make me an honorary citizen next. If I could speak bloody French."

And then the "good" general was gone and there was another general now that Christy Moran referred to as the "Mutineer". Gough the Mutineer, he called him, because he had led the mutiny of the officers in the Curragh camp, years ago it seemed like now, when he said he would not march his men against the loyal Ulstermen, should it be asked of him in a time of crisis, that time they formed themselves into the Ulster Volunteers to resist Home Rule. That all seemed like three hundred years ago. Now he was going to pick up where the good general had left off. That was the plan, anyhow.

"The best-laid plans of mice and men," said Christy Moran ominously, in a bad Scottish accent.

CHAPTER
EIGHTEEN

The whisper went round among the companies, and even if not everyone knew the name, soft words were said, and heads were dipped, in the proper funereal manner. But many knew the name, and many knew the story of the man in his fifties who had insisted on going up the line and into danger, a person with a thousand advantages, the brother, as Willie had put it, of "your man", the leader of the Irish Party at Westminster, whom Willie's own father had deemed a scoundrel. But it didn't seem so to Willie. The whisper went round and when it was said to Father Buckley, the priest openly wept. In fact, he burst into tears right in front of the corporal who said it to him. Then it became like a common death, like a person close to them all had died. For Willie Redmond was dead. He died in an old style, twice wounded, roaring at the disappearing backs of his men to keep going and watch out in the attack. Stretcher bearers attached to the 36th Division took him to their regimental aid post. Ulster accents eased him into death, minds that maybe before the war would have looked on such a person with traditional horror.

Willie Dunne bumped into Father Buckley in the shit-house. Of course, a shit-house had no roof, so could you call it a house, but there it was. The priest had his usual penance of mild dysentery, so Willie Dunne had to wait while the man strained over the hole in the ground, and shot out streams of thin yellow shit. At last relief seemed to return to the anguished features.

"I'm sorry for your trouble, Father," said Willie.

"I'll offer it up, Willie. Not much choice."

"Well, I meant, you know, that poor man dying, Father. The MP."

Father Buckley looked at him. His face broke into a smile.

"We were talking about him only the other day, weren't we, Willie?"

"Yes, sir."

"Everyone says he was a fine man. And he was. I had dinner with him one time, Willie. He was full of fun and stories. A most sincere and gentle man. You know I walked into Whytschaete myself to see what I could see. And there they were, back-slapping each other, North and South, and it was a grand moment. It was Willie Redmond's moment, if only he could have seen it. But he was killed. He was killed. That is the pity of it."

"Of course, Father."

"We have to keep our chins up, as the English fellas say. It's hard sometimes. But we've got to try. It'll all turn out right in the end. It's God's will."

"I hope so, Father."

"I hope so too, Willie."

But the talk didn't seem to be over.

"Are you all right, Father?" said Willie.

"I will be all right — when this bloody war is over."

"Of course," said Willie.

"Yes," said the priest.

The world and his wife knew they had done well and there was a queer little time when the whole division seemed to have the reputation of lions. There was more fancy training then, and more drummers pretending to be bombardments, and there were fellas dressed up as wounded men wandering about, and all sorts of mysteries. All this on the firm ground of summer, the firm ground of hopefulness.

As the rains came that August of 1917 the very earth of Flanders suffered a ferocious change. The whole country under Ypres dissolved. Field barriers melted, fields sunk away to flat quagmires, roads became memories. Horses, guns, carts, cars and mere mortal men found it difficult to walk over memories! The drear rain fired down day after day; thousands of guns were firing without cease. The beautiful system of dykes and drainage ditches perfected over centuries by the peaceable hands of Flanders farmers vanished. Huge lakes appeared on flat ground as if every little dip and depression were being glazed by God. The whole world turned black and brown, the sky, even the dreams of men. Puttees fell away after a week or two because it was impossible to keep anything dry. In Willie's platoon four men had hacking coughs all day and night. It was a highly mysterious change.

"What did we do wrong?" said Christy Moran, heavily superstitious.

When the whole country was turned utterly wretched and debased, their companies were marched up to the front. Everyone wore their long brown coats, and the big glistening hoods, and all the cloaks seemed to do was cook each man slowly underneath in a bath of uneasy sweat. They were almost glad to go, because while they squatted in those reserve areas, bits and bobs of the battalion had been sent up to do various tasks, and some said gloomily that the battalion was now only a few hundred lads. That was grievously frightening. Because they knew also that they were going to be asked to go for another little village, called Langemarck, before they were much older.

Under the hoods they thought their thoughts. Visions of home, streets of Dublin, faces, sounds and fleeting colours. All the long history of the war behind some of them, and the present chaos round them all. The roads sucked at them like hungry monsters, every step was a sort of wager. Shells landed liberally among them, so that often the struggling lines were broken by bloodshed and screaming. The poor lads of the Royal Army Medical Corps, stripped to the waist, hauled those morsels of humanity away if they were still breathing and gabbling and praying. The remnants were left to decorate the way. Hands, legs, heads, chests, all kicked over to the side of the road, half sunk in the destitute mud. And front ends of horses and horses' heads sunk in with filthy foams of maggots and that violent smell; horses that looked even in death faithful and soft.

Willie Dunne saw these sights, blinkered though he was by the hood. But you had to try to see ahead. How would he ever describe this to Dolly? He could not. She would wake screaming from her childish dreams all the rest of her life. It would topple a gentle mind over into craziness. How could a verdant land come to such an August? Even old Dostoevsky couldn't have imagined such a thing; no mind of any dreaming or waking person could have.

Timmy Weekes was trudging along beside him. He had Joe Kielty on the other side and a new man he didn't know, a frail little chap of nineteen. Nevertheless, he was keeping up well enough, that was the main thing. It had been intended as a march of two hours but already they were four hours going, in the bleakest dark that God had ever conferred on his strange earth.

"I was just thinking, Timmy," said Willie Dunne, "ould Dostoevsky would've taken fright at all this."

"Dante is the chap for this," said Timmy Weekes.

"Who's that, Timmy?" said Joe Kielty.

"Italian bloke," said Timmy Weekes, "called Dante."

"That's a nice, interesting name," said Joe Kielty.

"Or Tolstoy," said Timmy Weekes. The rain suddenly lashed into his face like it could make an angle for itself, so there was a pause. The wind was like bulls. "Now, Tolstoy wrote about wars. But not like this war. In his war you could still go home and fall in love with a lady."

"Can you not go home and fall in love with a lady?" said Joe Kielty, and the four of them laughed, a line of laughing men in the midst of a human nowhere.

"I wouldn't say no," said Timmy Weekes.

"A warm bed, a few bottles of beer, and a lass," said the new man.

"Now you said it," said Timmy Weekes.

Then they didn't say anything for a while, slogging on as they were.

"And how is it different now?" said Willie Dunne nevertheless. "That other fella's war and this ould war?"

"Well, maybe it i'n't so very different. Maybe not. Anyway, they don't write books about the likes of us. It's officers and high-up people mostly."

"So the battles maybe were the same?" said Joe Kielty.

"The same. Maybe so, Joe," said Timmy Weekes. "You put out a crowd of lads on the field, and the other side put out a crowd of lads, and you had musket shot and cavalry, and then the low lads like ourselves were shunted down the valley or whatnot, and fought like fucking lions, I suppose. And when everyone was dead on the other side, you had a victory. A victory, you know?"

"Well, and that's not the same with us, then, is it?" said Willie. "Because we only had a victory the one time, at "Whitesheet", unless you count Guinchy. And even then we were fucked to hell. Other times you had a rake of our lads killed, and a rake of the old grey-suited devils, and you wouldn't know who had won the fucking thing, sure how could you tell, boys?"

"Well, that's a difference, i'n't it, right there?" said Timmy Weekes. "But they might be adding us up after, and if more of us is left standing, then they might be calling that a sort of victory, i'n't that it?"

"Some fucking victory," said Willie Dunne.

"Some fucking war," said Timmy Weekes.

"And so say all of us," said Willie Dunne.

And that was strong talk. And that was all right for a while. But as that strange silence that could descend on you, even among your companions, descended on Willie Dunne, all ease and that tincture of happiness like the sweet juice in an orange left his brain. It began to throb with that all too familiar throbbing. A dash of grog might take that away. An ill thought, a curse, or a good sleep might also.

Christy Moran seemed to know where they were supposed to be, and after five hours of that "merry march", as he called it, he pitched them into some curious ditches. They may have been trenches once. The new officer was only a first lieutenant and he didn't know how to read the maps, so Christy was helping him along. It behoved them to tackle the trenches straight away because it would be daylight in a few hours, so even after their march they all started stabbing at the black soft clay with their entrenching tools, trying to fling the stuff back onto the parapet and parados. But it was like porter on their spades. They didn't know whether to laugh or cry, and did both generously. Still the rain cascaded with an intense passion that bespoke something that could think and breathe. It wanted to know every nook and cranny of every man, till every man was drenched and shivering.

The dawn came and stand-to was a sort of humourless jest. There were no firing steps, no duck boards, and, what was more imminent and sad, no breakfast to speak of. They nibbled at their iron rations, like rats themselves. Their trench was in full view of someone that bore a grave antagonism towards them, because the parapet was continuously strafed by buzzing bullets. Some crowd of geniuses somewhere had a mortar and were sending mortar bombs liberally over. Even when the shells exploded yards off, great chill sheets of filthy water came pouring victoriously down on their crowns. It was stupefying, withering. Willie Dunne could feel his very soul shrinking away in despair. Two days they suffered there, with the water to their knees, and not a bite came up behind them, not a scanty suggestion of fresh water, nothing. And always the ruckus of the shells, the machine-guns, the evil stenches. Even in the walls of the trenches hung the sad bones and fleshy remnants of other souls, as if some crazy farmer had sown them there, expecting in the spring a harvest of babies. At this point Willie would have believed anything. For those two days they pissed and shat where they stood, because the word "latrine" belonged now to another era. It was said that even the first-aid post in a trench behind, where Father Buckley held his station over the wounded, was a sort of pigsty of blood and entrails. And there was nothing anyone could do. Father Buckley had been reported to be roving about in the darkness, with a spade, and, even under that morass of shells above and in the vile muck beneath, had been carefully finding the dead, and, with

293

a few flashes of his spade, burying them into the entirely unstable ground, and praying over them with full and passionate prayers.

Willie Dunne never knew the first lieutenant's name but he led them into battle on the third day.

There was another tremendous expense of shells from their own artillery far behind which served to transmute three feet of mud into five feet of mud. Nevertheless, as the appointed hour Willie and his fellows rose up and started to grapple with the ground, for the ground itself was an enemy. The mud took a hold like very hands of their boots and pulled and held them. A nasty sucking noise, and they could hazard another step. There was in that place a veritable mile to cross to reach the objective that the Mutineer had in mind. To the right again in the miserable version of daylight the men of the 36th dragged their destitute forms through the same mud. Was this what poor Willie Redmond had in mind, thought Willie Dunne? It was only a brief thought. All his other thoughts were of wetness, violent noises, hurting joints. It was as if the whole battalion had been changed into hundred-year-old men.

Great numbers were falling. Others were finding where the quagmire was even more mired than other places and the mud was just swallowing them whole. The heads of men were being taken away by the low shells, and a million bullets searched out that struggling flesh, chests, groins and faces. They were fighting for nothing now, only breath and safety, a dream of safety, and after half a mile many would have settled for death, and did. The vilest fates were reserved for the wounded, half subsided in the mud, and receiving bullet and bullet again, as if all manner of human hope were now forbidden on the earth. This was a crazy walk of death, the terminus of all lives and wishes.

All about the German area they could see no trenches. Nothing familiar at all. At set intervals in the wild mud had been built neat little concrete houses, and the machine-guns were blazing out of them. No one could storm them, because the black morass forbade it. In all truth, Christy Moran didn't have a clue how to deal with them. He just pushed his platoon through, what was left of them, and in a low voice howled to himself in the howling air.

Willie Dunne, Christy Moran, Joe Kielty, Timmy Weekes, by some weird chance that they would never be able to explicate, came up to what Christy believed was the first allotted line.

"Where's the others?" said Joe Kielty, not expecting an answer.

"Did you see where that first lieutenant got to?" said Christy Moran with utter weariness.

Now the battalion in reserve was supposed to appear behind them in a bit and surge on wonderfully to Langemarck. Not a soul living seemed to be near them, nor a soul behind. All was a blank, black sheet of murderous nothing. It was daylight and the war had fogged the world.

Maybe it was minutes or hours but the air thinned a little about them and they saw that they were not in fact entirely alone. There were clumps of khaki uniforms all about. There seemed to be some hundreds coming behind, even thousands, as so greatly desired, and they could watch the shells dropping among them, and see in the distance the ruined soldiers falling. Every now and then Joe or Willie fired up the slope, when they thought they saw some leaping grey, like strange deer. Then a truly nasty thing — if such were possible of nasty matters further that day — happened. Willie's stomach felt as if it had fallen out of its place and dropped down somewhere into his feet. Because over the hill in front came line after line of grey uniforms, a sight of the normally invisible enemy in horrible formation.

The few clumps of their own British troops up ahead started firing at the Germans coming down. Then Willie saw a thing that amazed him. It was Father Buckley just ahead on the wrecked ground, with his stupid shovel, digging quietly beside a corpse.

"Father, Father!" he called, wild in the head from this addition of fright to fright.

"Shut up, Willie Dunne, shut up," said Christy Moran. "What in the fucking name of Jesus are you doing?"

"Father, Father!" he called.

The mass of German soldiers seemed to veer away down the hill to the left. They were stopping to kill everything in their path. Their own soldiers in the distance could be seen rising up out of lurking places and vainly trying to defend themselves. Some of the Irishmen tried old trench cudgels. Willie saw German and Irish with hands at each other's throats, both squeezing and yelling out strangled cries.

By some mercy of things the battered battalion started to come up behind. The new first lieutenant found them too, much to Christy's exhausted surprise, with some stragglers in tow. No one knew exactly what to do then, but it was true that they were now officially, as it were, relieved. The men who had just crossed that mile of destruction were screamed at by the remaining officers to go on up, and go on up they did. Christy and his companions started their weary way back. They weren't five minutes of the way done when a wild, strange sound made them turn. They looked back where they had been. There were hordes and hordes of Germans now, pouring down on the second wave.

There were dozens of the dead along the way at every step. The stretcher bearers had come out in groups of eight because of the mud. There were shouting, screaming men being ferried back roughly, and quiet faces with closed eyes.

Next day the dread truth was shared by the survivors in little groups. They knew one of the battalions had been reduced to one wounded officer. All the rest, those very men, Willie guessed, who had passed through them at the line and pressed on ahead at the behest of their officers, were dead or missing, believed dead. And yet orders kept coming to renew the attack. A mustard-gas bomb made a lucky hit right into the field headquarters of one battalion and turned three officers into green, smoking corpses, their skins eerily crackling and sparking in the ruined aftermath. And still along the lines of runners came the orders, to the dead and the dying and the wasted hearts, "Renew the attack, renew the attack."

"Where's Father Buckley?" said Willie Dunne.

"Killed in that pigsty of an aid post," said one. "He was there the whole day, giving the last rites to lads brought in. It was only a bit of corrugated iron, that fucking place. Shrapnel came right through and killed him. They buried him somewhere."

"But I saw him up where we were," said Willie Dunne. "I swear."

"He never left the aid post till they took him out to bury him."

"That's the saddest thing I ever heard," said Willie Dunne.

"Aye."

At least Major Stokes struggled down eventually to see them. Otherwise they were forgotten men, in an aftermath both insane and silent. By the time he reached them even he was covered in mud up to his armpits. He was bizarrely smiling when he came round the traverse. He looked about carefully at the strange arrangements.

"This is a terrible fucking trench, Sergeant-Major," he said to Christy Moran.

"Terrible, sir. But it's home."

The major laughed his odd, flinty laugh, like a sheep coughing in a mist.

"You fucking Irish. You always see the joke, at any rate."

"Yes, sir," said Christy Moran.

"Which one of you mud-men is my friend little Willie, Private Dunne?"

"I'm here, sir," said Willie.

Major Stokes came sloshing over to him. Willie was perched on a little makeshift raft of ammunition boxes.

It was odd. The major took off his tin hat and put it under his arm in an official kind of fashion. It was peculiar, the formality of it. Major Stokes' hair was quite white. It had certainly not been white the last time Willie had seen it.

The major kept his voice down now. "No hard feelings, Private?" he said.

Willie was surprised but he knew the answer straight off. He didn't really know what the major was talking about, but he knew the answer. It could have been a number of things, a number of dire things. But he knew the answer. It was the only answer in that place.

"No, sir. No hard feelings, sir."

Major Stokes gazed at him; it was the only word for it. He gazed. Maybe he meant to say something else, different things, maybe he would have said different things in a different place.

"That's very kind of you, Private," said the major. You couldn't just quite tell if there was still a hint of something in the words, a flavour of insincerity. But maybe that was his tone and always had been. Maybe at the age of two with his own mother he had puzzled her with that sardonic voice.

Anyhow, the major must have felt he had said his say and sloshed away again round the next bend to see the lads further along and how things were with them.

For fifteen days they stood in the water. The Royal Army Medical Corps boys had cleared the wounded and the dying, with a thousand curses and taking the name of the Lord their God foully and continuously in vain, but now the dire wasteland before them bristled with poor dead men and the foul air drifted against them. Liberal shells of gas and shrapnel and high explosive were thrown their way. The airplanes were all German in the sky, and they puttered down along the Allied trenches, throwing out bombs.

"This is a right fucking war," said Christy Moran. "A right fucking war all right."

Only in the dark of the night, the rain firing down, was there any semblance of safety, but it was a tricky, slight, little safety at best. They often thought that headquarters had forgotten them. That even their own supply battalion had forgotten them. Rare were the victuals that made it up to them; they had often to risk the horrible water that lay about everywhere if they were to have a chance to slake a thirst.

"We were heroes only a few weeks back. Now they don't give a kicking mule what happens to us. Bastards," Christy Moran kept saying.

The new first lieutenant did his best for them. He was cranking the field phone all hours of the day, half-begging for orders to get them out of there. There were only scarecrows and ragged souls of men left along that part of the line. It was a wretched state of things.

Finally there seemed to be some hope of being pulled back. It was said that a battalion of the Gloucesters were going to relieve them.

"All good things come to an end," said Pete O'Hara, and his damp, cold and hungry companions laughed. Not a man among them but hadn't thought once or twice of shooting himself in the foot, or eating a raw rat or the like, anything to be ferried away nicely. And what were they watching for now, only Death himself? If the Hun could rouse himself, there wouldn't be much to offer him by way of warlike spirit.

The Gloucesters never did turn up. Maybe the great Leviathans of that mud world swallowed them up. There was talk of new creatures fashioning themselves from this chaos, horrible, fanged whale-like monsters that could eat a soldier in two ticks.

They read the po-faced information in their soldier's small-books for the laugh, especially the stuff about keeping the feet dry and clean. And "clean dry socks".

"I like that bit best," said Willie Dunne.

There wasn't a clean dry anything for ten miles around, he thought.

Then Christy Moran pulled a rabbit out of the hat, for Willie Dunne, anyhow.

"All right, Willie," said Christy Moran. "You're not in debt and you're not on a charge, so I think I can spare you. Poor Father Buckley said I had to see pronto if I could get you a little home leave."

"What's that, sir?" said Willie.

"Furlough, Willie, I'm letting you go home on a bit of furlough, you lucky fucker."

Willie knew he wasn't due leave. Or had it been eighteen months again already? Had it been a thousand years? Despite the mud in his very arteries, despite the cold stone that had replaced his head, a tiny bubble of remnant joy surged up. He was going home, just for a bit. Father Buckley was still looking out for them from the grave, wherever his grave might be.

"Thank you, Sarge," he said. "I could kiss you, Sarge."

"Go way, you fucker, you," said Christy Moran. "I'm not your mother."

"You bugger," said Pete O'Hara. "Don't leave us here on our own."

"Sorry, Pete," said Willie Dunne.

"Bring us back a parrot then," said Joe Kielty.

"Rightyo."

When Willie was all packed up and his kit aloft his back and his gun in hand, and his greatcoat over everything else, and he wasn't in a position to stop him, Christy Moran reached in under the coat and put something in his top left-hand tunic pocket.

"Now," he said. "You keep that. Just in case I don't see you again."

"What is it, Sarge?"

"It's that fucking medal they gave me. I didn't know where to put it till this moment."

"But, Sarge, it's your medal, for gallantry, Sarge, killing those Germans and all."

302

"I don't fucking want it. You earned it just as much, you stupid cunt. Anyhow, Willie, it has a little harp on it and a little crown, and I reckon between the two it might get you home safe."

"Jesus, Sarge, I don't know what to say."

"Then shut up, Willie, and get going."

"Rightyo."

CHAPTER
NINETEEN

What a thing it was to be released out of there and ferried along by truck and train to places on the earth that were still firm underfoot. He stared out at that world, thinking all the time of his companions behind in that desolation. He found himself wondering what they would be gassing on about, and was surprised that though they were planted in a spot so evil, he missed them.

He was shocked to discover that England, as he passed through, looked and smelled the same. An Irishman passes through England and cannot think English thoughts. What lies between his home and Belgium? That England.

When he came into the lower hallway of the chief superintendent's quarters he saw Dolly straight away in a corner there, playing with a line of floppy dolls. He knew that his mother's mother made such dolls; he recognized them suddenly from his own childhood, green, white and blue woollen dolls, with painted cloth faces. He had forgotten such matters entirely.

"Hello," he said, "hello!"

The little girl turned her head. "Who are you?" she said.

"It's Willie," he said, "Willie, don't you know me?"

The little girl jumped up to her feet and raced across the cold flagstones to him. She creased herself like a wonderfully folding parcel into his arms, so that suddenly she was chest to chest with him, her heart beating, his heart beating. He was so glad they had been detrained in Amiens along the way and deloused and their uniforms given a good army clean for themselves. He had stood in a long line of civilian showers, the steam battering out of the cubicles, and those battle-altered men singing and shouting in the flameless inferno. What simple joy to be clean. What joy to have this little angel folded in against his cleaned breast.

"Oh, Willie, you look as old as Papa now!" she said brightly.

"You've grown up too, Dolly," he said. "What age are you now?"

"I'm nine nearly. Did you get my letter, Willie? I was hours and hours writing it."

"And a great long letter it was, Dolly, and you have no idea how glad I was to get it."

"I am sure you would rather have had biscuits, Willie," she said.

"I would rather have had your letter than any biscuits, Dolly," he said. "Are Maud and Annie above?"

"They are, they are, Willie. And not expecting to see you, Willie!"

"Willie, Willie," cried Annie and Maud, and it was true they were just like little girls with him too. Maybe they couldn't help it. Old times flooded back. They kissed him in turn and Annie roughly grabbed him for a few moments and looked sternly into his face. But she didn't say a word. She was crying though, her nice brown eyes brimming with tears and the tears darting down her cheeks. But she didn't try to wipe them away. She looked at him fiercely, and very slightly shook him, gripping the worn flannel of his sleeve.

He looked about the old sitting-room and there wasn't a mousehole out of place. If he had been lying asleep in some pitiful daylight in the line, and dreaming, it could not have seemed to him more real or more haunted, all in the same breath. He tried to imagine them here these last years, and he seemed in his mind's eye to see them flitting in and out of the rooms, as if his three sisters were a great crowd of women. It was a puzzling thought, and he put a hand to his head.

"Are you all right, Willie?" said Maud. "Sit you down there, man dear, and we'll make you a cup of tea."

"That will be lovely, Maud," he said, and started to cry himself. But they weren't tears of sorrow. They were other tears he didn't know the category of.

"How has it been out there?" said Maud, Annie still staring at him all the while. What age would Annie be now? Maybe fifteen. And Maud, surely seventeen by now. Did she have a boy to walk out with? Somehow he didn't think she did. And somehow he didn't think he should ask.

"Ah, it's just a war," he said. "You know."

"Well, we don't know, Willie, because we've never been!" said Dolly.

"And that's well and good," said Willie Dunne.

"We've had wars here too since you left last time," said Annie. "With scoundrels in the street and Papa distraught at every turn. And they say that there are men coming home from the war now, Willie, and giving their guns to those filthy insurgents, and saying that they lost them."

"I never heard of that, Annie," said Willie. "As you can see, I have mine safe and sound."

"I'm glad you do, Willie," said Annie.

"Oh, Annie, give over your old talk," said Maud, "and put that shepherd's pie back in the stove, and Willie, won't Papa be home now in a twinkle, and won't he be surprised."

When Annie stumped out to the scullery, Willie crept a little closer to Maud.

"I got your letter, Maud," said Willie.

"Oh, that's all history now," said Maud, but he knew from how she said it that it wasn't quite so.

"I'm glad," he said, anyhow.

The policeman was heard coming up the wooden stairs in his boots. He pushed open the door, Dolly heading for him like a swallow to its nest.

"Ah, Dolly, Dolly," he said. "Whatever would I do without you?"

He took off his cap and laid it on a bockety little table like a thousand times before. The circles and rounds of a life. He seemed lost and deep in his own thoughts. His face looked older, much more grey on his moustache, the cheeks lined and thin-looking. It was only a September evening and no one would stir a while yet to light a lamp, but nevertheless there was only a twilight in the room and streaks of grey Dublin light lying through it.

Then he looked across and saw Willie standing there, smiling as best he could. Willie didn't know what to expect, nor indeed what he had done exactly to bring Maud's letter to him in the trench. He had a fair idea but he didn't know exactly. But simple feeling rode over such thoughts and he couldn't help but smile to see his father's face.

His father said not a word. He finished putting his cap in its place and, holding Dolly by the hand, he moved across the gloomy space. He walked right up to Willie's chest, and of course he was a good foot taller than his son. The khaki uniform seemed stark alongside the trimness of the chief superintendent's black cloth and silver braid. The cuffs especially were elaborately decorated. Willie had never really noticed that before. He felt like water was pouring into him through a sewer-hole on the top of his head. He was being weighed down by it, whatever was the cause. He thought suddenly of his litany of vanished friends, and vanished faces that had not been friends but had vanished anyway. He thought of all those men of the 16th destroyed, hundreds upon hundreds. He knew he was beyond censure in his love and regard for them, although it had been difficult to honour them properly in their passing. It wasn't like the circles and rounds of life, it wasn't as if there had been time for proper eulogy and farewell, plumes of black feathers on funeral horses, cold gatherings in Mount Jerome or Glasnevin. He was a man of five foot six who had seen a thousand deaths. Now he stood an inch from the source of childhood comfort, the man indeed who had washed him tenderly like a child when last he'd been home on furlough. Well he remembered it, the big hands cleaning away the war. That could never be effected again, he knew.

His father let Dolly's hand go. He stopped a moment and maybe didn't know what to do. Then he lifted his right hand and shook Willie's right hand, leaning forward and lifting it from Willie's side and shaking it.

"There you are, Willie," he said. But the voice was hard and cold.

"Hello, Papa," said Willie.

Then the policeman did what to Willie was a horrible thing. He laughed as if there were something that he didn't believe, though Willie had said nothing. Maud was just coming in with the shepherd's pie on an old Wicklow dish, and she heard that laugh too, and looked at her father with a sort of cloudy fear swirling around her head.

"Have I done something to offend you, P —?" Willie couldn't even finish the word before the policeman spoke.

"They shot one of my recruits," said his father, in a surprisingly vague tone, "and brought havoc and ruckus to the city in the name of — who, Willie? Germany, they say. Through all these precious and important streets they put death and disorder. They put a mark on Dublin that can never be wiped away, a great, spreading stain of blood, Willie. And I read in a letter from my own son that he feels for them some stupid, ruinous feeling, that he has seen some bloody-handed gossoon killed in a doorway and wondered that he looked no older than himself. You stand here, Willie, in the uniform of your gracious king. Under solemn oath to defend him and his three kingdoms. You stand here in your own childhood home, your father a man that has strove to keep order in this great city and protect it from miscreants and the evil of traitors and rebels, for love of you all and in memory of your mother."

Oh, it was darker now in the room. There was a poison slipping easily through Willie's veins. The poison of disappointment and new horror. Never in all his days had he seen his father so chill and strange, the deep voice corrupted by anger, sounding like the terrifying voice of a stranger, of another. Never in his life had he even heard any such speech from his father, using words out of parades and ceremonies. Of course, Dolly did not notice, but ran over to Maud and leaped up onto her chair at the table.

"Sit down here beside me, Willie. I've been keeping your chair here all this time."

"It's a funny, dark world out at the war, Papa," said Willie slowly. "It brings your mind to think a thousand thoughts, a thousand new thoughts."

"I won't stand here and listen to your villainy!" shouted his father. "I have enough of villains and rogues out there in those streets. It is all under my care!"

"I know that, Papa. And that is a great thing."

"Oh, you say so, my little son? You say that. Of course, you don't mean it. Of course, you think everything I am and all I've done is a heap of ould nothing. A big heaped-up mound of scraps and peelings! That the hens can peck over! Isn't that it, Willie? With that treacherous gob on you! Now, that they might have killed me at the gates of St Stephen's Green, that that demon woman Markievicz might have marched up and shot her bullet into my breast and taken this life out of me, before I had to open a bitter letter and read those bitter words and feel the bitter bile loosen in the very centre of my body, so that I was crying in the darkness, crying in the darkness, for a fool and a forsaken father!"

Maud was openly crying, crying hot, plentiful tears, still holding the shepherd's pie. The heat of the dish had leaked out through her cloth and it was starting to burn her hands, but she didn't let it down.

"Will you not sit here, Willie?" said Dolly.

But Willie could think of no other thing than to look about him quickly one last time and, nodding his head to his father, and nodding his head to his sisters, go back down the worn stairs and out into the gathering dark.

That was the first thing on his list of important matters, that he had gone over again and again in his head on truck and train, wondering how things might be — and the second thing was Gretta.

He knew that dozens of letters from home went astray despite the best efforts of the postal service. He knew that many letters arrived half miraculously, and many arrived late. He told himself this religiously now, his father's words pounding in his head like the percussion of a great cannonade.

He went through the streets of his own city, up towards Christ Church. He didn't just have a general notion about the place; he realized he knew it in places stone by stone. As an apprentice builder he couldn't help but, in his heyday as a young man, gawp up amazed at the flying buttresses of the old, grey Protestant cathedral, and see where bits of it leaped the road itself. He used to think of the web of strong scaffolding required and the work of even erecting that, those vanished teams of fetchers and masons, mortar-batterers and the like. Stone upon stone, as with any building, the lowest to the highest. Stone upon stone, sitting on their beds, and snug and never a rocking motion. And he thought as he walked for the hundredth time in his head how like dancers the builders were, when things were going well and there was a lovely polish to their movements and a flowing stream of work. Well, they must all have been in high good form when they threw up that old cathedral, anyhow. The Protestants had two great cathedrals and the Catholics had nary a one, but he couldn't remember why that was, if he ever knew.

He didn't feel suddenly just as bad as he had done to hear his father speaking to him so, because he was approaching Gretta. How could he feel entirely wretched when he was coming near to where she was? Oh, the flood of battle and the tides of grief flowed through him and in him — but just as he traipsed along there under the cathedral railings, and turned down towards her doorway, he couldn't help but feel rinsed as a dusty tree in rain, he couldn't help it. When he thought of Gretta in that moment he thought all things could be put aside, put away. He would see the war out and when it was over he and Gretta would — by heavens, he would ask her now, he had been very stupid and tardy, he would ask her now again if she would consent to being his own true one. He was a grown man now, a grown man, and she would see him for what he was, and not mind it to the degree that she would refuse him. For that never would be so.

He moved up her ruined stairs. It was horribly dark because the house was squeezed in against Christ Church, and the windows on each landing looked like those dim paintings in old churches, lurking in the holy, lightless air. It might be Daniel in the lions' den, or the grave of Judas in the Potter's Field, you wouldn't know. He supposed you would need an old candle or something of the sort to have a proper look at things.

The door was always open into the great, fallen room of the long-dead bishops. The rags hung down from the dark ceiling just as always, with its myriad silent instruments in plaster. The families behind the partitions were murmuring and laughing; the glow of candles showed up the pitiful state of the "curtains".

And there was Gretta in her own strange light. Why, of course, Gretta herself was a candle, Gretta herself was a light. Gretta with her fine, white face as lovely as any stage singer's.

She was feeding a baby at her breast. He didn't see that immediately, but now that he stopped at the margin of her world, he saw the tiny child, he could even see the full, tight breast where it covered the child's face. Little hands opened and closed, opened and closed, and Willie could sense in the creature a depth of pleasure. He had lain down with Gretta but oh, so many months before. He was not so much a fool of a soldier that he couldn't count months.

"Gretta, Gretta," he whispered to alert her, as if she were in danger of a kind, and he must not wake or stir her enemies.

"Willie Dunne," she said, and wafted a thin blanket over her breast and the child's head.

"Is the child your own?" he said, perhaps desperately, because he knew she would not have milk otherwise. She was no wet-nurse, as far as he knew. Unless she had carried a child for him and lost it? Could such awful tragedy have occurred? Is that why she had not written? He would make it up to her a thousand times. Oh, Gretta, my Gretta.

"Well, it is my child, and my husband's child, Willie. You won't make a fuss now? I did write to you, Willie, and you never replied. And things go on as things go on, as my father will say."

"You wrote to me to say you wanted to be married?"

"I wrote to you, Willie, to say I had got that letter from your friend, and how was it so, and all the rest."

"What letter from what friend?" said Willie, feeling as she spoke as if he might have to go back out onto the landing and spew, she'd caught him so sudden. There was fear in his words now, fear worse than the fear of mere warring.

"I have it over in the drawer. Go and fetch it if you want, Willie. But you will know what it says. And you did not answer my letter. And I knew then you had done what it said. And Willie, whatever I am and whatever we were, I could not feel just the same after that."

"After what?" said Willie.

"Do you want me to say such things? Go and read it for yourself."

So Willie crossed over to the cheap little stand of drawers.

"It's just on the top there. There was no need to hide it. I told my father all and he advised me. He said he had said to you to know your own mind and you didn't. He said because we lived in these quarters it didn't mean we had to wait for men that went with whores. Sure Willie, there are whores enough all along Monto and Gardiner Street, you didn't need to go to Belgium to have one."

It was just a short letter with the address he would have put himself on it. It was written in long, snaking black scrawls, a curious document. The writer said he felt bound to inform her of the conduct of a certain Private William Dunne known to her, that he had to the writer's certain knowledge bedded a prostitute of Amiens notorious for disease and the writer felt it was his Christian duty to inform her insofar as he was in possession of such information which weighed heavily on him. It was a mournful duty which he had now performed. It was signed, yours ever, sincerely, A Soldier.

Even if he tried to lie to her now, what good would it do? She was married and she had the child. Even if he had received her letter, what good would it have done? He would have had to lie and would she have believed him, and if he had told the truth would he not have lost her anyhow? He was dizzy now with thoughts. He looked up from the awful letter and looked into her face. His own beloved whom he had rightly lost.

"I am sorry, Gretta. I am very sorry. And I am very sad to think I've lost you. I did go with a poor, ruined girl. And I did confess to a man now gone himself. And I never got any letter from you about it. And I would have walked over the cold deep sea to find you if I thought you knew about it. And if I caused you grief, and hurt your heart, I am so deeply sorry. I couldn't begin to tell what that war is, Gretta. I was even just thinking as I came down this way that all might be well in the end, because I loved you and we could be married."

To his astonishment, as he might only recently consider himself a grown man and might therefore know two good things in the world, she was crying. She was crying in that strange grey light of Dublin.

"You have a good man now, Gretta, to look out for you?"

"I have, Willie, a very good man. He's working with the Da. They're putting in the granite setts all up Sackville Street where they were disturbed by the fighting. My da slipped away from the Curragh camp last year because he said he'd rather be shot for a deserter than live as a British soldier. He needs to know his own mind, Willie, as you know. You won't be telling on him now?"

"No, no, Gretta. And that's well and good."

"I'm sorry, Willie, too, it turned out like this. I don't suppose it was such a very terrible thing you did, but at the time it broke my heart to read it. I hope it all goes well for you, Willie. I couldn't be against you, not you, Willie."

"I thank you, Gretta, I do. That is a comfort such as you couldn't imagine. Your father was right. I didn't know my own mind."

He stood there another while. He felt like a ghost, a person returned from some dark regions, no longer a human person. He felt like just wisps and scraps of a person. She was so beautiful sitting there; the child was meek and sleeping now. Gretta smiled at him her old smile, the smile he should have carried everywhere with him, if he was of any worth, and held up as a shield against the wretched temptations of a war. He turned away from that essential, living place, and out again into the glowering town.

He knew he would have to fetch up at some kind of dosshouse for that night, and did accordingly. It was full of tramps, and wrecked drinkers, and, ominously, other sad soldiers back from the war.

CHAPTER
TWENTY

He took the train down to Tinahely the next morning, because he had to do his duty by memory. At Westland Row station under the great canopy of iron and glass, he felt wearier than he ever had in the trenches. Some evil spirit had tricked the youth out of his body. In the night that same spirit had harrowed and raked him, and planted in him mocking seeds of granite and flint. At the centre of his body he thought something had perished. Like an old ash-tree he feared he would slowly hollow out, the rot taking him inwardly ring by blackened ring, until the winter wind came and blew him down.

Dublin was no longer like a city intent on the war. There were few uniforms about of men on furlough. In the streets he had seen troops, right enough, but they were soldiers about other matters, shipped in from England. Walking down Sackville Street, he had viewed the remnants of the uprising, the houses shelled away by the gunboats on the Liffey. Where the wide street had been torn up, right enough, there was a gang of men repairing setts, no doubt Gretta's father and husband among them. But he didn't look too long that way; he didn't want to see. The great street had been wounded in a cataclysm; it had erupted, spewing its mortar and stones to the heavens. They could put it all back stone on stone but there were many things that could never be put back.

In the corner of his eye he saw a little clump of boys in one of the side-streets that went down to Marlborough Street. He even saw the throwing arm of one of the boys shifting down in a throw, but he was still surprised and affronted when the stone hit him on the arm. He stooped and picked up the missile and it was a bit of granite from the setts, which a mason had cut with his hammer and bolster to make a piece fit. It was a little extra remnant of the city. The boys surged forward and the smallest and bravest of them ran out onto the pavement and launched such a gob of spit at him that he couldn't duck before it splashed against his cheek. The boys broke into wild laughter.

"Fucking Tommies, fucking Tommies, fucking Tommies, go home!"

He stopped on the pavement but he didn't feel inclined to run after them.

"I am at home, you little bastards," he muttered.

Of course, the little laughing group was skittering away down towards the Pro-cathedral. That was the church that stood in for a Catholic cathedral; it wasn't a cathedral in itself, it was instead of a cathedral. They were going to build a proper cathedral some day. That was where his father went to pray among the other Catholics of Dublin, loyal or not. He had sat there himself every Sunday with his three sisters and his father as trim and polished as a yacht. He could walk in there in his mind and sit down amid the smell of polish and the Italian statues, but in his mind the statues had been taken away and there were no ladies now to polish and scour the floor. Of course, that wasn't true, he supposed, things would go on a while longer, till another earthquake maybe shook the deep roots of the city, God knew when, and it all fell down. He wondered should he put the bit of stone in his pocket as a keepsake, but then he threw it roughly to the ground. Let it lie there to be thrown at another fool, he thought, another fool passing.

He got out at the little station at Tinahely, which had been put for some reason in an awkward place well below the town, maybe at the whim of a landlord. Maybe even the Fitzwilliams miles away over in Coollattin for at one time their power had stretched everywhere. For this was all country he knew. Not so many miles away lay the old realm of Humewood, where his grandfather had been steward. His grandfather was still alive and he wondered if he should go over to Kiltegan also, where he kept the vigil of old age in one of the lodges of the estate. But he thought, if his father was angry with him, how much angrier would be his grandfather, who had spent his whole life at the head of an army of estate workers, gardeners and farmhands, and was the vicar of the landlord on this earth, and as loyal as a wife. Of course, he was sure his father would have said nothing to him, because the two of them met only at funerals and weddings. In Willie's own presence the old man had often avowed that his son was a fool, and all his children were fools, but of those fools, James was the biggest of them. And he had put him into the police "with the other fools of Ireland". A fool, and the father of a fool certainly, was Willie's sad thought.

But the sunlight was easy in the hedges along the path; the rowans were heavy with their bright red berries. As he passed the gates down to Kilcomman church he found himself admiring the lovely trim of granite blocks, the expertise and the rightness of them, and the black gates as suitable as a suit. He wasn't exactly sure in his memory where the house of the Pasleys was, though he knew it was this side of the town, so he hailed the rector who just at that moment was inserting letters in the postbox, and asked him where the Mount was.

"Just up the hill there," said the rector. "You can see the roofs sticking above the beech trees."

"Thank you very much, sir," said Willie.

"Have you been overseas?" said the rector.

"Yes, sir. To Flanders, sir, these last few years."

"Are you going up to talk to the Pasleys?"

"I am. Because I knew their son, the captain."

"I was afraid you had more bad news. You know the other son's in France, too?"

"No, I didn't know that, sir."

"Ah yes. I am delighted to see you hale and hearty. We have lost seventeen men from hereabouts. Very terrible and sad it has been. And what is your name, Private, if I may ask?"

"Dunne, sir. William Dunne."

"Ah yes," said the rector, and Willie by old experience knew how the rector's brain was whirring, registering the name that would be unlikely to be a Protestant one, though the first name maybe betokened a certain deference to the powers that be. But, to give the man his due, his tone didn't alter. His own name was written in gold lettering just behind him as it happened, on the black notice that said the name of the church and the rector-in-charge. "Well, my friend, you will find them at the top of the hill. I'll bid you good day and God bless you."

"Thank you, Rector."

"Thank you, William, for taking the time to talk to me."

Willie felt curiously heartened by the words of the rector. In fact, he was close to weeping as he trod on up to the house among the trees.

He had enough sense to know he must approach the house from the lane that ran up to the yards. There was no purpose marching in through the fine gates and traipsing up the avenue.

He wondered then was he mighty foolish not to have sent a letter first, and how would he say why he had come? And why had he come, now he considered it? He had little idea but the notion of how the captain had stayed in him, the little history he knew of the captain still vivid in his mind. He was walking now in the captain's world that he knew nothing of. He hadn't even known he had a brother in the army, or had he? Had it seemed unimportant and had he just forgotten?

There seemed something vaguely unforgivable about that, in those days without forgiveness generally.

He knocked at the kitchen door just off the fine, trim yards. There were maybe two dozen outhouses of varying kinds, fowl houses and piggeries and turf houses, calf byres, loose boxes for the horses. It was a grand operation. And yet the house did not loom over him with grandeur or embellishment — it was low and simple, with a peaceful air. The sun was content to lie on the pack-stones of the yard; even the three sheep-dogs didn't bother with him, but stayed sleeping in their chosen suntraps on their chains. He knocked with his bare knuckles and after a little while he heard feet coming, and the door, which was already open a few inches, was pulled inward. There was a stout woman there in a blue overdress, just the same as his grandmother would have worn over in Kiltegan. He thought it must be a servant, the cook maybe, or the principal maid, because she was elderly enough.

"How're you doing, ma'am?" he said. "I'm looking for Mrs Pasley. My name's Willie Dunne and I was in the army with — with the captain."

To his dismay, he found he could not remember the captain's first name, but the woman rescued him, whether she knew it or not.

"George, you were in the army with George, oh bless me, come in, Mr Dunne, come in."

Then she drew him into the kitchen. It was like the kitchen of any farmhouse, with a big fire of turf and logs, and a scrubbed deal table, and the flagstones a little wet from the mop, and the old clock going at its work. But there was a door open into the rest of the house and Willie could see the genteel transformation there, with flatter plaster walls and pictures, and an old red carpet, and by another much bigger entrance a brass box of sticks and umbrellas. It gave him a strange pleasure suddenly to think of Captain Pasley walking there, and sitting, not as a captain but the son of the house, a farmer and a living man.

"Sit down there, Mr Dunne," she said, with true kindness. "We won't go into the sitting-room if you don't mind it. I have all the covers off the chairs and it looks like the end of the world. Let me give you some tea."

Her accent was a Wicklow accent but he didn't think any more she was a servant. The way she arranged her words and offered them was not the music of a servant, not at all.

"I'm very sorry," she said. "I haven't introduced myself. I am George's mother, Margaret Pasley. George was my eldest son. Now his father is down in the lower fields, but he should be up in a while, Mr Dunne. Did you come to, to — you're very welcome, whysoever you came, but — was there something to say to us?"

"No, no," said Willie, panicking suddenly. He had walked into rooms where maybe grief had been deep and constant. Yet her manner was bright enough. He was fearful now, treading in the shadows and the briars of the captain's own world.

"Did you know him particularly?"

"I did, I did, ma'am. Let me tell you —" But what should she let him tell her? She handed him the

325

beautiful blue china cup brimming with the soft coin of tea. He drank it with real thirst and drained it to the leaves.

"My heavens," said the captain's mother.

"You see," said Willie, "he was my captain in the first months of my service, and, as you know, he was —"

"He was killed, yes, at Hulluch. Were you there?"

Now she spoke with an eagerness like his unexpected thirst.

"I was," he said. "Not just in the moment of his death, because —" Oh but, again, how could he tell her that Christy Moran, himself and the others drew back, while the captain elected to remain? Was that why he had come? Not to say that to her but to himself? The captain had stayed and they had withdrawn — run away was the worse phrase for it. And the captain had elected to remain, though everyone knew it was only death to do so. And then coming back and finding the poor captain like a twisted hawthorn in the fuming trench. What was that? Not something to say to a mother.

"I can see," she said, "it is all happening still behind your eyes."

Then his eyes were full of tears again. What a fool indeed he was.

"Yes," he said.

"His commanding officer did write, you know. Yes, it was a good letter. He said he died bravely. I suppose they always say that. I didn't mind that, I wasn't thinking of courage in that moment, I was thinking I would never see him again. He was a very nice fellow, you know, a great friend to me. He was a bit stubborn and we had our differences, and he was very finicky about things, but — truly a fine son. You can tell me anything you like."

"But that's what I came to say, that he was a fine man, that's what I thought about him, and we had other officers since, and some of them killed too, but the captain, and I call him the captain, he was Captain Pasley, and —"

"You missed him when he was killed."

Willie Dunne said nothing then; why would he need to? He missed him when he was killed. He missed them all. He missed them when they were killed. He sorrowed to see them killed, he sorrowed to go on without them, he sorrowed to see the new men coming in, and to be killed themselves, and himself going on, and not a mark on him, and Christy Moran, not a mark, and all their friends and mates removed. Some still stuck in the muck, or in ruined yards, or blowing on the blessed air of Belgium in blasted smithereens.

He had come, he had thought, to comfort the captain's parents. How could there be comfort in a fool sitting in the kitchen with his tongue tied and his heart scalded?

"Do you know," said Mrs Pasley, "it means the earth to me to see what he meant to you. It does."

At length Mr Pasley was heard coming in. He entered the room gingerly because he was covered from head to foot in a grey dust. He looked like a grey ghost. His face might have been a carved statue.

"I'm going to have to have a good bath, Maisie," he said. Maybe the voice was a little like the captain's, the same accent anyhow.

"He's been liming all day," said Mrs Pasley to Willie. "This is a lad come from George's regiment, Pappy," she said.

"How do you do, young fella?" said Mr Pasley. "I won't shake your hand. I've been liming all day you see. Down at the Kilcomman end."

"It's a big job, that liming," said Willie Dunne.

"Aye, it is," said Mr Pasley. "It is."

After a fine old tea, it was time to be moving along.

"I'll walk you down the hill," said Mr Pasley.

"Ah, don't worry, sir," said Willie.

"Ah, I want to look over the hedge at the fields anyhow."

So the two of them strode down the hill again. At the bottom Mr Pasley went up on his toes and peered into the lower whitened fields.

"That's grand," he said.

When they got to the graveyard at Kilcomman, Mr Pasley brought Willie quietly in. He brought him over to a bright new stone, with its carving excellently done.

"There you are," said Mr Pasley. "Of course, his body doesn't lie here, more's the pity. But you know all about that."

It said the captain's name and that he had died "in the empire's service in the cause of righteousness and freedom". Willie nodded his head. He didn't think that Mr Pasley would be too sorry that Home Rule would not be coming after all, as people said. He didn't think he would be, no. In the cause of righteousness and freedom — and farming, they might have put, he thought. And liming.

Mr Pasley loomed beside him, looking down at his son's gravestone.

"Of course, John's still away, doing his best," he said.

Willie nodded and smiled. Then, almost without premeditation, he raised his right hand and laid it lightly on Mr Pasley's left shoulder.

"We called him George for to honour the old Queen's son," he said. "In those former days."

Willie softly patted the big farmer's shoulder.

Mr Pasley didn't flinch, or move at all, nor did he speak again for a minute or two.

For some reason they had given him a right old rigmarole of a journey back. He was to board the train to Belfast and cross from there. Maybe it was that the Ulster counties still tried to send soldiers, if they had any.

So he was on the platform in Dublin in the bright early morning, just stepping on. Of all the things in the world he expected to see, it wasn't the little scrap of Dolly coming racing down along the platform.

"Willie, Willie!" she called, "Wait, I want to say goodbye!"

Dolly arrived up at his legs with her usual force and gripped him.

"But Dolly, Dolly, you never came out on your own through the city, did you, Dolly dear?"

329

"I did not, Willie. Annie and Maud are after taking me!"

"But where are they, Dolly?"

"They're over back there by the gate."

In the distance right enough stood his two sisters.

"But why won't they come down too?" said Willie.

"They said you wouldn't mind if they stood back, and you'd understand."

Willie waved. They waved back anyhow.

"Of course and I do. I understand. Oh, Dolly, you're the best."

It meant the world to him after all. He kissed her, and hugged her, and the whistle blew then, and he kissed her again, and he kissed her, and then he stepped up on to the train.

"Goodbye, goodbye!" she called.

"Goodbye, goodbye," called Willie.

CHAPTER
TWENTY-ONE

When he got back, Christy Moran was very appreciative that he had gone down to Tinahely.

"You were using your loaf there," he said.

They had been tipped into a quiet sector and it was a time of tasks turning about and about, and mending the sides of things, and waterproofing the bottoms of things. They were in an old trench of the French and, as Christy Moran said, "it wasn't fucking Kingstown". It was no longer a continuous line, but what were called strong points established here and there, with many a gap between. But the machine-guns would cover those gaps if necessary, all firing from many points, so that a sort of weave of bullets could be imagined, like a huge magical garment that would protect them.

His birthday had come and gone like an ordinary day and there had been no parcel from home at any rate. "Like I had never been born!" he joked to himself. Twenty-one, though; he was privately chuffed to be so old.

Sometimes now and then in queer moments he seemed to hear his father's laugh — the bitter laugh that had frightened Maud.

There was a Christmas laid on all right, as if everything were still as it had been in the old world, but the little packets sent to them by the Queen had not the lustre and interest of former days. They sat together like the Ancients of Days in their huge coats and swaddlings and those that could still manage it prayed in remembrance of the birth of Christ, and those that could not sat in silence. Then 1918 came in, on dragging feet.

When the snow came it lay over everything in impersonal dislike. Noses and fingers were rubbed raw to keep the blood going round in them and in fast January one morning Christy Moran took a piss and it fell in a frozen yellow spike on the snow. You might attempt to speak a word or two and they too would be frozen into silence at the edge of the lips. They had a few old houses for billets, good old houses like Wicklow farmhouses but as if someone had gone in and scraped away every hint of woman, child or habitation. Though in truth they gloried in having quarters that shut out the bladed wind and drunken snow.

There was news from home that all the battalions there in reserve destined for Flanders were to be shunted to England. So Willie thought those boys of Dublin would have fewer targets for their spit and stone.

"They think we're all rebels now," said Christy Moran. "The bastards don't trust the fucking Irish any more. They think we're all going to rise up, lads, and slit their poxy throats for themselves. If someone doesn't get that rum up here in a minute, we might oblige them."

But Timmy Weekes, the Englishman, was as firm a mate now as Joe Kielty or Pete O'Hara. Christy Moran was in charge of the platoon just for lack of a spare commissioned officer. There was a terrible drop in numbers in the battalions, everyone remarked on it. Half strength as they were seemed almost a good thing by comparison. They tried to join up brigades and battalions but it didn't really make much difference. One of the rumours racing round was that the Yanks would be in promptly and make a difference. All those Irish lads that had gone out to America in the past, if they alone put on their uniforms and came out the poor Boche would find themselves clawing at the gates of Berlin to be let back in.

"I had three great-uncles and an aunt went to America," said Joe Kielty. "And I bet they had a few young ones in the interval. Yes, indeed."

Christy Moran looked at him for a full fifteen seconds and everyone laughed.

"I didn't say anything," said Christy Moran innocently, gazing about.

Of course, he wondered who had sent the letter to Gretta. He knew it could have been almost anyone, someone he had given offence to without meaning to, or even meaning to. Someone who might be long dead by now. He knew it couldn't have been O'Hara, though he had been on hand to witness his foolishness. It couldn't have been O'Hara, because he had all the manner and care of a friend. You couldn't do that to a mate of such degree, that was certain. So he didn't know who it had been. But the man who had done it he thought had ended his life just as effectively as the bullet of a firing squad. He was half glad he didn't know, because he knew if he did know he would be inclined to shoot that person. He would be inclined to take that person by the throat and squeeze the life out of him.

He did mention it to O'Hara. He said someone had sent a letter to his girl about the night at Amiens and she had wed another. O'Hara said such a man deserved to have his bollocks sawed off. He said he had heard of such things and he was inclined to think there was nothing worse a soldier could do to another soldier.

But as the year grew in days, every day brought fresh news that things might be stirring unpleasantly on the other side. Major Stokes for a while became more and more anxious and Christy Moran was forever plunging into the dugout when the phone was doing its bird-like ringing. When nothing seemed to follow these false alarms, Major Stokes fell silent accordingly. There was a sense that something was going to happen but as it didn't happen just then, it left a gap that could be filled with an odd fatalism. It was like waiting for the end of the world but at the same time planning for next year's harvest. They were doomed, but not just today.

There were always shrapnel bombs being fired at them, just to keep the conversation going, as Christy Moran said. One of the English lads had his foot severed. He was what Christy dubbed a sixteener, he wasn't eighteen anyhow. He was lying up the bank, his face the colour now of a dead dog-fish that the trawlermen might throw out in Kingstown Harbour, whitish-grey. The shrapnel had cut through the ankle quite clean. The foot lay just a mere inch from the leg. The boy was out for the count anyhow, luckily.

"Isn't that supposed to be attached to him?" said the sergeant-major curiously, in a dazed voice.

"It is supposed to be, sarge," said Willie.

"Well, put his boot back on him, Willie, will you?"

"It is on him, sarge. His foot is in the boot."

"Where's them stretcher-boys, where's them stretcher-boys?" said Christy Moran.

"They'll be coming up shortly."

"Would you tie a fucking turnakey about the knee," said the sergeant.

Then the stretcher-men came up, it was a sandy-haired lad called Allan from Glasgow and another man Willie didn't know. They loaded up the English boy.

"He don't look good," said the unknown man.

"You can say that again, Jimmy," said Private Allan.

"You're not going to leave that there?" said Christy, pointing at the boot.

"No point bringing it," said Allan.

So they went off and Willie and Christy and Joe Kielty were left looking at the boot.

"Better feck it up on the field," said the sergeant. "His dancing days are over anyhow."

"Oh, ho," said Joe Kielty.

The boy had left a deal of his blood behind him too. It made the eyes ache to look at it.

Then with mighty incongruity the sergeant said, in a funny little whisper:

"Happy days."

The terror that came upon them had been foreseen but what difference did it make, when it was like a plague of the Bible flung against them?

It was Joe Kielty on sentry duty that morning. A fog had been on the land since daylight, and Joe thought he was lucky if he could see ten yards ahead of him. It was like being under the sea. Then suddenly there was the violent swell and noise of thousands of shells going overhead, falling, Joe did not doubt, on their artillery somewhere behind. Then in short order the massive trench mortars started coming in, tearing away vicious yards of trench, burying and killing as they came. The violent ruckus was screaming down behind them and before them. Hour after hour they cowered and cursed, all the while surrounded by that strange, linen-thick fog.

Christy Moran knew quickly that he had only a dead phone in the dugout. He had a box with two pigeons in it for such an emergency, but when Timmy Weekes, who kept pigeons at home in Blighty, took one out on his hand, the white bird wouldn't go, wouldn't go for love nor money. Because Christy Moran was inclined to ask for assistance, as he felt in his old water that something evil was creeping up on them.

Even with the endless fall of shrapnel and mortar bombs, they peered out as best they could for whoever might be creeping towards them.

"First man to spot a German gets the coconut," said Timmy Weekes.

"What's a coconut?" said Joe Kielty.

"You don't know what a coconut is, you poor little man, you?"

"Of course he does," said Willie Dunne. "He's pulling your dirty leg."

"Right. Right," said Timmy Weekes.

So he and Joe Kielty were with their machine-gun and there was a lad from Shropshire to feed it and cool it with the waterpan. Truth to tell, he was a weedy little lad from Shropshire, and Timmy Weekes when first he saw him said for an instant he thought a rat had got into the trench disguised as a soldier. Be that as it may, they were glad of him as they stared ahead at the filthy fog in that clutter and amazement of shattering sound.

"Did you ever get a bad feeling?" said Christy Moran to Willie, as they stood crouched in against the wall, Christy taking the trouble to employ his notorious mirror. He was damned if he'd get a bullet through the head now after all he'd been through. Willie Dunne was sick with dread, it never was any different. And now that he had all the time in the world to think about what might be coming, his useless, unfriendly bladder let go again and he was standing it seemed for the umpteenth time in pissy boots.

The fog swayed in Christy's little mirror and it seemed after an hour or two that it was lighter and then there formed in it what looked like avenues of clear air, which would close and swirl at the will of some demon. Just as the barrage of mortar bombs ceased, he saw for a second in an opened avenue a solid mass, a pouring flood, of grey-uniformed men, moving along towards them at a queer old lick.

"Fire away, lads," said Christy Moran, mostly to his machinegun crew, but everyone got up on the firing step and did their best, although it was a tricky thing to kill a mist.

Other points in the defence arrangements were firing too, but at what was sadly debatable, because the fog had bunched up as foul and thick as ever. It was just that you knew they were there, those Germans, advancing, advancing.

"Fucking hell," said Christy Moran. "Oh, the fuck."

When the enemy became visible they were only fifty yards off. The machine-guns of three or four nearby points to right and left fired directly into them. There were, to their wild eyes, hundreds and hundreds falling.

"We're going to keep these fuckers off, lads," said Christy Moran. "Don't let them say nothing bad about us! Keep firing, Private Weekes, Mills bombs lads, and when they're close, feck them at the fuckers!"

Willie was firing and firing. His face was a bloom of sweat and the very sight of the Germans was an assault. The very vision of them was oppressive and terrible. You couldn't be more terrorized than this, not if a gun was put to your head and the trigger pulled again and again to find the full chamber.

Then of a sudden Christy Moran seemed to change his mind.

"Come on, lads, we're pulling back."

He said it in such a businesslike way, even in the midst of that furore, that Joe Kielty said: "Right, I'll cover you, lads!"

And Christy Moran, Willie Dunne, Pete O'Hara, Smith and Weekes went tumbling along the trench and into the supply trench, and as they belonged to a system of forward points, who were authorized to fall back, other sections of their company mingled with them, like a river gathering strength towards the sea.

They got into a wood they had not the name of, and yet the Germans were there too and came against them immediately. So they fired and they fell and they fought, and it was the second time in his life that Willie was so close to those soldiers. By whatever merciful chance, "nothing much to do with us", as Christy Moran put it, the attack on them seemed to be quenched for the moment. Then it was lying in against the trees and panting, and wondering if they should be digging like moles, and what the cure for that violent thirst might be.

Pete O'Hara had a hole in his side the size of a coconut. If only Joe Kielty hadn't remained behind, he might have shown him the size of a coconut, he thought.

It seemed to be evening now or nearly. Of course, the Germans were in such numbers they would soon find them out again. They wondered what was happening to the rest of the division, spread about in that disastrous place. The stench of gas moved about the wood like the children and spirits of evil. They had nothing to eat but the few stumps of iron rations they had with them. They had sucked their water bottles dry long since. Through the trees and beyond on a little slope, the sun had gone down, leaving on the lower sky a long, crisp mark of yellow-green light, very bright and lovely.

Willie Dunne heeled himself like a cart in beside O'Hara.

"By the good fuck, Willie," said O'Hara. "Will they know where to come and get us?"

"Who?" said Willie.

"Mammy and Daddy," said O'Hara.

"What's that?" said Willie.

"No, not Mammy and Daddy, no, I don't mean that."

"That's all right, Pete," said Willie.

"I'm going to die, Willie, I wish Father Buckley was here to send me off."

"They'll put a patch on that," said Willie. "It always looks worse than it is."

"It's all right, Willie, I've had my run. You know, I'm too fucking scared to be at this war any more. It's a stupid fucking thing to say, but I can't fucking do it."

"Well, and you have to, Pete. Didn't you sign up for the duration? Didn't you promise the King of England, Pete?"

"Ah, you're right, Willie, I should hang on, for him. You're making me fucking laugh now, Willie, that's not fair."

340

Then Pete O'Hara went through a few minutes of panting hard like a dog.

"Sure the King of England's not the worst. You haven't a drop of water, have you, Willie?" he said then.

"Not a drop," said Willie.

"You know it was me, don't you, Willie?" said Pete then.

"Go way, it wasn't, it was never you, Pete, you wouldn't do such a thing."

"I wouldn't do such a thing, and I did it, it was a foul thing I did, Willie, and I want you to know, if I could've called back that letter the very next day I would've, I would've, Willie."

Of course, Willie Dunne knew what he was talking about. Ah, he had known all along, but couldn't be thinking what he knew was obvious. This O'Hara had caused him the chief grief of his short life. The darkest and the chiefest among all the wretched griefs. For a moment he thought he might stick his hand into O'Hara's side and see how he liked it, pain beyond measure. He had lost Gretta for ever and ever, as Father Buckley would say, amen, and it was this bastard who had done it — this poor dying bastard, his friend.

"Why did you send that fucking letter, Pete, in your rotten black writing?"

"When I told you about that other poor girl, Willie, with no tongue, you remember, God forgive me, I was so fucking angry with you, I felt as small as a pin, indeed and I did, when you hit me. I said to myself —"

But Willie Dunne never heard what Pete O'Hara had said to himself. With his mouth open on the next word, with his eyes wide open, he died.

As the sun came up the shelling started again, though it was not directed absolutely at them. Them was Christy Moran and Timmy Weekes. There didn't seem to be anyone else.

"How's O'Hara?" said Timmy Weekes.

"Pete's dead," said Willie Dunne.

He put his head back against the tree behind and inadvertently knocked his helmet down forward over his face. Then he was in a moment of exhausted, calm stupor. Then a huge noise ate him like a whale. Then, as if in the next moment, he awoke in a rattling room, which was not a thing he expected. A rattling room it was, though, and he was strapped down to a seat — or was it a stretcher on a seat? — and he was trembling and shaking and he had a feeling that his breast was aflame and his legs were screaming at him with real voices.

He looked about him frantically. He was terrified. In the seats were a dozen women, beautiful young women in lovely dry and well-cleaned dresses. Dry dresses on a dozen lovely, lovely girls. But they were girls, they were girls, they were girls with no tongues.

Then it was all blackness and dark again.

CHAPTER
TWENTY-TWO

A little sweet-smelling nurse — that was what he noticed about her, the smell, not that he was much competition for sweet smells, as his skin healed — bathed him every day in some kind of stinking oil. That was, she rubbed at him with a sponge. Of course, the effects of the shell exploding so near him had done something to his engine, and he couldn't stop his head jerking about, and his left arm had a mind of its own, the mind of an arm that wanted to dance a jig all the blessed day.

Her father had a butcher's shop in Clonmel, she told him, which had aroused an interest in medicine. They were afraid to wash him in water, he supposed, in case his skin fell off like a dress. She rubbed him all over, but especially on the chest, where he had carried the main wash of the blast. By a miracle it had left his face alone. His helmet must have fallen down in front, he didn't know. But he was very glad of it, as it happened. There were scores of burns in that hospital that had turned nice-looking fellas into the fearful faces in a child's blackest dream.

Christy Moran wrote him a nice letter to say he was fucked if he would carry him so far the next time, and

343

hoped he was getting on well anyhow, and that it has been very sad about that business, and that that bomb may have fucked up Willie Dunne but it had killed poor Timmy Weekes.

"They say the old 16th has 'ceased to exist'," he wrote. "But Christy Moran is still here! The Mutineer was given his marching papers."

An officer did come round to see him. When Willie asked him about the battle he was told that a huge swath of the 16th was gone. The officer was from Leitrim himself, he said, so he felt it very keenly. But the Irish soldiers had not shown their backs. The French army had mutinied the year before, but you'd never see an Irish regiment refuse the fight.

There was a huge row at home, he said, about conscription that the government was trying to establish in Ireland. The officer said very bitterly that no one cared about the war now in Ireland, they didn't care if the men that were in already lived or died, and they certainly wanted no more going in. There were riots threatened and all sorts of wild disobedience. It was like Russia now, the officer said. It was like Germany itself, except the German people had some excuse to resent the endless war, since they were starving in their shoes.

Mothers in Ireland said they would stand in front of their sons and be shot before they'd let them go, and that was a change, the officer said. They could raise one hundred and fifty thousand men immediately, he said, and that was a great number and would win the war. But the Nationalists wouldn't stand for it. Said King

George could find lambs for the slaughter in his own green fields from now on.

Whoever said that, it was well enough said, Willie thought, but didn't say it out loud. What was the point?

The officer expressed immense satisfaction that the Irish Convention — Willie didn't know what he meant — had failed. Home Rule, he avowed, was a dead duck.

"Poor Father Buckley wouldn't like to hear that, sir," said Willie, his words thrown about like a baby's food.

"Who, who?" said the officer, for all the world like an owl. "I tell you, Private, your contribution has not been unavailing. The Sinn Fein is on the rise, but when the war is over, we'll go and show them what's what. When the war is over we'll show them what we think of their treachery."

But now Willie's head and arm were shaking so badly the officer couldn't see the point of comforting him further, and off he went, his duty accomplished.

The newspaper that the little nurse read to him said it was thought the 16th hadn't fought well. It was feared they had thrown down their arms and run at the first sign of attack. Even Lloyd George had said something the same. So it wasn't just the parlour maids; it was the master of the house as well. You couldn't trust the Irish now. Hadn't fought well! The sorrow of such a phrase! Willie would have shaken his head at that except it was already shaking.

Only King George himself seemed to have a good word for his Irish troops. That fella had a heart anyhow, Willie thought.

There was no point saying anything about it. Something had come to an end before even the war was over. Poor Father Buckley. The aspirations of poor men were annulled for ever. Any fella that had come out in the expectation of Home Rule could rest assured his efforts and his sacrifice were useless. For all that his father would think of it, Willie thought that was very sad. Very fucking sad. And very mysterious.

The doctor, who was in his own opinion a great wit, had greeted Willie Dunne with: "Well, here's the Sinn Feiner." There wasn't wool enough in the basket to knit socks for those feet.

In a month or two the top layer of skin was healing pretty good. He knew in his bones he was lucky. He had stood there, a human person, right in the middle of a bomb, and though it had lacerated his arms and legs, and burned his breast, all the scores and marks were slowly disappearing. In his delirium under morphine the streaks and fierce red blotches looked to him as if hell were painted on his body, the city of hell and all the roads leading to it. Slowly, slowly, under the ministrations of the little nurse, the map of hell faded.

Then the day came when the little nurse put her hand against his heart.

"You have a tattoo here, Private?" she said.

"No," he said. "I was never a sailor, Sister."

Sister seemed a very pleasing thing to call another person.

"Well, you do, Private. It is very small but I am sure you do. A little harp and a little crown."

Willie couldn't think what to make of it. He was days and days thinking about it, as he hadn't much else to contemplate, and he tried to peer down his chest and see the little yokes, but he couldn't keep his bloody head still enough.

A few days later, the little nurse brought in a mirror for him to see them with. Willie looked in the mirror with his jumping eyes and saw his bearded face. It was a thick, black beard the like of which even a Wicklow hill-farmer might fear to sport. He laughed at himself. He laughed. His head lashed about and he roared.

Then the little nurse turned the mirror inward and he glanced at the little marks. It was a harp and a crown, right enough.

"Oh, Jesus, I know what that is. It's Christy Moran's medal. By Jesus, Sister, the heat's after branding it into my skin. The heat of the explosion. I had it in my pocket there."

"Did you ever see the like?" she said, shaking her head, but in her case with perfect control. "Well," she said. "You'll carry that to your grave. I have no oil will wipe it off. It is just like you'd brand a young calf."

"I don't mind them at all, Sister, not at all."

"Well, who would ever have thought?" she said.

"They'll never believe us, Sister."

"And they will not," she said. "They will not."

She had only come in for something small, the nurse, his sweet-smelling nurse with the hair the colour of conkers.

"Will you — will you," he began with difficulty, like his head was being pitched about like a football kicked away out to sea.

"What, Private?" said the nurse.

"Will — you — will you — hold me?" he said with a gasp, and many a stupid-sounding splutter. He was no better than an idiot like that, well he knew it. He would have no world at all like that, for ever more.

"I can't do that," she said. "It isn't allowed at all."

"Please — please — please," he said, oh, his chin jutting, and turning, and turning, eyes darting, and darting.

"All right," she said coldly enough.

And she gathered him into her arms. She was wearing a blue overall over her white dress, against the spits and all the rest. It occurred to him then that she was spat on by him, just as he had been spat on and stoned by those boys of Dublin Town. She gathered him in.

He closed his eyes and Gretta's face slowly filtered in. All the ache and murder of the last years just for a moment ceased — ceased to write itself in the history of his addled blood. He hung suspended, beautifully aloft, somewhere, he knew not where, with Gretta's face, her breast, her arms about him. He was surprised by the soft silence, as if his brain had been a noisy place lately. Curiously, to him, the face was not her face now, but the face he supposed as it might be in times to come — the trim contours of the jaw were no more, the eyes were hooded, she was altered by time and how he wished he was to be the man to comfort her in that and

348

avow to her that no lessening of youth would bring a lessening of love. How he wished he was to be the man who would be old beside her, and herself old. Going about the town like two old lizards.

"I'll just hold you now a few moments," she said. "In a motherly way, mind."

"Oh yes," he said. Motherly.

Then the tender miracle happened. He would have to call himself the Miraculous Dunne after that, like old Quigley himself, God rest him. Oh, God rest him, and God rest them all. His own body was suddenly strangely at rest, and deliciously.

Her breasts were pressed against his arm, he couldn't help noticing. They were small and hard and cold, not at all like Gretta's. She seemed to him suddenly a sad person, a saddened person, a sad nurse. Maybe her sadness had cured him. Could it have been? he wondered.

St George's Military Hospital,
Shropshire.
June 1918.

Dear Papa,

I have been in hospital a while in England but you are not to worry, I am better now and am being sent back to the war. We were left in trenches a long while near Ypres and everyone was tired and then there was a bomb. I was not injured but I began to tremble and could not stop, so they took me to England. I was here a good few weeks. Now I can hold a pencil again and write to you, Papa. In these last days I have been thinking a lot in my bed and I have been thinking about you and Mam and the old days. I was thinking how strange it was when Mam died that things were still pleasing to a child and that was because you bestirred yourself and were a good father. I was lying there thinking how it might have been, two young girls and a boy and a baby girl into the bargain. So how did you manage all that? It was a wonderful thing to do, to hold us to you, and make all those teas, Papa, and find time to play with us, and when you did give out it was for good reason. Do you remember, Papa, the time you took us on the Liffey ferry over to the Great South Wall? And how you knew the old captain in the old house and we all went up to his lookout room at the top of the house and looked out over the river? And you showed us the red lighthouse and the green lighthouse? And how sunny it was that day, and we walked along past the sentries on the wall, and you showed us the long buttery stones the seawall was made out of, and when we got to the Pigeon House we all had to sing that old song you had taught us, "Weile Weile Waile", you put the four of us up on the steps there, and you said, "Sing for your mam now." And the gulls were very surprised. I was lying in bed and wondering why you did that. As a child nothing seems strange. Now that seems very strange and wonderful. I am going back to the war and will not be home I think till next year. I wanted to say in this letter that I have been thinking about all that has happened to me, and many another thing. And how some of those things

350

made me start thinking in a different light about things, and how that offended you so grievously. And I understand why. But it cannot change the fact that I believe in my heart that you are the finest man I know. When I think of you there is nothing bad that arises at all. You stand before me often in my dreams and in my dreams you seem to comfort me. So I am sending this letter with my love, and thinking of you.

Your son,
Willie.

Start thinking in a different light . . . Some of his new thoughts offended even him. It had nothing to do with kings and countries, rebels or soldiers. Generals or their dark ambitions, their plus and their minus. It was that Death himself had made those things ridiculous. Death was the King of England, Scotland and Ireland. The King of France. Of India, Germany, Italy, Russia. Emperor of all the empires. He had taken Willie's companions, lifted away entire nations, looked down on their struggles with contempt and glee. The whole world had come out to decide some muddled question, and Death in delight rubbed his bloody hands.

You couldn't blame King George, God knew. You couldn't even hardly blame the fucking Kaiser. Not any more. Death now had a hold on the whole matter.

And his loyalty, his old faith in the cause, as a man might say, a dozen times so sorely tested, was dying in Willie Dunne. An ember maybe only remaining, for his father's sake.

★ ★ ★

She shaved him so gently it was like being shaved by a human smile. She lathered up his whiskers and with a blade as sharp as marram-glass she took off the black beard. She pushed the strands together in a little sheaf and put them in what she called the "Hair Box". What she did with them then he didn't know. His friend from Clonmel.

CHAPTER
TWENTY-THREE

It was almost a jaunty, happy thing to go back to his regiment, what remained of it. All in his youth and prime, like the song said. To the extent that a man with a broken heart could be happy. To the extent that a man with the soul filleted out of him could be happy. Since the things he had wished for were no more, he wished for nothing. He breathed in and out. That was all. That was where the war had brought him, he thought.

There was a terrible lack of new Irishmen now in the army. You could hardly meet another fella in transit. It had all dried up, those thoughts and deeds of '14. It was all a thing long done and past. No one now thought it was a good notion to kit up against the Kaiser and go to Flanders. The 16th was gone the way of all old, finished things. He read again and again in the paper that the Irish that remained couldn't really be trusted. So they had stuffed the gaps in the 16th with what English and Scottish and Welsh they could muster. An Irish soldier these days might as soon run as fight. The Mutineer himself in fact said it, and he should have known better, their own general. Ceased to exist! And then to be blamed for that themselves. That was a test of loyalty anyhow, to hear a thing like that, never mind a rake of Germans rushing at you. But Willie heard it said on the trains; he could smell that opinion almost in the sea air of Southampton. Better forget about the Irish. They always had been a strange crowd, anyhow. Well, that was just an old song of those days. It wasn't "Tipperary" any more and "Goodbye Leicester Square".

Between your own countrymen deriding you for being in the army, and the army deriding you for your own slaughter, a man didn't know what to be thinking. A man's mind could be roaring out in pain of a sort. The fact that the war didn't make a jot of sense any more hardly came into it.

He was twenty-one now. That was a grown man, right enough. He couldn't cross back quick enough. It was very strange to him. All the "valleys of death" he had been through, all the fields of dead men, all the insane noise, and wastage of living hearts, you would think would have deterred him mightily. He didn't understand the war in the upshot, and he had thought to himself a dozen times and more that no one on earth understood it rightly. And he certainly didn't desire it and he feared it like the hunted animal fears the hunter and the hounds — but all the same he grew happier the closer he drew to his friends. A sort of happiness he feared he could have nowhere else. If he thought of Dolly, indeed, he felt tearful. If he thought of Gretta he felt as if he must stop breathing and die. Indeed, he could cry at the shortest notice, queer little things set him off, a fag butt thrown on the ground, the whistling of a lonely bird, he had to stop and collect himself, let the crying stop, and the shaking stop. He didn't really care if anyone saw him. That wasn't important. If it looked like cowardice, it looked like cowardice, and that was that. He knew that it was just that he was a man with bits of himself broken. That's all it fucking was. In those moments he was as weak as a newborn lamb; the weakest soldier in Germany could have killed him with his breath. But still he hurried back along the ways of the war, and with a curious pride he came into the place where his new platoon was set, and gave Christy Moran a glad hello, and received one back, and an embrace.

"I thought I would not see you again, Willie," said the company sergeant-major.

"I don't blame you," said Willie Dunne. "Are there any of the other lads I know here now?"

"These are new lads now," said Christy Moran. "Geordies, they call themselves, each and every one. They talk so dark they might as well be fellas from the Galway islands."

But then Willie saw a familiar face.

"Sarge, Sarge, you didn't tell me Joe Kielty came through."

"Ah, yes. You can't kill Joe, Willie."

Willie went over to the Joe Kielty who had been smiling across all the while. He took Joe's right hand in both his hands and shook the hand.

"Joe, you must be the best gunner in all of Flanders."

"Ah, not so bad."

"The best gunner, my God."

"The best runner, anyhow," said Joe Kielty, laughing.

"Come here a minute," said the sergeant-major, and Willie followed him to a dugout. Christy Moran ducked in there and came out again carrying a thick book that Willie thought he recognized.

"I sent all of Timmy Weekes' things back, like you do, and I hoped his father and mother wouldn't mind it, but I kept this back. I was going to send it on to you in a while. But you're here now, Willie, and can take charge of it."

It was the Dostoevsky that had made that winter near Ypres well-nigh bearable. Willie didn't cry then. He felt proud, somehow, and loving towards Timmy Weekes. The King of England was a gentleman and his soldier Timmy Weekes was, too. The war was a fucking folly and it had ruined the lot of them and even the living were ruined, and it would never be any different, but Timmy Weekes was a gentleman.

"Thanks a lot, Sarge," said Willie Dunne.

"I just thought you might like to have it," said Christy Moran, in elegant tones not entirely characteristic of him.

"How in the world did you get out of that, Joe?" said Willie next day, crouched down together in the daylight in a manner that now seemed immemorial.

"Ah, well," said Joe, "it just came round in a handy way."

"How so, Joe?"

"I was trying my best to kill those poor fellas, rushing towards me. I was going along not so well, when somewhere behind them they began firing these huge shells, big mortar jobs that fell straight down from the blessed heavens, and they came short of me anyhow, and killed a rake of their own fellas. You lads were gone a good half-hour and there was a big gap in the lines coming at me, and I thought to myself, Is that enough time now to give you? And I saw this great horde of grey jackets come streaming in the distance, yelling like madmen, so I said to myself, It is! and went galloping off after ye, but it was days and days till I found the sergeant."

"You deserve a big medal for that, Joe."

"Ah, well," said Joe.

The summer of 1918 passed and Major Stokes was found hanged in a little haybarn three miles from a recent battlefield. His fine black motorbike was found neatly propped outside. His note to his wife mentioned the stresses of the war and apologized for his apparent cowardice. He put on record his love for his three sons. He hoped they would be spared such a war in the future. He didn't mention Jesse Kirwan.

Now the regiments of the Yanks had done their long training and were putting their polished toes into the blood and wastelands of the war. It was their coming in — and the very resplendent look of them, fellas that seemed inches taller, and wider, and stronger, and generally larger, like giants in a storybook fed on beef and turkeys — it was their coming in that eased the anxieties of the government, and so feared conscription was let go by in Ireland. There'd be no new hordes of

Irish lads following in behind, against their will or willingly. Whoever was out there already was all there was, and all there would be, of Ireland now in the fields of Flanders.

And yet those were soon the days when the army surged forward, lost many more thousands to Hades and heaven, offered here and there the long-desired sight of the cavalries cantering over spreading farms — in their dull khaki certainly, but the horses putting out the flags of their manes, and all those men surging at last on those epic creatures, and the grey and darkening men of the Kaiser driven fiercely towards Germany.

And here and there along the roads Willie's lot shared the way now and then with American units, astonishing tall lads, they seemed to him, any one of which his father would have been proud to have as a son, if height were the measure of a true son. King Death maybe eyed them differently. Why, in the space of a few weeks they lost three hundred thousand men, it was said, and that was a dire slaughter to equal any of the suffering nations.

They passed on and on through Flanders. And that was almost the first time in the long years that Willie got a tincture again in his heart of the impulse that had brought him out, to put his hand to freeing old Belgium. And he was astonished to feel it again.

All that wild day they pressed on after the fleeing Hun. But it was a strange business, that fleeing. They never did see the vanishing army, hastening back to their

358

homeland. What country would they find there? What greeting would they have? Maybe they will be stoned, maybe they will be greeted like heroes. Maybe their country too had changed behind them and was no more, was another country altogether. Starving in their shoes, the officer had said. It was rumoured the old Kaiser would be killed, or he would pack up and go and be Kaiser no more. The men generally would have liked him to be captured. Maybe to be hung up alive in a public place and his guts put out for himself! After all the sear death and dark griefs he had brought to the nations!

As they followed in the wake of the German divisions, moving it must be like deer and rabbits back through the unopened woodlands, the neglected fallow fields, it was dismaying to Willie to see everything had been levelled and destroyed. How had they found time to crush down the buildings of Flanders, to burn the aching fields? They feared to drink from the rivers and wells for dread of poison. It had been a war of kingly poisons, in the air, in the memory, in the blood.

Past every building Willie in his mind built them up again, he forced himself to see the scaffolding poles lashed up, and the masons and the carpenters come again, and everything being made anew. They would be busy hereabouts, the armies of the sacred building trades.

He could feel the ending in his bones. He followed Christy Moran like he had done now for three years. He was light in his bones, the sergeant-major, he hadn't changed much. He still whistled brief Dublin songs and still muttered to himself, cursing and coining dark phrases. He could have been put, Willie thought, to be King of Ireland. He could not be discouraged. If the Boche had had him for Kaiser . . . The wrong men were up and the wrong were down. That thought had turned Russia on her head, and made the brave French fellas down guns and tools in '17. A thought that had brought out the men in Dublin, and that had killed Jesse Kirwan into the bargain.

He knew he had no country now. He knew it well. Finally the words of Jesse Kirwan had penetrated deep into the sap of his brain and he understood them. All sorts of Irelands were no more, and he didn't know what Ireland there was behind him now. But he feared he was not a citizen, they would not let him be a citizen. He would have no pride to be walking through Stephen's Green, he would not have the mercy of youth or the hastening thoughts of age. They may stone him too when he returned, or burn the house of himself to the ground, or shoot him, or make him lie down under the bridges of Dublin and be a lowly dosser for all the rest of his days. He went on through the widening farms. He had fought for all this in his own manner. He had crouched in the murderous trenches, he had miraculously — so said Christy Moran — come through the given battles, and almost alone of his comrades he was alive. No, he did not understand Jesse Kirwan entirely, but he would seek to in the coming years, he told himself. At least in the upshot he would try to know that philosophy. But how would he live and breathe? How would he love and live? How would any of them? Those that went out for a dozen reasons, both foolish and wise and all between, from a world they loved or feared, but that equally vanished behind them. How could a fella go out and fight for his country when his country would dissolve behind him like sugar in the rain? How could a fella love his uniform when that same uniform killed the new heroes, as Jesse Kirwan said? How could a fella like Willie hold England and Ireland equally in his heart, like his father before him, like his father's father, and his father's father's father, when both now would call him a traitor, though his heart was clear and pure, as pure as a heart can be after three years of slaughter? What would his sisters do for succour and admiration in their own country, when their own country had gone? They were like these Belgian citizens toiling along the roads with their chattels and tables and pots, except they were entirely unlike them, because, destitute though these people were, and homeless, at least they were wandering and lost in their own land.

About midday they came to a hilly place where it seemed a contingent of some Bavarian soldiery had decided to make a stand. At least they were trying to hold a rickety bridge, or so it would appear in the distance. Someone read the map and said it was called St-Court. They must have had a few pieces of artillery with them too, because there were big shells being lobbed suddenly into the woods behind. Strangely, the force and nature of the old war returned. Perhaps they would all dig in again, and be at this for another

361

thousand years. This would be their country for ever more, these few hills, this bridge, these autumn-tormented trees. He would ever look out on here from a neat trench that he would make with his entrenching tool, and they would fashion, him and Christy Moran and the other lads, some nice revetments from the hazels in the wood, and keep everything as trim as they could, and pray for good weather. And those Germans in the distance would become a rumour, the ghosts of a rumour, another world, but a close world, the dark moon to their bright sun. And so it would be for ever and ever more.

Darkness fell and the guns continued to fire, the fierce yellow lights going away some kilometres behind. They were such big guns, they could fire back ten Irish miles if they wished. Perhaps that was why the Germans had stopped, because they were loath to leave their guns. Perhaps they had been forbidden to leave them. Perhaps they had no officers left and they did not know what to do, except fire and fight.

Then as the slight coin of the moon appeared above the hills, like something thrown in a game of penny-push, everything went quiet. He and Christy Moran and about three hundred other men were spread about, waiting for orders to come up from headquarters now so far behind. There would be a runner scurrying through the dark world, to reach the colonel and ask what to do. He could see the officers gathered in a little lean-to, like a shepherd's hut. Maybe they would decide for themselves. No doubt they would wait for first light and push on then against the little bridge. Maybe they were bringing up their own artillery along the muddy roads.

A local owl sounded across the river marsh. Willie could see the rushes with their thick brown heads. They would be sinking now into winter soon, feeling the fingers of the frost touching them greedily. He could hear the human music of the river, and see the pleasing pewter of its colour as it pushed along between its incurious banks.

Then he heard singing from the German section. He found he knew the tune well, though the man was singing in German. Perhaps he was singing now in an ironical frame of mind, for the song was "Stille Nacht, Heilige Nacht". Silent night, holy night. The song of that first, far-off friendly Christmas truce in '14. It was not a night that was holy. Or was it? The voice was as simple as the river, it seemed to Willie. It came from the throat of a man who might have seen horrors, made horrors befall the opposing armies. There was something of the end of the world, or rather, he meant, the end of the war in the song. The end of the world. The end of many worlds. Silent night, holy night. And indeed the shepherds were in their hut and their flocks were scattered round about in these lovely woods. The sheep lay down in the darkness fearful of the wolves. But were there any wolves in the upshot? Or just sheep against sheep? Silent night, holy night. Stille Nacht, Heilige Nacht. Heilige, holy, a word he had not looked at in his mind since Father Buckley was taken. Holy. Could they not all be holy? Could God not reach down and touch their faces, explain to them the meaning of their travails, the purpose of their long sojourn, the journey out to a foreign land that became a sitting still among horrors? So far, so far they had come that they had walked right out to the edge of the known world and had fallen off into other realms entirely in the thunder and ruckus of the falls. There was no road back along the way they had taken. He had no country, he was an orphan, he was alone.

So he lifted up his voice and sang back to his enemy, the strange enemy that lay unseen. They shared a tune, that was still true. A single shot marked its own note in the easy dark, hushing the busy owl.

Joe Kielty caught him. Joe Kielty didn't want him falling to the ground, although a small man mightn't have far to fall.

Willie saw four angels hanging in the sky. He did not feel it was unexpected. They might have been painted there, old Russian icons. Angels of God, of earth, or just extremity, Willie couldn't know. One had the face of Jesse Kirwan, one Father Buckley, one his first German, whom he had killed, and one Captain Pasley.

Maybe in the passing drama of the earth some of them were given lesser lights. But all of them were captains of his soul.

A soul in the upshot must be a little thing, since so many were expended freely, and as if weightless. For a king, an empire and a promised country. It must be that that country was in itself a worthless spot, for all the dreams and the convictions of that place were discounted. There was nothing of it that did not quickly pass away. Nothing of worth to keep. Some thirty thousand souls of that fell country did not register in the scales of God.

Under that heaving swell of history was buried Willie and all his kindred soldiers, in a forgotten graveyard without yews or stones.

He saw four angels, but angels in those days were common sights.

Dublin Castle.
October 1918.

My dear son Willie,

I thank you for your letter of the last instance from the bottom of my heart. I liked to read your letter and what you said. I want to go and see Father Doyle now up in Wexford Street because I know I have done a stupid thing. I was forgetting that about the old days. My head was getting full of stupid dark thoughts. I was forgetting the easier things to think. How I love you, Willie, and what a good son you are. How you did go out to fight for Europe as you said, and how brave you are to be there. And if it was bad here these last years how bad was it out in Belgium? No one knows but you, Willie. I had no right to be getting cross with you. But that is all over now. I have read your letter over and over and Willie I have learned something from you. I will not be so stupid again and I will ask God to forgive me. Will you forgive me, Willie? Forgive an old man stuck in other days. I lived

365

my life in the service of the Queen and when she was dead of the two kings that came after. I wanted to keep order in this old city but in answer to your question I also wanted to remember your mam and do what she bid me which was to look after you all. I cannot have the first thing make me forget the second thing. I must always as far as lies in my power look after you all though you are in your prime now and maybe I am not the man I was in those old days. When you come home Maud and Annie say they will make a tea for you you will not forget. Dolly will make the rooms look good she says. You won't find us cold ever again. I am sorry Willie and there is not a man alive should not say he is sorry when he does wrong. So I am sorry. Keep safe Willie and I am so glad to learn you are over the trembling.

Your loving father,
Papa.

This letter was returned with Willie's uniform and other effects, his soldier's small-book, a volume of Dostoevsky, and a small porcelain horse.

When Dolly, some years later, emigrated to America, she brought the Dostoevsky with her as a keepsake.

Willie's father's world passed entirely away in the coming upheavals. In the upshot he lost his wits and died a poor figure indeed in the County Home at Baltinglass.

Somewhere in the earth of Flanders Christy Moran's medal still lies. His medal for gallantry — "gallivanting, more like", he had said. It had been seared black by the old explosion.

Maybe the helpful, acidic earth has eaten into the blackness and the quiet medal is clean and brown, showing, if only to the worms, its delicate design of a small crown, and a small harp.

They had to bury Willie as quickly as they could because now the Germans had broken away at last, and they were obliged to follow.

They put him in near the spot where he had fallen and got up a wooden cross with his details on it. Joe Kielty said a few heartfelt words. Christy Moran was anxious that the particulars were correct, and for safety's sake he made a note on his map of the position of Willie's grave, in case everything got swept away.

Then they went on without him.

William (Willie) Dunne, Private,
Royal Dublin Fusiliers.
Killed near St-Court,
3 October 1918.
Aged 21.
RIP